Also by

Reading the Landscape: poetry
Incunabulum: a novel
Second Chances: true stories of living with Addison's Disease
Ordinary Domestic: collected short stories
Creative Writing Prompts to Feed the Imagination

with Eileen Munro
As I Lay Me Down to Sleep

White Spirit

Carol McKay

Carol McKay (signature)

Pp

The PotHole Press

Published in the UK by
The PotHole Press
Hamilton, UK

www.potholepress.co.uk

Typeset by The PotHole Press, Hamilton, UK
You can learn about Carol McKay by visiting
her web site www.carolmckay.co.uk

ISBN (Print) 978-1-910033-13-5
ISBN (ePub) 978-1-910033-14-2
ISBN (Kindle) 978-1-910033-15-9

This book is a work of fiction. Any resemblance to actual
persons, living or dead, events or places is entirely coincidental.

About the Author

Carol McKay co-wrote the Scottish bestseller *As I Lay Me Down To Sleep* with Eileen Munro, published by Mainstream in 2008, and was interviewed on BBC World Service about her ebook *Second Chances: True Stories of Living With Addison's Disease* in 2013. Her prize-winning short stories and poems are widely published in anthologies and magazines. Carol won the Robert Louis Stevenson Fellowship in 2010 and taught creative writing through The Open University between 2004 and 2018. PotHole Press published her post-pandemic novel *Incunabulum* in 2020, and her poetry pamphlet *Reading the Landscape* was published by Hedgehog Press in February 2022.

Chapter 1

Vomit rose in his throat again and he retched. Bile clung to his lips and oozed up his nose. He lurched as the man shrugged him further over his shoulder. It felt like there were plastic ties on his wrists, biting into him. Ties round his ankles, too. How could he cut them? He didn't even have his schoolbag.

He couldn't see a thing through the hood. Maybe the man had drugged him. His head was pounding.

The man said he had something for him. In the van. Inside it. He'd never suggested they go inside it before.

The boy tussled again, bucking his body. He should have thought about the warnings. A growl came from him: an angry, whining, animal sound. 'I trusted you!'

'Enough!' the man said. 'D'you want another cuff?'

That was it! He'd met him to test the new game. That's all he'd wanted. He'd gone in the van with him to that new place. That room. And the man had thumped him. Where had that come from? His jaw stung at the memory. Oh but there was worse.

He had to stay awake. He had to shout so this guy would let go of him. It was crazy. Where was he taking him? This kind of thing didn't happen to him. His pals at school would be looking for him. His mum would wonder where he was.

Where was he? In the country? It didn't sound like the town. He thought he heard a bird cry. A buzzard, high up, looking for a field mouse. A shrew, a baby bird, a young pine marten. If he shouted for help, would anybody hear? In summer, the hills were full of people. But it was October.

The man tripped. They both toppled sideways and landed hard. The boy scrambled, but the man seized him.

'My mum's got money,' the boy whined. 'I won't tell her what you did. I won't tell anybody. I promise.'

They must have gone off the track. The ground seemed softer, shifting under them. There was a smell, now. Undergrowth. Dead leaves. Fallen pine needles. They'd gone into the forest. That was it. The boy whimpered. His mum would never find him. His neck was rubbing against the coarse stitching of the man's uniform. What was going to happen to him?

His mum would find out he'd lied to her. She'd find all that stuff the man had given him.

The man shrugged the boy up and off his shoulder and he thumped on to the ground. All the breath came out of him. He sucked in air to get his breath back. It was weird through the hood. He was desperate to pull it off, but his arms were trapped by his own body weight and the ties tore into his skin when he tried to cleave his wrists apart. 'Help!' he shouted.

Hands gripped him by the shoulders and rammed him against the ground. There were sparklers in his head.

'Shut up!'

The man yanked the hood off.

That face above him. A halo effect from the sun behind. Dappled light through yellow leaves. The man's shape dark; his familiar face blacked out.

'I won't tell,' the boy whispered. 'I won't tell anyone. I promise.'

Rough fingers under his chin, brushing beneath it, stroking his neck. The man's breath quickened again, but this time it was different.

'If I take your bindings off, you won't fight, will you?' he said. 'You'll do as I say?'

'I won't fight.'

The hands moved to the boy's sweatshirt, lifted it and slid under it, slowly moving over his skin, his nipples and collar bone; into the

2

dips below his shoulders.

A whistle sounded. Bird call or human? The man's head moved, his eyes peering into the forest. Beyond, far downhill through the trees, the wide loch would be brimming.

The man took a knife from his pocket.

'What's that for?' The boy struggled to sit up. The man pushed him over, shoving his shoulders against the tree roots, smearing his face into the leaf mould. He was cutting the ties! The boy felt the tug as each tie was severed. 'I knew you wouldn't hurt me! I knew you liked me! You do like me, don't you?'

'What?' A pause. 'Don't say that!' A low groan. 'Don't say it –'

The man gripped him by the shoulders and smacked his head on the roots – once, twice, three times – till the boy's vision filled with blood and the whole world disappeared.

Chapter 2

They could see the blue lights cycling through their sequence ahead of them. Allan MacIntyre pulled his Alfa to the verge behind the uniform car and he and Jane Coburn got out. It was a typical still day in early autumn. The birch leaves were yellowing on the hillside yet the pasture was still green, all the way down and across the wide valley. With the sky clear, Loch Ness below them pooled still and deep, and deep blue. Back on the hillside, it hadn't rained for weeks, so the ground was dry and the copper and yellow leaves that had already fallen crumpled under their feet.

'What a place to die,' Allan said. A look passed between them. 'I never get used to this bit.' Hands on his hips, Allan breathed in lungfuls of fresh air as they waited while PC George Smith, the first responder, approached them.

'Hello, Sir. Ma'am. It's the body of a young male – just a boy, really – half way up the hill in the thick of the woodland. Age about thirteen? Looks recent. The elderly woman who found him's a bit shocked.' He nodded his head towards the second police car. 'She's in the back there with PC Welsh, Sir. Do you want to go and speak to her first, or see the body?'

'We'll look at the scene.' Allan checked up ahead where the road curved to see if there were any other vehicles parked there, but there were none. 'Scene of Crime officers on their way?'

'I asked for them straight after calling you.' The PC held his arm out to indicate the direction then led Allan and Jane across the single track road, across a narrow draining ditch clogged with yellowed grasses and thistles festooned with fuzzy seed heads.

4

'One day, I'll get a job where I can sit with my legs crossed, in a tight skirt and high heels,' Jane said.

'Filing your nails and touching up your lipstick?'

'You bet.'

'You chose the wrong career, darling.'

Jane shook her head in the direction of the PC. 'You know, Boss, you can't get away with that anymore. One of these days some woman's going to sue you. And it might just be me.'

'Sue me?' Allan said, pausing for breath and turning his attention from Jane to the young man and back again. 'You started it!' he carried on climbing up the bank.

Jane caught the PC's eyes. 'Don't worry. He *is* just joking.'

The route they were taking was steep and full of tussocks. Grasses were bent aside and some of the mossy patches were smeared with foot falls – plenty of signs of someone passing in a hurry. Allan stopped and rested his hands on his knees. 'Did you say the woman who found him was elderly, Smith? What possessed her to choose this route?' he looked back. They'd climbed twenty metres from the roadside.

By now, the PC was a couple of metres ahead of him. He slowed and turned to answer. 'I think this is her route out. A bit pell-mell and frantic. She told PC Welsh she'd gone for a stroll up the roadside and then took the forestry track.'

'I was wondering.'

'She's about 65 or 70.'

'Fitter than you, by the sound of it,' Jane said. 'You ready?'

Allan got his breath back and they continued upwards. The young PC had to slow down to stay with them. 'You'll need to try out the new gym up on the top floor, Sir,' he said, tentatively joining in with the banter.

'I have tried it. That's the trouble!' Allan registered the way the PC was grinning down, past him, to Jane Coburn. 'Quit it, you two. D'you think I can't see you?' He paused, one foot on a rock and his elbow leaning on his raised knee. 'I'll be writing your end-of-year

5

assessments, remember. What happened to the days when DIs were respected?'

'Aye-aye, Sir,' Jane said, behind him. 'Want me to go ahead so you can get your breath back?'

He snatched a glance over his shoulder at her. She was still grinning. 'I'm not decrepit yet.' He looked uphill to the young policeman. 'Is it much further?'

'About the same again?'

'Jesus.' He searched in his pockets for a bar of tablet and broke off two squares. 'Want a bit?' he asked the others. The PC shook his head. Jane accepted.

'Tablet?' There was a note of disbelief in her voice. The sweetie was basically sugar melted in milk with a vanilla pod waved over it.

'Need a wee sugar buzz to help me tackle this mountain.'

'Ah, southern softies!'

'Aye, they don't have terrain like this in Balornock.'

It was battlefield humour. Funny how the mood changed as they drew closer. Allan could tell they were near by the way the PC slowed down and his movements became more reverential. He talked less, with eventually a quiet, 'Just up ahead, Sir,' before shoving aside some thick fronds of juniper to let the DI in to the small clear patch where the body had been found. Another PC was taping off the area.

The boy's body was naked, soft and pink like a newborn, and the yellow birch leaves above him allowed the sun through to dapple his skin. His face was screened by vegetation. There were no signs of clothes or anything else – no bag or carpet that might have transported him. Nothing to identify him, either, though a boy this age would certainly have somebody looking for him.

The PC waited where he'd arrived while Allan and Jane moved round the perimeter of the closed off area, not wanting to move onto the scene itself before SOC had a chance to do forensics.

'Jesus. What a fucking tragedy,' Allan said, his voice quiet. A leaf fell close to the boy's body. It was incongruous – savagery in a place of beauty. 'No knife wounds or bullet holes by the looks of it,' Allan said. 'But there's blood.'

Jane sighed. 'Yeah – there's been some kind of a struggle, Sir. See the red patches round his neck and under his armpits?'

'What age do you think he is? Thirteen? Fourteen?' From what they could see, the boy had tufts under his arms and scrubby ginger pubic hair. His genitals had developed.

'Yeah – early secondary school.' Jane said. 'Wee soul. Not the best way to dodge out of it.'

Allan felt a wave of exhaustion hit him. He knelt down and put his hand on a rock, using it for support while he leaned in for a closer view. 'That's a scar on his stomach. An old one – might help identify him. And look at this, Jane. This is where the blood's from.' The boy's nose was mashed and his face and hair were smeared with blood and dirt. 'Is it just me, or does his neck look kind of awkward, too?'

'Could be,' Jane said.

Allan's phone rang and he jumped. 'What is it, Ross?'

'Hi Boss. There's been some kind of fire overnight in the bins at the Inchmarsh Industrial Estate.'

Allan looked at the corpse in front of him. 'So? Is it out now?'

'I think so,' Ross said.

'Right. So what are you phoning me for? It'll be kids' stuff.'

'Maybe not,' the younger man said. 'Looks like it might have been some kind of explosion. Maybe deliberate, or maybe something combustible in the bins themselves – something that shouldn't have been there.'

'Inchmarsh?'

'Yeah – the bins at the back of the Q-buster Distribution Company.' There was the sound of Ross clicking through his computer screens. 'Electrical and electronic goods distributors, mostly. Want me to check it out? The woman that called in was pretty flustered. So the beat boy says.'

'Have we got anything on the company? On file?'

7

'I don't know. The call's just in.'

'Check it out, then. Don't be long. Do the usual and file a report.'

'Right, Boss.'

Allan frowned at Jane as he tucked his phone away. 'Ross.'

'I guessed that.'

He pushed himself upright and brushed dead leaves from his palm. 'Okay. Finished here?'

Jane looked around. 'I think so. Absolutely no sign of ID.'

'Nope. But someone will miss him.' They stood silent for a moment. 'We'll see what Helena Finlayson and the lab have to say.' Allan shifted his eyes from the pale boy to the PC. 'Right – let's have a word with the woman who found him.'

The route down was gravity-assisted and took half the time. Back on the road, the SOC wagon had arrived and the team were suiting up in their whites. Allan hailed them with a wave and walked over to give them his impression. They promised to get photos to him and a preliminary report asap. Two ordinary cars drove by in the short time Allan was talking to them. The media would soon get hold of the news of the police being all over the road, so they had to get at least some info out there, even if just to stall the public and put off the excitement seekers. And buy time to identify the boy.

Back at the police car, Jane Coburn was talking to a PC Allan didn't recognise. When he approached, she straightened up and acknowledged him. 'Ready to talk to the witness, Sir?'

'Absolutely,' Allan said. 'And there's no need to be quite so formal – PC...?'

'Welsh, Sir. Anna Welsh. I'm new,' she said. 'Thank you, Sir.'

Allan nodded.

Irma Russell was sitting in the back seat of the police car. When he opened the door, he saw a woman in her mid-sixties, sitting upright with a lightweight backpack on her lap. There were two expensive-looking jewelled rings on her fingers. Her eyes were brown and unblinking, and her mouth was pinched, but other than that there was no sign of emotion.

'Ms Russell?' he said, and slid into the seat. 'I'm DI Allan MacIntyre. I'm sorry to keep you waiting. I understand you've been through a harrowing experience, and I'm sure you'd like to go home as soon as possible. Thanks for staying here so I can ask you some questions.'

The woman nodded.

The car radio screeched and PC Welsh leaned in through the front door and turned it off.

'Right.' Allan repositioned himself on the seat. 'I've been to see the boy's body.' He glanced at the woman. 'Not pleasant. Can you tell me, in your own words, how you found him? Take your time.'

Her voice took him by surprise. A white settler. It was rich and deep, with southern English vowels and crisp consonants. He found himself studying her as she talked. She had that self-assurance that came from old money and private education. Not that you'd know it from her grey dufflecoat, whose fake-horn toggles she began to toy with as she moved her tale from a stimulating walk in the uplands on the look-out for red kites and squirrels to finding a red-headed boy, roughed-up and naked in a sunlit glade.

She glanced out of the window, catching her breath, then looked back at him. 'He looked so – fresh – it was inconceivable he might be – he might not be breathing.' She shook her head, making her bobbed grey hair swish from side to side. I mean – obviously, he was lying there naked, so I did wonder what I'd stumbled into.' She licked her lips. 'I'm not a squeamish person. I was raised in the country. I walk regularly. But I never, in all my life, expected to find a dead boy.'

With that, the corners of her mouth twitched and turned down. Allan clamped his hand over her wrist and gave a squeeze. 'Thank you, Ms Russell,' he said. 'I think we'll give you a break. Have you given your details to PC Welsh?' The woman nodded, dabbing her nose with a cloth hankie. 'We'll have to get back to you for a full written statement. You won't be going anywhere, will you, over the next few days?'

9

'I'll be here till Saturday. I'm on a retreat till then. Though I have to say, it's not turning out the way I expected.'

'No. Right – well, I'll be sure to get back to you before Saturday. PC Welsh will take you home, now. And please – can I ask you one thing? Difficult, I know, but until someone comes forward to identify him, please don't talk to the media, and be very careful who you do talk to.'

'Of course, Officer – ?'

'MacIntyre. DI Allan MacIntyre. Here's my card. If you think of anything – anyone suspicious you noticed on the way up the track, for example – get in touch with me. I'd appreciate it.' He shook the woman's hand firmly – his grip a degree or two less firm than the one she gave him – and stepped out of the car.

The sun was still shining. He took his phone from his pocket and checked the time. What had happened to lunchtime? No wonder he felt wiped out. His hands shook as he broke off another couple of squares of tablet. He sucked them greedily as he walked back to his car.

Jane Coburn was waiting for him, jingling the car keys, concern in her eyes. 'Another sugar buzz. You okay, Boss?'

Chapter 3

Khalil Buchanan studied his phone then glanced at the sky.

It was dusk and the traffic was busy. Two lanes were backed up in each direction and Khalil dodged between crawling, growling cars and traffic islands as he walked home from the supermarket. The two bags he was carrying over one wrist didn't feel heavy yet, but the milk and potatoes, and tins of beans and soup would weigh him down if he took too long.

The car brake lights glowed red and the streetlights were coming on. They were still mostly sulphurous orange on this main road, though the streets off it had more sky-friendly LED lighting, directing the white light down to the pavement instead of up to pollute the sky. It made it easier to distinguish stars from blinking aeroplane lights. Once, he'd even seen the International Space Station.

Khalil turned right and walked along past the charity furniture outlet shop and the plumbing merchants, then past the discount supermarket. He paused for a minute to look at their display of fireworks. The shop's bright lights flooded the pavement, illuminating flattened chewing gum splodges, cigarette butts and sweetie wrappers. Khalil was more interested in his mobile. A plane passed overhead, and he stared up at it, craning his neck to make out its winking wing-tip lights and get some idea of its livery. Difficult, given the level of light from the shop. Quickly he checked his phone again, thumbing through screens. He didn't see the two figures till they blocked his path.

'What's in the bags, Khal?' They stepped close: breathing

distance. One towered over him, hard bone and muscle.

'Nothing.' Khalil drew himself up. Gripped the bag handles.

The tall one pinned him by the arms and the other frisked his pockets. 'Any fags?'

'I don't smoke.'

'Blow? Eccies? What's in the bags?' He dragged them from his fingers.

'Shopping. Bob's messages.'

'Old Bob, eh? Still being his bumboy?'

'Just doing his messages.'

'Aye? Wee bottle of vodka? No – he wouldn't ask you to get that, would he?' He took the milk out and drank from the bottle, spilling it on the pavement.

'That's Bob's.' Khalil snatched at it, but the tall one held it out of reach while the other grasped Khal by the elbow and spun him. The first raised his hand high and let the milk stream out, a white fountain splashing on the pavement. Two men walked by, heads turned away, shoulders hunched inside heavy jackets.

The tall boy tossed the plastic bottle aside. 'Who you talking to on your phone, Khal?' he said and snatched for it.

'Leave it!'

He shoved Khal's chest. 'Snapchatting your boyfriend?' He wrestled it from his hand and stared at it. 'The fuck's this? Aeroplanes?' Like an alarm, the phone rang and the boy jumped then said, 'Khal's phone. Who's calling?'

'Who is this? Put Khalil on, please. I'm his mother.'

'Hold on, Mrs Buchanan, he's pulling his pants up.' The other boy jeered.

Khalil lunged, tore at the boy's hand to loosen his grip. The phone hit the pavement and flipped.

A red Alfa pulled up at the kerb and Allan MacIntyre stepped out. 'Ah, no you don't,' he said. He clenched his fists in their jackets and shoved the two apart. 'Two against one's never right.' The boy in his left kicked his shin. 'Ouch, ya wee bastard,' Allan said. He twisted his arm up his back and murmured in his ear. 'Want to see my ID?'

'Naw!'

'No?'

'Naw!'

Allan notched up the pressure. The boy squealed. Allan released him, springing him forward. 'On your way, the pair of you!'

'Who d'you think you are!' The boy spat. 'Some fucking Jedi?'

'Yeah, yeah,' Allan said, hands on his hips. 'More trouble, you looking for? On it bring.' The boy hesitated, still squaring up. Allan feigned a boxing move and the boy winced. The DI nodded. 'Think I can't take you?'

The boy switched attention. 'You're fucking dead, you.' He jabbed the air near Khalil with his finger. 'You'll not get away with it.' His pal upended the bags and the two loped off, yelling from a safe distance, 'You're done for. We'll get you.'

'Dead brave, eh?' Allan said, watching the two as they stalked off. 'What a pantomime.' He turned to ask the remaining youngster, 'You okay, son? Did they hurt you?'

'I'm fine.' Khal picked up his phone. He shrugged off the older man and turned away. 'Still there, Mum? Stop worrying. I'll be home in five minutes.' His voice shook. He flashed an ungrateful glance at Allan as he slid his phone into his pocket. By now, Allan was squatting to pick up the shopping. Khalil gathered up the rest. There was nothing he could do about the milk, except maybe ask his mum to give old Bob some of theirs, but she'd some guy coming to visit her. He nodded to the man who'd stepped in, turned his head up towards the sound of a plane high above him before crossing the road and setting off home at a jog.

Chapter 4

It was the kind of street Allan felt comfortable in. Two storey flats and semis surrounded by gardens and thick privet hedges, rose bushes or wooden fences. It was the kind of street he'd grown up in – the kind that were former council houses, most of whose occupants had pounced at the chance once the 'right to buy' had come in. Who wouldn't want to own the home they'd been renting for twenty or thirty years or more, and own it for a knock-down price? The trouble was, most of the originals had moved on once they'd got this toe-hold on the property ladder, and they'd sold to private landlords. The result was houses with broken windows, missing roof tiles and half-stripped cars in the front lawns.

Still, Allan thought as he pulled on the handbrake outside Lorraine's house, this one was well looked after. It didn't surprise him about Lorraine. She might be a single mum, but she'd put the fear of death into anyone who tried to damage or downgrade her neighbourhood. If not the fear of death, the fear of electrocuted testicles.

He'd met Lorraine three weeks previously. A woman of a certain age. No hang-ups. Free and easy. Ach, shite. What was he talking about? He rubbed his eyes and forehead with the fingers of both hands. He shouldn't admit to this, but after Emma Gough, easy-going Lorraine was exactly what he was needing.

Allan checked his teeth in the rear view mirror. His face was getting thinner – or 'leaner' – and that summer tan was holding out, giving him a celebrity look, or so he liked to think. It was a tan that had lasted longer than usual: a fact he put down to the hours he'd spent, walking along in the mid-day sun in Andalucia when he should've learned from the locals and avoided it. He'd had a lot on his mind and it was nothing to do with work. No. He'd split up from Emma. Ah well. Long term relationships. Who needed them?

A couple of six year olds were watching him from the pavement, so he resisted the urge to wink at himself in the mirror, reached behind him for the bottle of wine, and stepped out of the car.

'You two not heading off to bed? It's nearly dark,' he said to the two girls, who stared at him without speaking, one of them running the palm of her hand up the point of her nose. 'Don't stay out too late, now, d'you hear me?' He watched as they scooted off back along the street the way they'd come.

Allan locked the car and put his hand on the gate at Lorraine's path. It was a semi-detached house, and most of the windows were in darkness. Only the two upstairs bedroom windows were lit. Allan had been in one of them, once, and hoped there might be a second time tonight. It had been a tough day, and, yes, he'd been tired, but a shower and change of clothes had freshened him up and you couldn't let the job impact on the rest of your life. Or that was the theory.

He cleared his throat and leaned on the doorbell. It was one of these silent ones that didn't ring at the door, but soon he saw a light through the bubbled glass panel and there she was – the door opened and she bobbed her head round with a big smile. It was a smile you had no choice but to reciprocate. Just the sight of her made him feel buoyant; she was that kind of human being. She pulled back the door to let him in and as he stepped inside he put his free hand round her waist and pulled her up against him, enjoying her softness as he kissed her lips.

'Get in before they all start talking about me,' she said, grinning, and shutting the door behind him.

The house was warm and filled with good smells. Allan followed her into the kitchen, watching the swish of her backside moving inside the dress she was wearing. 'You look nice,' he said,

15

putting the bottle on the table and snuggling in at her. 'Fancy a quick one before dinner?'

'What are you like!' She twisted to face him and pushed her arms up round his neck.

He kissed her deep and long. 'Hmm?' There was a noise behind him and Lorraine abruptly pushed herself away.

'Here's my boy.' She flicked a glance at Allan. 'You didn't get to meet him when he was away at his cousin's. Khalil – this is Allan. Allan – Khalil.'

Allan recognised the boy straight away, but Khalil's eyes were issuing a warning that Allan mustn't mention anything that had gone before. So Allan held out his hand and said, 'How're you doing?'

Khalil just glared. It was like checkmate. Then he slid into his seat, checking his phone.

'Er ... The "no phone" rule?'

Khalil scowled, leaned up and slipped the phone into his pocket.

'Yes, Allan, this is my son – my very polite and well-mannered son. Though you might have to take my word for that.'

Allan kept his hand extended. Lorraine set out big bowls of dahl, raita and chapattis.

'Khalil!'

Eventually he took it and shook it. The handshake Allan gave was firm, and he didn't release it till Khalil said, 'Hiya,' because that meant the teen-beast was tamed and they could move on.

'Sit! Sit!' Lorraine said, so Allan pulled out a chair and examined the spread.

'Smells amazing.'

'Oh, it's nothing special. Just everyday food. I hope you enjoy it! Tuck in. Do you know how to – ? Khalil – show Allan how it's done.'

Allan almost laughed at the expression that came over the boy's face. That was all he needed – having to show some middle-aged white guy how to tear up and eat a chapatti using the correct hand.

Lorraine was jiggling and fidgety. 'Just use your fork if you feel

16

more comfortable! Make yourself at home!'

She was pushing her front out and wiggling from side to side in a way her son clearly found revolting. Allan almost had sympathy. You shouldn't have to watch your mother making a play for a man. To make matters worse, Allan put his left thumb in the stew and sucked it clean and Khalil sank his forehead on to his hand. When Allan met Lorraine's eyes, she started laughing. Then he laughed. Just a single laugh that found a way out despite his best efforts to treat the boy seriously, and before he knew it, he and Lorraine were laughing in one of those bouts that are hard to recover from, all because he was too clumsy to be able to tear off a strip of chapatti one-handed. The lad did not look at all comfortable.

'Sorry, Khalil,' Allan said, straightening his face and trying to compose himself and regain that air of solidarity. But when Lorraine helped him scoop up dahl, he dribbled it down his cleft chin like a four-year old.

Khalil bumped the tablespoon and sprayed dahl on Allan's shirt sleeve. And then his phone beeped and he fished it out of his pocket to look at it and Lorraine said, 'Oh for goodness sake!' and the laughter died. Lorraine jumped up for kitchen towels to clean up the spill and Allan said, 'Don't worry about it,' but her hands were shaking.

'Ahmed's coming over,' Khalil said.

'You mean – is it alright if Ahmed comes over?'

Khalil shrugged.

'Well, okay.' Lorraine drilled her forefinger on the table. 'But not till we've finished dinner.'

Allan saw the simple pleasure and innocence in the boy's rich brown eyes when he answered, 'He's only going to stay for a couple of hours while his dad's at the mosque for a meeting.'

The rest of the meal was more relaxed. Allan asked Khalil a few questions about school, and sport, and he told the boy a few facts from his own teenage years in Glasgow, cherry picking the funny things, like flour bombing passers-by from the fourth floor of the high flats, or the time his pal challenged him to throw his laced-up trainers round the wires dangling between streetlights, because he'd heard that was supposed to attract drug dealers. They'd waited, half hidden in the bushes, but no dodgy-looking guys in big motors came, and then they couldn't figure out how to get the trainers down, so he had to tell his mother someone mugged him for them, though they only cost a fiver from Primark. Half an hour later, the doorbell rang and Khalil excused himself quite politely, obviously pleased to be released from the third wheel role he was serving with his own mother.

'Thanks, Allan. He enjoyed that.'

'Ach, he's alright. Relieved to get away from us.' Allan grinned, and toyed with his napkin. 'And I don't blame him. Ahmed's the cavalry.'

Lorraine smiled. 'Yeah, I embarrass him. Still, Ahmed's a good lad. Good company – safe company. They're not all like that.'

Allan didn't mention the incident outside the off-licence, just nodded in agreement. 'It can't be that easy to be in his situation.'

'What, mixed heritage? He's well used to that.'

There was something a bit clipped about the way she said it. 'Okay. Good.'

Lorraine lightly squeezed Allan's arm with her hand. 'Sorry, I didn't mean that to sound so snippy.'

'No, that's okay,' he said. 'I've not got any kids.' He winked. 'Not that anyone's told me. So anyone that can raise any fifteen year old boy on their own is an Amazonian as far as I'm concerned.'

A little voice in Allan's head goaded him for the way he was sucking up to her. Flattery. If food was the way to a man's heart then he was clearly hoping the way to hers was by buttering her up about her spotty adolescent.

Lorraine sipped her wine. 'Well, it can be difficult sometimes. I think he gets issues at school. And to do with his dad. But I just try to support him.'

Allan nodded. The last thing he wanted was to get serious or talk about some previous man in her life, so he pushed his plate forward on the table and said, 'That was delicious.' He'd slipped off his suit jacket. Now, he folded up his white shirt cuffs, exposing his tanned forearms. He leaned them on the table and watched Lorraine clear the plates away.

'I'm glad you liked it,' she said. 'Just something simple, but we think it's tasty.'

As he watched her he could hear the boys in the living room. It sounded as if they were playing on a games console. Lorraine came closer and he pulled her onto his knee. 'They sound busy,' he said. He sought her soft mouth and she moved hungrily on him. 'Can we take this upstairs?' he breathed.

Her pupils were dark and her eyes were gleaming when she glanced up from him towards the living room door. 'What, really?'

'They wouldn't hear a bomb going off under them.'

'I don't know,' she said. 'Let me think about it.'

'Go on. What is there to think about?'

'Mmm.' She returned his grin. 'Okay, but we'll have to be quick.'

Chapter 5

Thompson crushed the can and tossed it out the open window into the bushes. He shouldn't; he was the first to condemn it when he saw the embankment decked with plastic and aluminium detritus in the daylight, but this whole situation irritated the shit out of him. The lights he was stopped at were fixed on red. It was dark; it was well past rush hour, and there was nothing coming from any of the other roads at the junction. He was the only one waiting. He revved the accelerator, edging the vehicle forward as if that was going to make the lights change any faster. It didn't. He braked hard with both feet on the pedals. Why didn't they vary the timing depending on the number of cars at the junction? They could keep count with all the cameras they had everywhere. Modern fucking Big Brother's Watching You society. Another surge of fury rose in his chest. Couldn't design their way out of a paper bag, don't get him started on a plastic one.

He pinched his phone out of his inside pocket, squinting up at the lampposts to check no cameras had sight of him now. Looked at the screen. No new messages. He thumped the heel of his hand off the rim of the steering wheel. Still no messages! Here was the main reason he was angry. Angry? No. He was livid. That ingrate had total, selfish disregard for anything but acting out his own sordid fetishes. And here Thompson was, having to cover up for him.

Well, he'd done it. This once. But it better not have screwed up his own plans.

At last, the lights changed and he took a right, heading away from the city, feeling the tightness in his chest ease as he moved the vehicle forward.

His plans weren't ready yet, but they soon would be. Just a little more patience. Patience, and practice. He'd use the pervert to his own advantage.

On the left-hand side of the street was the huge building of the new academy. A palace of glass. He slowed down and lowered his head so he could examine the building through the passenger window. All those lights left burning overnight. It defied logic that they were vaunted for their energy efficiency. Rage came over him again.

He pulled over to the pavement, the better to check the entrance layout. It was too new – and too important – for him to be able to rely on Street View. He'd need to find a way in in daylight. Find a way to check it out, without anyone seeing him. He breathed out heavily. He couldn't let that bitch humiliate him anymore. It was one thing when he was a kid. But starting on him again now? That wasn't on. Not now he *was* somebody. He caught sight of his hair in the rear-view mirror. That would have to change, too. It was too long, too thick, too obvious. His appearance could easily draw attention to him, so he'd have to be careful.

From a distance, on the other side of the school building, across the playground, came the sound of fireworks. They'd been in the shops for weeks. Some youngsters had already got a hold of them, and he watched the cascade of red and white flashes ignite and burn to ash in their descent through the dry air.

Fireworks. They didn't know what was coming to them. He took out his phone again and sent another text.

He'd keep himself out of the limelight for now. Everything was in hand, or soon would be. He'd get his own back on Fanny W.

Still no reply from that self-centred piece of shit. But one good turn deserved another. Thompson would insist he cover up for him. Whether he wanted to or not.

Chapter 6

'Don't fall asleep!'

Allan opened his eyes, Lorraine's face close to his.

'How long was I out?'

'Not long. The boys are still downstairs.'

She was smiling. He grinned back. 'Do you think they heard us?'

'I don't know. Did we make any noise?'

He squeezed her again and kissed her nose. 'You certainly did.'

She kissed his eyelids. 'Then I must have enjoyed it.'

'Yep. We'll need to do it again some time.'

'Aye,' she said. 'But not now. Now it's a cup of tea and away home with you.' She sat up on him, taking the duvet with her. 'Time for me to get back into mother-mode.' Her skin was soft pink; the weight of her breasts made them droop; her nipples were raised and dark. He reached for her, but she pushed his hand away. 'No, that's it. Time to get up.'

'Treat them mean, keep 'em keen?' he said, watching her get up and dressed.

She grinned, pulling down her dress at the back.

She went downstairs first, and he went into the bathroom. As he washed, he looked at himself in the mirror. God, she'd taken it out of him. An enormous yawn overtook him and he rubbed the corners of his eyes. It must be just after nine, but it had been a long day. When he went downstairs, Lorraine was in the kitchen, setting out mugs for tea against the background cacophony of the kettle. The living room door was still closed and the same sounds were coming

22

through it, so he guessed they hadn't been missed, which made him happy. It meant they could do it again sometime then he'd get back early to sleep in his own bed. He'd had enough of creeping out of warm beds in the middle of the night.

'Thanks for tonight,' he said, putting his arms round her from behind again.

She threw a warm smile over her shoulder and stirred the cups. 'My pleasure. And I mean that! Now, will you take these into the boys for me? Do a bit of bonding?'

He opened the door with his elbow and edged in sideways, picking up an instant change in the atmosphere. The games console was connecting with the big flat screen TV on the wall, but it looked like it was playing a demo. The two boys were sitting on the couch, engrossed in one phone, though it was quickly disappeared on to the floor at the side of the couch.

'Hot chocolate, lads?'

'Cheers,' Ahmed said.

Lorraine came in and laid a big plate of doughnuts and a bowl of crisps on the coffee table beside the cups. She introduced Allan to Ahmed, and the boy shook his hand immediately when offered. The four chatted for an innocent quarter of an hour or so till Ahmed received a call to say his dad was outside. Allan couldn't resist. While Khalil and Lorraine saw Ahmed to the door, where he put his shoes on and bade them goodbye, Allan lifted Khalil's phone from where it had been tucked in under the sofa. One eye on the door into the hallway, he pressed the on button. It asked for a pass-code. Someone had told him long ago that most people's default number was 1234. He punched it in, but it didn't work, so he tried the sequence in reverse. Still no joy. Then he remembered seeing the boy draw a squiggle over the numbers. He looked around, saw a game logo on the TV screen and tried that. It got him in on the second attempt.

There, on the screen, was a map, and over it were lots of little images of aeroplanes. Each edged slightly forward while he watched; each had a number on it. When he tapped one, the full details came up – where it was heading, what kind of plane it was, what cargo it was carrying. As he read, a text announced itself on the top portion of the screen, accompanied by a notification sound. There was no time to read it.

'What are you doing?' Khalil's voice was accusing. 'That's my phone. You've no right to look at it.'

Lorraine was behind him in the doorway. Her brows were down, disapproving. What right did he have to snoop on a fifteen year old's phone? Was he a perv? It was all there in her eyes. Khalil he was less worried about.

'Sorry – I thought it might have been Ahmed's. Here – no problem.' He handed it over. The boy left the room a streak of anger.

'That was a definite no-no,' Lorraine said.

Allan held his hands up. 'Mea culpa. I won't do it again, promise.'

She wasn't appeased. 'He loves that phone. His dad gave him it.'

'Yeah?' Allan held her eyes. Then made out he was conceding. 'Fair enough. I shouldn't be such a nosy bastard.' She was still frowning. Should he mention the boy found dead? It would be in the papers soon enough. 'It's just this case that's come in. A boy killed. Not much younger than him. Sex attack, too, by the looks of it.'

Her mouth opened. 'A boy? Here?'

'Sorry – I probably shouldn't have mentioned it.' He pulled a face he hoped would ease the atmosphere. It did. She came over to him and put her arms through his to cuddle him. He pecked her cheek. 'Anyway, don't worry about it. And tell Khalil in the morning I'm sorry.' He kissed her hair. Yawned again, despite the tea. 'I think it's time I went home.'

Outside, he waved to her from the gate, waited till she closed the front door and then he got into his car, knackered. Shagged out. Was it just that? He put the key in the ignition, seeing, as he did so, Khalil at the window of his bedroom, the lights out, his mobile in his hand, and his eyes on the sky.

'Strange kid,' Allan said to himself as he turned the key.

As he pulled away from the kerb, he thought of that other strange kid he'd seen today, naked on a mountain. Poor bastard. Somebody would be frantic, looking for him. A block or two further on, Allan pulled over and took out his phone to see if any of the team had messaged him to tell him the boy's parents had reported him missing. But there was nothing. Allan tucked the phone back inside his jacket pocket and pulled out again, heading for home.

It had been a long day. After a two-hour sleep, he woke up, lay on his back and thought through everything that had happened. He lived again the hard climb on the makeshift rocky path up the hillside, saw the police tape fluttering and that young boy lying there, pink and innocent, with the bones round his eye sockets crushed. A boy not much younger than Khal and Ahmed. Somebody, somewhere, knew something about it.

Chapter 7

Ross looked as if he'd been at work since before daybreak. There were two paper coffee cups on his desk which were empty apart from milky scum, and his electric shaver case lay open. Ross himself, clean-shaven, was engrossed in his computer. All perfectly normal, then, Allan thought as he saw him through the glass wall that separated the corridor from the open plan office.

'Morning, Ross. *Semper* vigilant, I see.'

Ross stirred from his position of total concentration, tipped one of the cups to see if there was anything left in it, sat it down again and stretched his arms up above his head. 'Morning, Boss. *Semper vigilo*, as always.'

Allan slipped his jacket over his chair and sat down. The chair was new, like the building, and still had cellophane covering the seat. 'Any news from last night?'

'Nope. About the boy? Nothing. About the fire? Couple of things. Want to know now?'

Allan checked his watch. 'Let me grab a coffee. The others should be in any minute. Meeting in fifteen?'

As Allan drank his coffee, he skimmed the morning's headlines. Nothing had got out so far about the boy's body, but the media would soon be on it and he was surprised the departmental media man hadn't door-stopped him on his way in. He made a mental note to take pre-emptive action and go and see him after the morning briefing.

In the incident room, Jane Coburn was wiping down the white board. 'Morning, Sir,' she said.

26

'Jane.' The DS was tiny, and her hips and shoulders moved from side to side in opposite directions as she reached up to wipe the board. As Allan perched on one of the high stools and watched her, he scolded himself for not paying more attention in science lessons at school. 'What is that thing about every action having an equal and opposite reaction?' he asked her.

She turned to see him, her brown trouser suit jacket and white shirt returning to their position now she was no longer reaching up. Her eyes narrowed. 'You having a go at me already this morning?'

Allan laughed. 'Never. How're you doing, anyway?'

'Good. Good!' she said and sat down to wait for the others. 'You?'

'Never better.'

'Oh. Because I thought maybe the gym was getting too much for you, given that I never see you there despite all your promises, and the way you were gasping up that hill yesterday.'

'Aye, well. There's a time and place for everything.'

Ross and Sam joined them, and after a squabble over biscuits, they were ready to start.

'So.' Allan moved to the front of the room, to stand beside the white board. 'Two incidents. Totally separate. One minor, one major. Let's get the first one out of the way so we can concentrate on the important one.' He looked at Ross. 'News on the bin fire at the distribution centre?'

Ross flicked through papers and passed one to Allan, which he scanned as Ross read to the others. 'Yesterday morning's fire in a rubbish container at Inchmarsh Industrial Estate. Phoned in by Cathy somebody or other, the office manager.' He glanced up. 'I didn't catch her name. She was in a bit of a palaver with anxiety.' He ran his finger down the printed report. 'Sam and I went for a look and had a word.'

'And you still didn't get her name?' Allan interrupted.

'I told you – she was jittery. Talked nineteen to the dozen and half of it was unintelligible.' He flicked his eyes to Sam for corroboration. 'Anyway, she'd turned up for work at quarter to eight in the morning and parked her car at the other side of the warehouse, but it was only when she opened her office window that she smelled smoke, went out to investigate and found smoke billowing out the bin. It was too hot to handle, and she'd come out without bringing a fire extinguisher, and she was frightened it was going to spread to the building or one of the cars –'

'– even though she couldn't see any flames?' Jane said.

Ross nodded. 'Even though she couldn't see any flames. So she phoned in and it was virtually out by the time anybody got there.'

'CCTV footage?' Allan said.

'Not checked yet, Sir,' Ross said.

'Okay. Thoughts, team?'

Sam said, 'We reckon it's probably kids. This Cathy woman said they'd never had any trouble before and she's worked there ten years, since the company was down in the town centre.'

'Okay. So, Ross – you check out CCTV and Sam can speak to Forensics. You did call them?'

Ross blushed. 'Well – no, because we thought it would be kids.' He lowered his brows, seeing his boss's frown. 'But we got them to wheel the bin out of the way so no-one else would put anything in it.'

'Right – that's something. Sam – get someone from Forensics to bring it in for a look. Okay. Thanks, guys. Now – this other case. Jane, fill us in.'

Jane twisted in her seat to face the others. She licked her finger and separated the pages she'd printed, passing one to Allan. 'So.' She looked round her colleagues, sensitive to the air of expectation, uncomfortable at feeling slightly excited. She hadn't investigated many murders. None of them had. She took a breath to compose herself. 'We'd a call from a woman attending a retreat at Abriachan. She was walking in the woods and discovered the body of a boy, aged approximately 12 to 14, naked, recently deceased, bruised and bleeding, with no obvious puncture wounds, but blood on his face, blunt force trauma to his face and possibly a broken neck.' She glanced at Allan. 'Still waiting for confirmation of cause of death.' Her eyes flicked over to Sam, who sat with his hand over his mouth. Ross was tapping his lips with his pen. 'Looks like a local lad – white, ginger hair, well enough nourished as far as we could tell – but no one's claimed him yet.'

'Nothing to identify him?' Ross said.

Jane shrugged. 'Nothing. Well, apart from an old scar on his belly. He was completely naked. He was either dumped there, naked, or the killer made damn sure to take every stitch away with him.'

'No phone or anything?'

'Nope. So we're waiting for the phone call. Although, obviously, the pathologist might be able to identify him. Sometime.'

Allan nodded. 'Surprising there's not been a call already. Boy that age.' He looked round the team. 'Might be a looked-after kid. But somebody'll be missing him sooner or later.'

'D'you want me to check with the schools, Boss?'

Allan nodded his head from side to side, weighing it up. 'Check looked-after children's homes first. Sound them out – see if anyone's been missing overnight.'

The meeting broke up and Jane had just started pulling up social work contact details when the office phone rang. She answered, listened for a while before telling the caller to show someone into an interview room and hung up. She breathed out noisily through her nose then picked up her notebook and phone and went over to see Allan. 'Front desk phoned, Sir. There's a Mrs Jasmine Brooks here to report her son's missing.'

Interview Room 2 was down a flight of stairs and along at the end of the corridor. Allan felt he was walking to an execution. It was the quieter of the new headquarters' interview rooms, and the one they used for more intense enquiries. So far, it had only been used a few times, but the stairway down to it, and the corridor, echoed the tick-tock of their footsteps, and although the room itself was brightly painted with lemon-coloured walls and mock-terracotta floor tiles, it had an atmosphere that unnerved even seasoned officers. It might have been the furniture.

'I hate this place,' Allan said and scowled to Jane as they looked in the viewing mirror from the control room next to it. Jasmine Brooks was sitting in one chair at the metal table, her hands clasped in her lap, and her chin pulled in tight to her chest. She'd a paper hankie clutched in her hand. 'We should've ditched that furniture. We've imported all the angst it's soaked up over the years at the old office and brought it here.'

Jane pulled a face. 'You're needing a holiday, Sir.'

He sniffed. 'You might be right, but it won't be today. Let's get this over with.'

He pushed open the door and extended his hand to Mrs Brooks. 'Good Morning. I'm DI Allan MacIntyre, and this is DS Jane Coburn. Thanks for coming in.' He and Jane crossed to the other side of the table and sat down. The woman across from him was petite and compact, with hardly any meat on her bones. Her hair was more blonde than red, but she had the same translucent skin Allan had last seen on the hillside in dappled sunlight. She was a bit younger than him. Early thirties. 'I understand you've come about your son?'

Her pale blue eyes glued themselves to his and she licked her lips. 'My son Jamie. He didn't come home last night. He isn't answering his phone and none of his friends know where he is. The man at the desk said to tell you what he looked like. What he was wearing. I've brought in a photo. Most of my photos are on my phone, but this is his school one.' She lifted her bag from the floor and as she unzipped it and picked out a white envelope, Allan and Jane met each other's eyes and looked back to the young mother. Her trembling fingers pulled out the glossy picture of a smiling ginger-haired boy. 'This is Jamie.'

Allan reached for the photo and studied it briefly. It was just a head shot. This boy's face was clear-skinned and freckled. The boy they'd found on the side of the hill had a bloodied face, bashed out of shape.

'Mrs Brooks,' Allan said. He put the photo on the table in front of him. When he leaned forward, he felt the chair rock under him. It was the one that had lost the rubber cup from the bottom of one of its tube-metal legs. He swallowed. 'Can I ask you when you last saw Jamie?'

Mrs Brooks wiped her nose. 'The day before yesterday.'

'Two days ago?' Jane looked at Allan. 'You left it two days before reporting it?'

Mrs Brooks' pale skin flushed. 'It's complicated.' Her eyebrows were barely discernible, but pulled down, they hinted at fear. Her lips were thin, pressed together. 'He should've come straight home from school but he didn't. But sometimes he does that – goes to a friend. Or to his dad's.'

'But you've checked there? And he's not there?' Allan said, conscious again of the chair's bare metal leg clicking against the terracotta floor tiles as he moved closer to ask his question, then back. He pulled the chair forward, scraping the metal leg across the tiles.

The woman shook her head. 'His dad hasn't seen him.'

'And his friends?'

She shook her head again. 'None of them. Unless they're in on it. That he's hiding.'

'Does he often hide?' Jane asked.

'What?' Mrs Brooks seemed surprised that the attention had turned to Jane. 'No – he doesn't. But he's thirteen.'

'Meaning...?'

'Meaning it's a difficult age. That he's beginning to answer back. Not tell me where he's going or who he's going out with.'

'Absolutely,' Allan said, nodding slightly to let the woman know he had this. 'Mrs Brooks, so we can build a picture, can you tell me – does Jamie have any identifying marks?'

She frowned. 'What do you mean?'

'Well, any scarring, or...'

'He had his appendix out a couple of years ago.' She looked from

one to the other. 'It was an emergency, so it was a big scar. Biggish.'
She gestured to the place on her body.

Chapter 8

The scar clinched it. Allan cleared his throat and rested both elbows on the table between himself and the boy's mother.

'Mrs Brooks – Jasmine,' he said, and then he pulled his hands in close to him after all. 'Did you come here by yourself today? Is there someone waiting for you in the foyer, or in the car?'

She frowned, gripping her handbag. 'Why do you want to know?'

Jane leaned forward. 'Or is there someone we can contact for you? Someone close?'

'My mum lives with us, but she's not here.' Her head spun to Allan. 'What is it? What's going on?'

Allan steadied his voice. 'I'll have to ask you to prepare yourself for bad news.' He waited a moment. 'Yesterday morning, we found the body of a young boy in Abriachan Wood.'

She jolted upright. 'The body?' She touched her hair. 'No, but that won't be my boy.'

Allan and Jane waited.

She rubbed her mouth then gripped her bag again. 'In Abriachan Wood?'

'Yes.'

'Yesterday morning? But Jamie would be at school.'

'This boy matches Jamie's description. We haven't had confirmation of his identity yet, but he matches Jamie's age and hair colouring.'

She shook her head. 'No.' She drew in a big gasp of air. 'No. No, no – he'll be messing about with a friend. Playing a game.' She

33

looked from one to the other. 'You know what they're like.' Her voice inched up in pitch. 'Not my boy.'

Allan picked up the boy's photo and studied it then met her eyes. 'This boy has a scar on his abdomen.'

That was when she crumpled. The air came out on a thin wail that began almost inaudibly but grew in intensity, her mouth remaining open, her body beginning to rock forward and back, forward and back, unswallowed saliva already beginning to drizzle from her bottom lip.

'Mrs Brooks!' Jane said.

Allan had to get out of the room. His heart was racing and the breath had been sucked out of him. Even his hands were shaking. He pushed his chair back from the table, cursing the metal leg for scraping along the floor tiles again. 'DS Coburn will look after you. She'll make sure we've got your details and let you know where we proceed from here. Jane?'

Jane was already out of her chair and had wrapped her arms round the mother's shoulders. She was cooing comfort. She nodded to Allan.

Shit, he couldn't deal with this. He closed the door to Interview Room 2 behind him and paced off down the corridor. Where was he going? Why couldn't he cope with this? He pushed the door into the toilets and hung over the sink, splashing water over his face. What the hell was wrong with him? He dried his face and hands and coldly appraised his reflection in the mirror. He looked fit enough. He still had that healthy tan. So what the fuck was wrong with him? He never used to be like this. Maybe he should just stop skipping breakfast.

He went down to the cafeteria, but it was rowdy and he couldn't face socialising, so he bought crisps and an apple and took them back to the office to eat. There were two things he needed to do. Apart from getting a grip of himself. He needed to see the pathologist, and he needed to see the media man. He crunched into the apple. Shit. What a mess he'd left Jane to deal with. But Jane knew her stuff. She'd arrange for the mum to be looked after. They could go to interview her properly once the mum had a chance to take it all in. They'd need to run identification. Jane could do that. Allan just needed to speak to Helena Finlayson about cause of death. And speak to the media man. Once he'd got this food in him. He twisted open the water bottle and drank deeply from it.

You know what they're like, the woman had said. The power games they play. Kids. To explain why she hadn't questioned when he hadn't come home. It reminded him of Khalil.

Allan fished his phone out of his jacket pocket and thumbed through the screens. 'Hi,' he said.

'Hey, how are you?'

Lorraine's voice sounded relaxed. He felt his weariness melting. 'Good,' he said.

'So, why are you phoning?'

He could hear machinery in the background. She would be working. 'Just wanted to hear your voice.'

'On a school day?'

He swivelled in his chair. 'I was just thinking about last night.'

'Uh-huh. And this is what cops do when they're on duty?'

What the fuck was wrong with him? 'Nah, it's just – that boy I told you about.' His eyes scanned the car park outside, and the landscaped gardens, and, beyond that, the rounded sandstone walls of the castle on its hill visible in the distance against the blue sky, but he wasn't really seeing them. He couldn't tell her about Jasmine Brooks and her dead son. Shouldn't tell her. What could he tell her? 'Just, it's hard.'

She chortled.

Through the glass, he saw Jane walk along the corridor. He raised an eyebrow to acknowledge her. He'd need to ask her how she'd got on with Mrs Brooks. To Lorraine, he said, 'Are you free tonight? Can I come round about seven?'

Arrangements made, he hung up and turned to Jane. 'Everything okay?'

'Yeah – I see why you needed to hot foot it away. And here I was, concerned you were taking it badly.'

'I needed the loo. Honest.'

She pulled over a chair and sat across the desk from him. 'Are you okay? You're a bit shaky these days.'

'Me? I'm fine.'

'Okay.' She sized him up then let it go. 'So, who's the new woman?'

He was just about to slip the phone inside his pocket, but he switched it on again, looked up Instagram and showed her a couple of photos of Lorraine, strawberry blonde, curvy and vivacious.

'Very nice.'

He winked and slipped the phone away. 'You jealous?'

'You bet. The best looking ones are all straight.'

'You need to get out more – out of the burgh. Meet some new faces.'

'Then again, I could just wait. You're bound to turn her.' Jane's eyes went to the car park, where Mrs Brooks was in the back seat of a police car, being driven away. 'This is shite, isn't it? I hate these bastarding criminals.' She met her boss's eyes; shared an acknowledgement; sighed. 'Anyway, I asked PC Welsh to see her home. Told her we'd be in touch very soon for information – and about identification.'

'Right.' Allan straightened up the sheet of paper she'd given him at the morning briefing. 'Check out family, friends and so on. I'll need to speak to Media and Helena now.'

~~~

Jason Bonar knew his stuff. He'd had fifteen years in the police force in the far south and was well versed in knowing what to leak, when to leak it, and how to manage media expectations. He was in a meeting when Allan knocked on his door, but he knew the DI wouldn't have come up in person to interest him in the departmental sweepstake, so he quickly cleared the junior staff from his office and invited Allan inside. The room was warm with body heat and smelled of coffee and mints. Jason was in rolled-up shirt sleeves, his heavy arms covered with dark body hair. His palm was moist when Allan shook it. He pointed to one of the chairs vacated by the team. 'Have a seat. Coffee?'

Allan shook his head and quickly told him what they knew. It wasn't much.

Jason whistled out a long breath. 'So, a thirteen year old boy, dead in the woods. Predator at large in the community. That'll go down well with the tabloids.'

'Won't it?' Allan said. 'Lock up your daughters. Or your sons, in this case.' He passed over Jamie's photo and an information sheet with the boy's full name and address.

'We'll go with the standard thing. More details when we know them. Police officers at schools and so on. You'll do a press conference? With the parents?'

'Heading out there as soon as I've spoken to Helena Finlayson. I'll be in touch.'

On his way back to his office, he phoned Finlayson.

'Hi. Any news for me?'

He heard the rustle of paper. 'Unfortunately, not really. Just preliminaries. It'll be later today before I can do a full PM.'

'Too bad. I'm seeing the mother again later.'

'Well, he was definitely murdered. Probably within twenty-four hours of when he was found.'

'So that makes it Monday daytime, when he should've been at school?'

'I'd say between 12.00 and 6.00pm. Can't be any more specific for now. I haven't even looked at his stomach contents yet.'

'I might come round with one of my new boys and observe, if you're okay with that.'

'New boy?'

'Yeah – an experienced officer, but new to us and never seen a PM before.'

'Okay, bring him round. Let's say three o'clock?'

He paused at the door into the office. 'Sorry, Helena. I'm going to push it. Any word on cause?'

She clicked her tongue. 'Give me a chance! We're looking at strangulation, but a heavy beating, too.' She paused. 'And anal rape.'

Chapter 9

Allan rang off and checked in with Sam to warn him about the afternoon's post mortem. Then he and Jane headed off for an early lunch before going to see Jasmine Brooks. While they ate, they discussed tactics, or at least, their aims for the visit. The woman would be a mess, and they had one chance to do things right.

The Brooks family lived in a modest terraced house in one of the established housing estates in the city. Its tiny front garden was laid down to grass, but it had a park bench under the window, with coloured metal butterflies fixed to the wall above. Two hanging baskets swung in the slight wind off the hills, their flowers wilted and thinned out. There was only one window downstairs, and its blinds were closed.

Allan and Jane stood outside the porch and rang the doorbell. After a few minutes, they heard someone open an inside door and saw movement through the frosted glass. There was the sound of a key turning in the lock and the door opened with a wet sound, as if this front door wasn't usually used and the sun glued it shut. A woman in her late fifties or early sixties showed no surprise to see them, and didn't look at their ID when they automatically offered it.

'Come in,' she said. 'Jasmine's having a lie down. I'll give her a shout.'

They followed her inside. The porch gave directly into the living room, and there was a flight of stairs up the opposite wall.

'Have a seat,' the woman said. Her hands flew about the edges of her sleeves while she talked. 'I'm Jasmine's mum, by the way. Jamie's gran.' She turned as if to shake hands, but didn't. Instead, she fished an already saturated paper hankie from the sleeve of her jumper and dabbed her nose with it, then her eyes. She screened her eyes with one hand, took a breath to steady herself and fixed a look at them with her eyes gleaming. 'That lad was a good lad. Never a bit of bother. You'll need to get who did it. We're devastated. Devastated.' She shook her head. 'But you sit down and I'll fetch Jasmine.'

For all that she was slim, she leaned heavily on the banister as she climbed the stairs, leaving Allan and Jane where they were standing. They looked around the room. There were photos of the ginger-haired boy in an athletics strip, holding a small trophy in his hand and with a wide smile on his face. There were his school photos, ranked through the years from primary to early secondary. The only other photos in the room were of Jamie with his mother and grandmother.

'An only child,' Jane said.

'Why does that always make it worse?'

They heard voices above their heads then the floorboards creaking, and soon two sets of footsteps came down the stairs.

'Mrs Brooks, thanks for seeing us again so quickly,' Allan said, approaching the younger woman with his hand out again. Her hand was cool and feeble in his. 'Do you feel well enough to answer some questions? We'd like to be able to build an in-depth picture of the circumstances around Jamie, leading up to what happened yesterday.'

Jasmine nodded. Like her son, her skin was translucent, but she went beyond that, appearing flimsy and insubstantial. She slipped onto the couch.

'I'll go and get the kettle on,' her mother said, and disappeared through the door under the stairs. Soon they heard the kettle and clinking of mugs.

'What do you want to know?' Jasmine said.

'Well, maybe you could tell us what kind of boy Jamie was – let us get an idea about him.' Allan indicated the photos. 'I can see he

40

was keen on sport.'

The mother's eyes moved listlessly over the frames. 'He was.' She reached for a clean tissue from the box. 'He liked running.'

'Was he a popular lad?' Jane asked. 'Did he have lots of friends?'

Jasmine shook her head. 'No, he was quite quiet.' She met Jane's eyes. 'He had a few close friends who'd moved up with him from primary school. Boys that had got to know him. But they all kept themselves to themselves. They looked after him when he was bullied.'

'Was he bullied recently?' Allan asked.

'Erm... Well, I had to go to the school a few weeks ago to see his guidance teacher because his results were down and he was – I thought he was becoming withdrawn, as if he might be getting bullied again. He was bullied in first year. Because he was ginger. If it wasn't that, it would've been something else. They jockeyed for position because they were all new to the school. That's what the teacher said. But she said she didn't think he was being bullied this time round. Just losing interest in his school work for some reason. I don't know why – he always liked science, but his results had plummeted. I was worried.'

Jamie's gran came through with a tray and set it down on the small table in front of them. 'Too interested in computers and gaming, like the rest of them.'

Jane smiled a half-smile to the older woman.

They had tea and took down some details of who Jamie's friends were, and what clubs he'd belonged to. Then Allan said, 'You mentioned something about his father. Did he have regular contact with his father?'

Jasmine crimped her mouth and looked over at her mother. 'His dad and I separated years ago. About five years ago. Just because we really weren't getting along.' She reached up and rubbed at her forehead then dropped her hands back into her lap. 'Well, actually, that's a lie. He had a girlfriend and I told him to get lost. So he did. There were other things, too. We lost contact with him for a while.'

41

'Left them without a bean,' her mother interrupted.

'Mum,' Jasmine said, hushing her mother with a look. 'No, after about six months he got back in touch with us, and we sorted out maintenance, and access, and since then everything's been fine. Jamie loves him.' An anguished expression crossed her face. 'Loved him. And he loved Jamie. I'm in no doubt about that. He wouldn't touch him.'

'I'll say that about him,' the gran said. 'Robert wouldn't hurt a fly, but if he was going to harm anyone it would be me.'

'Okay, thanks for that. We'll need to get his details. Have you informed him?'

Jasmine nodded. 'I phoned him from the police station. We're going to meet up.'

'But, Mrs Brooks, if I can just ask you,' Jane said. 'At the station, you mentioned that you didn't worry straight away about Jamie because you thought he would be at his dad's house. Did you phone his dad to find out?'

She was nursing her mug. She sipped from it then jolted it back down on the table, overcome by another wave of grief. She covered her eyes with her hand and they could hear her struggle against the sobs.

'Take your time.'

Jane passed her a hankie. She wiped her eyes and nose with it then looked at it as if she'd lost all sense of what she was supposed to do now. Eventually, she crushed it in her palm. 'I phoned all his friends but he wasn't there, so I left it another while then phoned his dad, but he didn't answer. He works shifts and I thought he must be at work. I thought – if Jamie was mad at me and he'd gone to his dad's, like, as a way of getting back at me...' She struggled to keep from sobbing. 'If he was trying to get back at me he could be at his dad's but just let the phone ring and ring to worry me.' She blinked again. 'I'm sorry.' She regained control. 'We'd had a falling out. Jamie and me. Nothing major. It was just about him staying up into the night playing games online and not sleeping. I think that's why he wasn't concentrating well at school.' Her voice went up an octave. 'I can't believe the last thing we did was argue.'

She leaned over to her mother, who wrapped her in her arms. Allan watched as Jane noted down details of the conversation. Surreptitiously, he checked his watch. Then he said, 'Mrs Brooks, have you any idea of anyone who would want to hurt Jamie? Or can you think of any possible reason for him to be singled out? Think about the last few weeks. You've said he wasn't sleeping, and that he wasn't focused at school. That there might be bullying. Could there possibly be anything more sinister? Any other unusual behaviour, or new friends – older friends, maybe – that you picked up on?'

She listened and considered what he said but shook her head. 'Just what I said about school.'

Allan nodded. 'Okay. If anything occurs to you – or if you think of anything when you see his dad – please get in touch with me. I will, of course, have to see him, too.' He gave her his card. Then he told her Forensics would appreciate access to the house, with a particular interest in looking at Jamie's bedroom. He asked if he and Jane could have a look now.

'Of course,' she said, and led them upstairs.

It was a typical boy's bedroom, with a modest flat screen TV on the wall and a games console in front of it. The bed had a duvet cover in the colours of the local football team, which his mother hastily tried to tidy up until Allan asked her to leave everything as it was until Forensics had been there. She wrapped her arms round her waist instead. Allan picked up the boy's schoolbag and browsed through it. 'Did he not usually take his bag to school?'

'Yeah, that's strange,' she said. 'He always took it. Usually.'

Allan took out a jotter. English. He frowned and put it back in the bag.

'Look, Sir.' Jane lifted a pillow by a corner, revealing what looked like a top of the range phone under it.

'Where did that come from?' Jasmine reached for it, but Jane stopped her, conscious of forensics. Jasmine glanced towards the bedroom door. 'Did you get him that, Mum?'

'Not me!' Gran shook her head.

'Maybe it was from his dad?' Jane suggested.

'I doubt it. He's got another two kids under five.' Jasmine looked up into Allan's face. 'That looks well out of our price range. As far as I'm concerned, the only phone Jamie's got is my old pay-as-you-go model. I was saving up to get him a new one for Christmas.'

Gran started to say something, but then she changed her mind.

'What?' her daughter asked her.

'No – it's nothing.' She shook her head. 'Nothing.'

'I think we'll bag this and take it over to Forensics straight away. Jane'll give you a receipt for it.'

They spent another few minutes looking over Jamie's things. When his mother excused herself and went to the toilet, Allan asked the older woman if there was something she'd wanted to tell them. 'It doesn't matter how minor it is. Best to get it out there, just in case.'

She fingered her lips. 'It's just when I saw that phone under his pillow,' she said. Her eyes went to the door to check her daughter couldn't hear. 'I was bringing his clean clothes up after I'd ironed them, and the door wasn't shut properly, so I heard him speaking to someone.' A strange expression came over her face. 'Okay, I'm a nosy besom, and I stood and listened for a minute. I thought maybe it was a wee girl friend or something. You know.' She shook her head at Jane, who gave a half smile of encouragement. 'Anyway, it didn't sound like he was talking to a girl. It sounded as if he was talking to an adult.'

'Can you remember anything he said?' Allan asked.

Her eyes scoured the walls. 'Not really. It was more just a feeling. But the thing is, there was something I didn't like, so I opened the door and he was on that phone.' She pulled out her soggy tissue and dabbed her nose. 'He cut the call straight away and buried the phone. When I admired it and asked him where he'd got it he said he was trying it out for someone. Road testing it.' She looked again towards the bedroom door. 'Yeah, that was the expression he used. Road testing it. I didn't tell his mum, but I got the distinct impression he was "road testing it" for some man.'

Chapter 10

Allan called back into the office to drop Jane off and pick up Sam before attending the post mortem. He spotted Sam through the glass, intent on his paperwork. He hadn't been involved at this level before and it was important to take him.

Helena Finlayson's lab was on a different site, so they had to cross town to get to it. It was a fine autumn afternoon, dry and mild, and people were out in the streets in their summer jackets. Sam was quiet, looking out of the window as they drove along the banks of the Ness. The wide river pushed its way from the sharp cleft between hills that formed Loch Ness. On it went, through this most northerly city to the Beauly and Moray Firths and beyond to diffuse its waters into the North Sea. Here, in the city, the hills were left behind. The landscape was open, and the trees on both riverbanks were yellow and orange against the backdrop of blue sky.

Allan drew the car up outside the austere older building which housed the mortuary.

Helena was writing a report on screen when they arrived. Her half-moon glasses were mid-way down her nose, making her look older than she really was. She swept off her glasses when Allan knocked twice and opened the door.

'I wondered when you'd show up. Come in.' She secured her glasses on the neck of her vest top by tucking one leg inside it and held out her hand.

Allan shook it perfunctorily and introduced Sam. 'Helena, this is Sam Abouwaye. Sam – Helena. Sam's been with us for a couple

46

of weeks, but this is his first big case.'

The two shook hands warmly. 'Pleased to meet you. Don't take this the wrong way, but let's hope we don't see too much of each other.'

They walked down the long green corridor. As Helena unlocked a heavy door, Allan could see the young man was tense. He'd been quiet all the way over in the car, and in the weak strip light in this old building, his skin gleamed with a thin layer of sweat. 'You going to be alright with this?'

'Going to have to be.' He wiped his palms on his jacket.

Helena pushed through the door and held it open for them, then pulled her lab coat closer round her. The chill clutched at their sides. The body store had large refrigerated units along one wall. Helena unlocked one of them and drew out a tray at waist height. The body came out head first. Even Allan was relieved the boy's head was covered by the white cloth. It gave him time to prepare mentally. Using two hands and extreme tenderness, Helena peeled back the shroud and met Allan's eyes, waiting for his reaction.

Allan scanned the boy's face. The nose was crushed and bloody and there was bruising at both eyes. The lips had swollen and burst. Yet he seemed unreal. Frosted. The lid of one eye permanently cracked open.

'At this stage, I'd say the probable cause of death is strangulation, but there's lots of damage to the head as well as the neck.'

He and Helena stepped away from the body towards the other wall, where there was a desk and writing facility. She pulled out her preliminary report and began to go through it with him, but Sam caught her eye. 'Don't touch him, please!'

Allan had a glimpse of the young officer's dark hand reaching for the boy's red hair.

'Sorry.' Sam folded his arms.

'Don't worry about it,' Helena said. She smiled at him – a polite smile – and pulled up the cloth over Jamie's face again then pushed the tray back into the fridge. 'I'll get the techie to lay him out next

door. Why don't you two go and watch from the viewing platform?'
She looked at Allan. 'You know where it is.'

Allan kept a grim silence as the two men walked back along the
corridor.

'Really, I'm so sorry, Sir,' Sam said. 'Total rookie mistake. I think
I'm just anxious. Seeing him like that.'

'Yep, it's hard. And it doesn't get any easier.' Allan stopped
at a door marked Observation. They pushed through a second
door into a brightly lit, clinical room fitted out in white tiles, harsh
lighting and stainless steel sinks and surfaces. The technician was
transferring the boy's body to the central table. Helena Finlayson
came in, gowned up and wearing wellingtons. The techie began to
arrange an array of bowls and cutting equipment.

'If you need it, there's a sick bag there,' Allan said, giving Sam a
wink.

'No, I'll be fine.'

The two of them stood in the observation dock, looking through
the screens, which meant they didn't need to get gowned up. It
also offered them a slight emotional distance. It was hard not to be
moved by the tenderness Helena showed as she combed with slow
strokes through the boy's ginger hair, or the way she examined the
pink scratches on his white skin.

She looked up to the observation booth. 'Definite signs of
penetrative sexual abuse.'

'Long term?'

Helena considered this. 'I wouldn't think so. There's intense
trauma to the membranes, but it's all new – no sign of healing.'

Out of the corner of his eye, Allan saw Sam's hand go to his
mouth, but it wasn't because he felt sick. And the young man was
stoic while Helena cut into the boy and removed his stomach and
organs.

Allan's phone rang. It flashed up Lorraine's name. He felt a mix
of guilt at the intrusion and a sense of relief to have an excuse for a
break. He took it outside in the corridor.

'Something's come up – I can't see you tonight after all,' she said. Her voice sounded flat.

'You okay?'

'Yeah, yeah. Just – there's something I need to do. Something I need to check up on. Family stuff. It's complicated.' There was a pause. An awkward silence.

'No problem,' Allan eventually said. 'I probably wouldn't be in the best frame of mind anyway.'

'No? Bad day?'

He looked at his shoes. Yet again, he was feeling drained. 'You could say that.'

'Did you get any more word on that boy? On what happened to him. Or who did it?' She sounded as if she was holding her breath.

He scratched his head. 'Nah, still ongoing. In fact, I'd better get back.'

'Well, don't work late. Go home and relax. Have a bath or something. I'll give you a call and see you soon?'

When he went back in, Helena assumed he was being called away, and he didn't disabuse her. Sam looked like he'd seen enough, anyway.

'I'll get a full report to you as soon as I can,' Helena said. Her words were faintly muffled by her mask, and she nodded a goodbye as the two men quietly left the room.

'How can anyone do that to a kid?' Sam said as they headed back to the car.

'The perpetrator or the pathologist?' Allan joked.

'Both. It's inhuman.'

'Sadly, it's all too human,' Allan said, and they drove off in silence.

Chapter 11

She couldn't bear him to come to the house. Couldn't bear it. She said she'd moved on, but how could she move on after what he did to them? Even if it was years ago. And now this? She had to confront him. Had to know if he did it.

She waited till it was dark. Too many neighbours twitching their curtains. She arranged to meet him in the city centre. Took the bus and got off at the station. Already, music was blaring out the pub doors. She pulled her coat around her, partly from cold, partly for concealment. Tugged her collar up and sank her chin in it as she passed the so-called gentlemen's club. She didn't want any of these lechers seeing her. 'Don't go,' her inner voice said. 'What's the point? What will you say? What if he hits you?' That wasn't going to happen. If it did – she was ready for him. She could feel the weight in her bag, slung over her shoulder.

She just needed to know. And to punish him.

The sky had cleared and the air was savage. She was too early. The library was open, so she went in, passing between the grand entrance columns. It was a mistake: too bright; too visible. Even at this time, tourists were using it as an unofficial waiting room for the station. More pleasant than the real thing. An older couple in walking boots and purple jackets were trying to understand the coffee machine. A woman in her early twenties was roaming the aisles, wheeling a small case behind her. A local, white hair yellowed with neglect, and jacket just as greasy, sat with his body loose in the comfy seats, half asleep. In for a heat. The staff were involved in a craft activity in the children's section. Bright and airy, it used to be her favourite. Their family favourite. Tears pricked the corners of her eyes. Acid tears. That bastard.

The tourists moved away and she bought a latte, the liquid scorching her fingers when the thin plastic rim flexed in. She'd only sipped half when she realised it was time. She set the still hot cup down beside a column on her way out.

The entrance to Market Brae Steps was in the gloom: somewhere she'd never have walked alone in the dark. She kept walking, past it, glancing up the steep ascent to check it was empty. It was. She paused as if she was looking in a window. Turned back. The steps went up in three sections, a dozen steps each. There was no sign of anybody on them. She checked over her shoulder, partly out of long habit – fear of the bogey man – and partly for reassurance she hadn't been seen.

The lampposts were lit on the stairway, but their light was feeble. She wasn't feeble. She steadied herself with a hand on the railing. Gasped, with the effort of the climb, or with the prospect of confronting him. The lane bent to the left. She looked to the right, checking the shops in the old mews were clear and nobody was lurking. Bridal boutique. Barbers. Tanning salon. All empty.

He'd come from the top. She knew that. There was a car park up there; a posh residential area. Not that he lived there. A multicultural centre. She'd taken visitors up to the top for the view it gave over the city. 'City'. It was just a big village, really. A mini version of Edinburgh with its tenements and closes.

She paused for breath, and to clear the debris from her mind. She thought about the weight in her bag – the thing she'd grabbed to teach him a lesson.

She'd told him to meet at the bottom of the steps – in the street. It was a lie.

At the bend half way up, she waited. Tucked in beside the old wall. Below it, on the other side, there were bushes. The back gardens of the pubs and lower tenements. It was gloomy here. The old buildings, in a curve opposite, didn't have any lights. So he

51

wouldn't see her. No one would see her. She tucked herself in to the rough right angle and waited. Unzipped her bag and fingered what she'd brought with her.

She checked her phone. Where was he? Deliberately late as a method of control? She clamped the skin inside her cheek between her teeth and bit down.

Feet on the stairs – coming downhill towards her. She shrank against the wall, a twig scraping her scalp through the hair. Was it him? He turned the corner, heading left, away from her. Yeah, she recognised his body shape. The dark hair and features. He'd something in his hand, but it was just a bottle of water. She called him.

He stopped. Took a moment to register her. 'What are you doing here in the dark?' he said, heavy brows furrowed. 'I thought we were meeting at the bottom?'

'I needed to see you.' Her voice was half-volume, heart too fast to hold steady.

'Aye, well, why don't we go down and get a coffee?' He tucked the bottle of water in his pocket and peeled away, expecting her to follow him.

'No.' She gripped his sleeve. 'Here.'

He sniffed. His head moved barely perceptibly from her hand on his sleeve to her face, his features indistinct in the darkness. 'Not want to go to a café?' He hesitated. 'We can talk about it?'

'No.' Hate curdled. Heartburn. 'Was it you?'

'What?'

'Did you do it?' She dug her fingers into his forearm. 'Answer me!'

'Do what?'

'Kill him.' Her voice broke. 'Do those horrible things to him!'

He snatched his arm away, grabbed hers and shoved her against the wall. 'Is that what you really think of me?'

'Do you blame me?'

He leaned his weight on her, bending her over the rough stone wall, his knee between her legs, his heavy feet blocking her. Her bag dangled useless, out of reach. She shoved against him, too weak to push him off. 'Get off me!' His breath was in her mouth. She twisted to the side. Rammed her shoulder and hip against him. 'Let go of me!' she squealed, shoving.

He tried to pin her arms, but she was like an octopus. 'Stop wriggling! This is crazy.'

She curled towards the ground, his hand back under her chin, the other arm round her back. 'I don't believe you.'

'I'll let you go and we can talk.'

'No!' She surged from the waist and burst out from his arms. Stuttered a few steps backwards into the lane.

He straightened. Drew breath. Stared at her.

'I know you did it!' she said. 'I just know you did.' Her hands shook as she drew the weight from her bag.

Hands on his hips. Panting. 'What the fuck are you up to?'

She squeezed the trigger.

He roared. It went on and on as the liquid stung him. Mould cleaner. It was all she'd had. She wished it was pure bleach. Pure acid, burning into him: punishing him. Trembling, she thrust it back in her bag and rushed off on unsteady legs back down the way she'd come.

Chapter 12

Allan dropped Sam off at the office and checked in for any news. It was only just after six, but it had been a long day and it was too late to start anything, so he headed home, stopping off for a bottle of red wine and kebab on the way. The last of the sunlight was vanishing and his house was cold, in darkness. He switched on the TV and closed the curtains, ramping up the heating and sitting on the sofa with his jacket on till the room warmed up a bit or the wine kicked in. He woke a couple of hours later to canned laughter from some reality show, sweating with the heat and unsure where he was. He threw off his jacket and shoes, poured himself another glass of wine and sat down with his iPad to check the news. Before long, he'd moved on to what had become a habit: searching symptom checker websites to try to figure out what was wrong with him. So far, it looked like pernicious anaemia, diabetes, heart failure, and Lyme disease. Combined. No wonder he didn't have energy for the gym.

Next morning, after adding insomnia and caffeine addiction to the list, he headed to work. He met Sam on the way in. 'Yesterday didn't put you off, then?'

'Nah. Back for more.'

'Glad to hear it,' Allan said and patted his young DC on the back. He checked his emails then called the team together for the morning briefing.

'Right, email from Jason Bonar this morning. Jane, can you arrange for a car to pick up Mrs Brooks for a media appeal some time early afternoon? She can bring her mother or – maybe better

54

– the boy's father with her.'

'Sure, Sir.'

'We'll need to interview him anyway. Find out where he was when Jamie disappeared and rule out whether the phone came from him or not.'

'Okay dokes.'

'Did you arrange formal identification?'

'Yesterday.'

'Excellent. Usual procedure for the media thing. Jason should book the room and so on, so just liaise with him, but keep me informed so I know when to turn up, yes?'

Jane nodded and made notes.

'So – preliminary data in from Helena Finlayson confirms Jamie Brooks was sexually assaulted with penetration, close to the time of his death which is now estimated at Monday lunchtime. The contents of the boy's stomach suggest he hadn't eaten lunch. The fact we found his school bag at home suggests he either didn't go to school that day – though his mother and grandmother assured us he did – or he slipped out, maybe at lunchtime, maybe to meet someone he knew, maybe not. The mother tells us Jamie experienced bullying when he started at this school, though it's not been so bad since then. Still, the boy was going through some teenage rebellion – typical stuff, not doing what he was told, playing one parent off against the other – and that's why she didn't report him missing straight away. He's been known to disappear without texting his mother and turn up safe at his father's house. That's the background. Apart from that, he's a "good boy". That's what his mother thinks, and his gran.'

Allan checked his notes.

'Sam, can you check known paedophiles, at liberty and anyone just out of jail?'

'Will do, Boss.'

'Any word on that fancy phone under his pillow, Jane?'

She turned wide eyes to him. 'We only lifted it from the house yesterday.'

'True. Push them on it, will you? In fact, no. You've got enough to do. Ross – you handle that, will you? Get it off them as soon as. I'd rather you went through whatever data and phone records there are on it. Make it a priority.'

'What, over the fire at the distribution centre?'

Allan looked confused.

'The fire in the bin at Inchmarsh Industrial Estate.'

He ran his hand through his hair. 'Forgot about that. Yes – the boy's phone takes priority. Definitely.'

There was a pause while the team waited for Allan to continue, but he seemed to have lost his thread. 'Do you need another coffee, Sir?' Jane teased him.

'Intravenously. Yeah, sorry – bit of a sleepless night. Anyway, no sign of anything back from Forensics about blood or DNA or anything. Still too early for those. So – questions?'

'What about the boy's clothes, Sir?' Sam said.

'No trace of those at the scene. This is a killer who cleans up after himself. What do we think of that?'

'I'll look into previous MO when I check out the paedophile register in case that shows up,' Sam said.

'Good. I'm going up to that retreat at Abriachan to interview the woman who found the body.' Allan ran his finger over his notes. 'Irma Russell. I'll do that this morning.'

'Sir, what about the gran mentioning Jamie speaking with a man on the phone, and denying it?' Jane said.

'Let's hope Ross turns up trumps on the phone, as soon as we get it back from Forensics. I suppose there's a chance they'll pick up prints from it, though who knows how long the boy had it. Meanwhile, Jane and Ross, contact the head teachers at the two other secondary schools in the area. Let them know about the murder.' He looked from one to the other. 'Okay it with them that you and routine officers will be at the school gates, providing security and asking if anyone knows anything. You'll need to arrange to pull up CCTV as well.'

'What about the school Jamie went to?' Jane asked Allan.

'I've a contact there. I'll take that one myself.'

Chapter 13

Traffic on the road that followed the line of the Ness for several miles was light, and the October sun slanted on the water surface and turned the trees on the hills around it golden. As the land rose and the buildings were left behind, Allan felt he was shedding a skin. Though he'd grown up a city boy, comfortable among the tall tenements and high rises of Glasgow, he'd had childhood wanderlust, disappearing for hours at a time into the microcosm of the city's canal and river network and exploring far into the countryside. When the post had come up in Inverness, he'd seized the opportunity. Well, there was the other stuff it was good to leave behind, too, like shedding a skin of a different kind.

He drove without stopping past the forest where the boy's body had been found, slowed as he crested the hill and sounded his horn to warn anyone approaching on this single track road from the opposite direction, then drew briefly into one of the passing places as the view opened out in front of him.

He switched off the engine and opened the window, revelling in the silence punctuated only by the caw of a crow and the bleat of a sheep. Ahead, in the air, a hen harrier hung, black-tipped wings barely flickering before it dived, plummeting through the air. To Allan's right was deciduous woodland – the slender, creamy trunks of birch trees drizzled with yellow tear-shaped leaves; to his left, a field sloped down towards the valley, and the white buildings of the writers' retreat sat squatly on the land. A light wind tugged at tufts of wool snagged on the fence's barbs. This early in the morning, the valley still held woolly twists of white cloud, below eye level, soon to disappear in the strengthening sun.

Allan checked the clock on his phone. He'd have to make this quick so he could get to the school in good time. He started his car and turned into the stony farm track, the car bumping unevenly down to the buildings of the retreat.

He introduced himself in the office and was shown into the farmhouse kitchen. The member of staff went into another room and soon returned with Irma Russell, who looked calm and unruffled by what she'd been through, or by the prospect of reliving it in an interview. She smiled broadly to him, and the member of staff suggested they have coffee then go to the hay bale studio for privacy.

'Good idea,' Irma said. 'Please – sit! What'll you have? Do you prefer tea? There's green, and various herbals.' She indicated a whole shelf of jars and packets.

'Coffee's good for me,' Allan said, pulling out a chair from the wide pine table and sitting down. 'Can't get enough coffee in the morning.' There were peach-coloured lilies in a vase in the table's centre, and sunlight glowed on the waxed pine dressers and wicker baskets that stored tablecloths and napkins, and an assortment of breads and biscuits.

Irma scooped coffee grounds into a cafetiere and filled it with steaming water from an ultra-modern urn. She brought it to the table with mugs, sugar and milk, then took a plate of cake from one of the fridges on the opposite wall. 'Orange almond cake. Delicious. The staff made it last night. Would you like a slice?'

'There goes my waistline,' Allan said. The cake was topped with chocolate and smelled delicious.

Over coffee and cake, they chatted about the Centre. This was the third time Irma had been here, so finding the boy had been a sudden and horrific change to her routine. From the room beyond, there were sounds of laughter and chairs shifting. Sensing the mood alter, and having finished his cake, Allan suggested they move to the studio.

Carol McKay

They walked across the grass towards the little round building. Its walls were sharply white and it was topped with a round roof made of blackened thatch. Inside smelled strongly of the residue from its wood burning stoves. There were dust motes in the rays coming through the wooden-framed windows, and a fine layer of ash surrounded the slate fireplace, along with baskets of kindling. There was a coal scuttle, too, and chunks of quartered tree trunks were stacked on shelves. On the fire surround, cloaked in ash, lay a pair of very long, very thick padded and blackened mittens for use with the tools for loading wood into the stove. A small fire had been lit, presumably by the staff member who'd suggested they move there, but the room was much bigger on the inside than the impression given from the outside, and the air was chilly, so they pulled their chairs closer to the fire.

'So, Ms Russell,' Allan began, setting his coffee mug down on the hearth and reaching into his pocket for his notebook and pen. 'You gave us some details at the scene, but I wondered if you'd remembered anything else.'

'Not really,' she said, and pressed her lips together. She peered into her mug.

'It's quite normal to run over situations like this in our minds. To torment ourselves with the image. Have you been sleeping well?'

She looked up. 'Oh don't worry about that. I tend to lie awake at night anyway. That's when I write.'

He nodded. 'And have you written about this?'

She gave a single laugh and tossed her head back, shaking her near-white hair. 'Half a notebook full. Not a prompt I'd have chosen.'

'Is there any chance I could have a copy of that? There might be something you've remembered during the night and jotted down and not realised you haven't mentioned it to us. If you see what I mean.'

The faint lines in her face deepened. 'Well, my notebook's private, but I suppose I could photocopy some of it.'

'I'd really appreciate that. Then we can leave you to get on with enjoying your retreat in peace.'

She went up to her room and brought the notebook down. There were twelve double pages and he glanced furtively at his watch as she photocopied them. When she passed them over, she said to him, 'Incidentally, Mr MacIntyre. I hope you don't mind me saying this, but do you keep well?'

'Sorry?'

She held his eyes. 'I noticed you were very out of breath on the day we found the boy's body. And yet you're hardly carrying any excess weight. And your hands are cold. And you have a rather peculiar tan.'

'Do I?' he laughed and inspected the backs of his hands. 'I was in Spain. Burned myself.'

'I see.'

It was bizarre to be on the other side of the interrogation.

'Well, I just wondered,' she said. 'I have a friend, you see – well, I had a friend, a special friend – who had a health condition we didn't spot until it was too late.' She blinked a few times, holding her breath, then inhaled sharply and shook her hair again. 'Well, it was a long time ago. But you remind me of him. You could humour me and get yourself checked out.'

'Please don't waste any time worrying about me, Mrs Russell –'

'– Miss –'

'Miss Russell.'

'It's Addison's.'

'Addison's? Not Russell?'

She blew out through her nose. 'No, it's Russell. Miss Russell. But the condition is Addison's.' She put her hand on his arm. 'Something to tuck away in the back of your mind.'

Chapter 14

It was mid-morning break when Allan arrived at Thistlebank Academy. He parked some distance along the street outside the sturdy-looking perimeter fence, and cast a wary eye over the seagulls who were squawking and diving, their yellow beaks wide, ready to grasp any crust, chips or biscuits eleven to eighteen year olds left unguarded. Then there was the guano. The path up to the school was spattered with it, mixed with the ubiquitous trail of chewing gum.

As he approached the office, he noticed Khalil and Ahmed standing by themselves, up against the wire fence, quite apart from the other boys, but when he called over a hello Khalil returned his attention to his phone. The reaction jarred, but Allan reasoned he'd probably have done the same thing himself if his mother brought men home. If she'd lived long enough.

At the front door, Allan had to buzz the intercom and explain who he was before he could be admitted, and then show his ID. Once inside, he asked to see the head teacher, and had to wait till she could be summoned. He stood, hands in his trouser pockets, in the corner of the high, extensive atrium which seemed to be at the heart of the school. Things had changed since the chalk and dust, and timber floors and door frames of his day. This was light and airy. There were posters on the near wall – something about being 'plastic-wise' – student artwork and typed paragraphs presenting research about some big climate change investigation the kids had been doing. There were four different bins for recycling, some with cans and plastic cups from the water cooler spilling out on to the floor around them. And there was some kind of meter that was flashing numbers.

Above the general echoing sounds of school life came the tapping of high heels, and there was the headie, bustling towards him. As she approached, he realised she rustled, as well as bustled.

'DI MacIntyre, I see you've found our S4 climate change and sustainability project,' she said as she approached him. She tapped the wall beside the flashing numbers. 'Look at that! That's the energy we're producing from our solar panels. We're very proud of what our young people have been doing. They've achieved quite the high profile in the local press for their work on it! Not that everybody's been happy about it, but what can you do?' She reached down to pick up some of the garbage around the bins then wavered as if she couldn't quite work out which bin each should go into, before laying it all back on the ground again. She dusted off her hands. 'You can't please all the people all the time, and some people are never happy.'

She held out a chubby pink hand that jolted a static charge through him. 'Frances Wallace.' Silver bangles on her wrist jingled, as did the three silver chains she wore round her neck, draping over the undulations of her bust. She wore a fitted shiny dress in colours that dazzled.

'Thank you for seeing me,' he said.

Her eyes examined his. 'Unbelievable situation,' she said, clutching her own hands in front of her waist now, but otherwise not moving. She smelled of Chanel and bacon. A curious combination.

'Can we talk somewhere?' Allan indicated around him, implying that the middle of the school wasn't ideal for confidential conversation.

'Of course!' She pointed the way to her office. 'Tea?'

'Thanks, but no,' Allan said, and explained about the coffee and chocolate orange cake.

She closed her office door behind him. 'Make yourself comfortable.' She told her secretary to hold calls and allow no interruptions. 'Now,' she said to Allan, 'I'm all yours. Where do we go from here?'

Allan crossed his legs. 'First, I'm not sure what you know, so let me tell you what we do.'

Frances Wallace nodded. She clasped her hands on the desk in front of her. 'All I know is what Mrs Brooks told me. That Jamie was found dead in the Abriachan woodlands.' Her voice almost broke.

'He was found on Tuesday by a woman walker. We think he was abducted – or went with his attacker willingly – round about lunchtime on Monday and murdered quite quickly after.'

'Horrifying.'

Allan raised an eyebrow. 'Can you confirm he was definitely in school on Monday morning?'

'I'll find that out for you. Anything else?'

'We'll need to find out his last movements here, and speak to his classmates, maybe his teachers – anyone he would've come into contact with.' He looked out of the window. 'Do you have CCTV surveillance?'

She sighed. 'Sadly, yes.'

'My officers will need to go through that. Do the children have individual lockers?'

'Yes – but we have a master key for them. I'll get the janitor to arrange access to that. You'll probably want to speak to Jamie's registration teacher. She'll have picked up if anything was bothering him.' She wrote some notes on an open pad. 'Can I ask you something?'

'Of course.'

'I'm obviously concerned with school security, and morale. I've already got counsellors in to help the children come to terms with it. But could you address an assembly?' She squirmed forward in her chair. 'I need someone from the investigation to reassure the children they're safe. And the parents.'

Allan nodded. 'When are we talking?'

'The sooner the better, especially for his year group.'

Soon, Allan found himself addressing two hundred thirteen year olds, reassuring them the police were doing everything they could to discover what had happened and to keep them safe, and he told them police officers would be stationed in the school playground. 'And if you have any information you think can help us – you need to tell us.' He thought about the way Khalil and Ahmed had turned away from him, keeping themselves to themselves. 'You might think it's disloyal to Jamie if you talk to us about him, but – believe me – nothing you could say would be interpreted that way. Nothing at all. And anything – the smallest detail, any old thing you half noticed and thought seemed a bit strange, or wrong – get in touch with us.'

Mrs Wallace spoke up then, reassuring the children anything they said would be welcomed, and reiterating that they were safe, but shouldn't take risks. 'I'll have a letter ready for you to take home to your parents at the end of the afternoon.'

As soon as the head teacher stopped talking and the children began to file out of the assembly, the noise levels in the atrium rose in a wave of excited chatter that assaulted Allan's ears. Mrs Wallace had stopped to talk to the janitor, and while he waited for her, Allan scanned the hall, looking at all these normal kids in their uniforms, and all these teachers directing them to file out row by row. Then he saw her. Emma Gough. Her hair was dark and much shorter than when he'd last seen her. Her eyes were dark, too. She'd always had a thing for dark eyeliner. Allan recalled watching her in the mornings, layering on the black with a wand.

'Ready?' Frances Wallace was by his elbow. 'The janitor can show you inside Jamie's locker now.'

'Er – can we leave that for now? I'll get my team out and coordinate with Forensics. We'll need to set up a base where we can interview the children, and the teachers and other staff.'

'No problem! I'll get a room sorted out for them.'

On his way out, Allan asked the woman at the reception desk what class Emma Gough taught, and she directed him to the first floor in the orange wing. Allan thanked her and strode through the atrium, hands in his trouser pockets. He didn't know quite what he'd say, and as he knocked on her classroom door he silently cursed himself for stirring things up again, but a contact was a contact.

She opened the door, saw him, and turned to the class. '2B – I need silence from you. Full concentration on your reading.' The noise level began to rise as she pulled the door wide to leave the room and she spun round again. 'I said "silence". I'll be on the other side of this door. So – shush!'

The door was self-closing and heavy, and Allan stepped back as it swept her out of the class towards him. Despite his reservations, it did feel good to see her. Not that he'd let her know that.

'Allan!' she said and rested her hand momentarily on the lapel of his jacket.

Her face looked younger, fresher, than he remembered. Maybe she'd given up drinking. He couldn't smell any from her. She smelled good. Looked good. She stood almost as tall as him. He glanced down to see she was wearing heels. He couldn't resist taking in her figure. Well, it was a fitted wool dress she was wearing.

'So good to see you,' she said, 'though obviously not like this. What are you doing here? Is this official?'

'Semi,' he said, then, suddenly self-conscious, he ran his hand over the top of his head. 'I mean – we'll have to interview you formally, but I saw you in the assembly so thought we could have a quick word. You were Jamie's English teacher?'

She nodded.

'I recognised your name from his jotter.'

Her eyes sparkled at that then her attention was drawn to the classroom. The noise was building again. 'Wee buggers. Listen to them.' She looked back to Allan. 'I was Jamie's teacher, yes, and I do want to chat, but now's not a good time.'

'Okay. Shows how little I remember about secondary school.' He took out his card and tried to pass it to her. 'If you think of anything that might help the investigation, can you call me?'

She refused the card. 'I know your number, Allan,' she said, perplexed and frowning. 'Why don't we meet later? Have a proper talk?' She did the old thing she always did – parted her lips and gazed up under her lashes at him, somehow sinking down a little, despite her heels, to enable her to do that. Every time, he fell for it. Every time. But not this time.

'I don't think so. We'll keep this official. My team'll be at the school running interviews, so if there's anything strikes you, you can let them know.'

'Too bad. But if you change your mind... I'd love to hook up. Find out how things have been going for you.' She looked him up and down. 'You're in great shape.'

He stepped away, scratching his head and half smiling. 'Right – I think your class needs you. And it's time I was somewhere else.'

He was conscious of her standing there, holding the door handle, watching him as he moved away. When he turned back to see if she was still looking, he saw the door sweep shut and heard her hollering at the children, voice as dark as her eyes and that aspect of her personality that had simultaneously attracted and repelled him.

Chapter 15

When Allan arrived back at the office, Ross was engrossed in CCTV footage. There were dirty mugs on his desk, and papers were piled everywhere. How he could concentrate with so much clutter around him, Allan couldn't guess, but Ross's powers of concentration were known to all. In fact, it took Allan three goes to rouse him from the screen.

'Sorry, Sir,' Ross said, sitting back in swift guilt. His eyes were red and watery.

'Which school is this?' Allan peered, trying to recognise the scene.

Ross stretched, fists clenched at his shoulders. 'No, no – this is the bin footage. I've not got to the schools yet.'

'Bins?'

'Inchmarsh. The Industrial Estate.'

'Christ, I keep forgetting about that.' Allan drew over a chair and perched on it. 'You better give me a rundown.'

Ross raised his eyebrows and turned back to the screen. 'I've not long started. The woman reported the fire early on Tuesday morning – about 7.45 – but it was well alight by then so I've been checking back.' He looked at Allan. 'So far, the big news is two foxes and a cat.'

'Par for the course,' Allan said. 'How far back have you gone?'

Ross checked the screen. 'Two or three hours.'

Allan watched the footage play for a moment. It showed the empty car park in darkness, with just some patterns of grey and orange light from the streetlights. It jumped on repeat through several camera shots, synching through the three CCTV surveillance points in different parts of the industrial estate. 'Hold on, I'm not getting this,' he said.

'What d'you mean, Sir?'

'There's no sign of a fire, there. Look...' He tapped the screen at a shot of the bins only to see the image change again to a longer view. 'There's no fire there. What time is that?' He squinted at the time signature in the corner. '5.38? You've missed it. You need to come up nearer the morning, surely? To when the fire happened.'

'Ah, but that's it,' Ross said. 'That's what's making me bleary-eyed.' He leaned round to focus on his boss. 'There's nothing. I've been over the time frame from 6am till 7.45 when this Cathy woman reported it. Three times! And there's nobody there.'

Allan waited.

'Like – one minute there's peace and quiet, and the next shot of the bins, they're on fire.'

'So, has the footage been tampered with?'

Ross looked back at the screen. 'I don't think so. The time signature doesn't jump.'

'Are you telling me somebody managed to get in and out with a lit rag or something in the time it took for the camera attention to switch to the two other views across the car park? Were they on jet packs or something?'

Ross shrugged. 'That's why I'm going back earlier in the night.' He looked at his boss again. 'To see if someone set it up earlier.'

'What d'you mean?'

'Like, detonated it remotely.'

Allan stared. 'A bomb? In Inverness?' Allan clapped his subordinate on the shoulder. 'I think you've been watching too much high octane television. It'll just have been kids fannying about. On skateboards or something – going too fast to leave a trace. Is there any other footage you could pull in? From the streets around?'

Ross sighed. 'I can try. Will I give up on looking earlier, through the night?'

Allan had stood up by now and was pushing the chair back at the other desk. He registered Ross's red eyes and pasty complexion. 'When did you last stretch your legs? Go and get some air, and something to eat. Then see if you can source some other footage from the neighbourhood. I know you do a good job on this kind of thing, but we've got other priorities. This is taking far too much time just for a bin fire. Check any other footage you can get your hands on for the time just before the fire, and if you can't find anything, we'll take stock from there.' He laid his hand on Ross's shoulder. 'And sort out those mugs before you re-discover penicillin.'

Over the couple of hours, Allan briefed his DCI, got the go-ahead to pull extra staff on to the school investigation, and brought their supervisors up to speed. Then Jane told him Jasmine Brooks and Jamie's father had arrived for the media briefing. Allan felt his stomach turn over. He loathed these things, but the killer was out there and the public had to know about it. As he walked to the lift to head to the media room, he was aware of his legs and belly trembling. He fished in his jacket pocket for tablet, but the sweetie wrapper was empty.

Jason Bonar was already there, speaking with the journalists and testing mikes. 'All set?' he asked Allan.

'Jane's on her way up with the parents.'

The local press and TV journos milled around the room and as the scheduled time drew closer, Jason asked them all to get into their seats. The room was warm with so many bodies and the camera lights. Jane led in Jasmine and Michael Brooks. They kept their heads down as they filed into their seats behind the long table. Allan rose to shake their hands, aware of the instant cacophony of camera shutters set to 'continuous burst' so the journalists wouldn't miss a second's changing facial expression. Any make-up Jasmine had put on had been cried off. Michael was acting strong but his stoicism was betrayed by the red bags under his eyes.

'Ladies and gents, thanks for coming,' Jason said.

There was a further cacophony of shutter clicks and dazzling flashes as he introduced the panel. It was completely oppressive and Allan rued the day it was decided these performances were necessary.

Jason handed over to Allan, who outlined what they knew – or what they were prepared to say about what they knew – and asked the public to report anyone suspicious. Then he handed over to the parents to give their statement. It was the usual.

'Everybody loved my Jamie. His teachers loved him. His friends...' Cameras flashed as she raised her eyes from the tissue clenched in her lap. 'He was the sweetest, most wonderful – '

She looked at her former husband. The two sat, not touching, joined only by this huge loss they were suffering.

Jasmine sobbed. 'I can't bear to be without him!' She looked straight at the journalists and the cameras flashed again. 'My Jamie didn't deserve this. He'd everything to live for.'

There was an uncomfortable silence.

'Please help the police find out who did this to our son,' Michael Brooks said, his voice devoid of anger; too broken for anger yet. 'Somebody knows who did it to him. Please turn him in so he can't do it to anybody else's baby.'

It was harrowing. Melodrama at its worst. At its worst because it was true. After that, it was over. Some on the floor were eager to ask questions, but Jason truncated the session and shepherded the parents out. While Jason talked to them, Allan steered Jane by the elbow, moving her gently out of earshot.

'You'll interview the dad?'

'All set up, Sir.'

'And the mother?'

Jane looked back at her. 'Tea, I think. Bit of an ordeal.'

'Yeah, I hate these things.' Allan clutched his stomach. 'I'll need to get something to eat. Keep me posted?'

'Sure thing, Sir.'

He stopped off at the cafeteria for chips, salting them till they looked snow covered. After that, and a mug of tea, his stomach

71

Carol McKay

settled and the shakes he'd felt in his legs disappeared. As he ate, he thought about Emma Gough and wondered if he should've arranged to meet up with her but decided on balance it was better to let the PCs handle it. He checked his phone and sent a message to Lorraine, asking if she was free tonight. She replied straight away that she was, so he was in a happier frame of mind when he returned to the office.

'You're looking better, son,' he said to Ross, who was nowhere near young enough for such a biological relationship. 'Any news?'

'Yeah! I pulled in some footage from a petrol station just outside the industrial estate and found this.' He switched between windows on his computer and played a clip.

Allan moved in closer to get a better view of the jerky black and white footage. It showed two boys. He peered at the screen. Was it his imagination, or did they look familiar? He snapped his gaze back to his assistant. 'Get that enlarged and printed. I want to see their faces.'

Chapter 16

Allan stopped off at home to shower and change. He shaved and dabbed his skin with something astringent that stung like fuck then turned his chin patchy puce and white. It looked bizarre against his weird tan. He grabbed his leather jacket and car keys, trusting the walk to the car would cool it down.

Lorraine didn't seem to notice, anyway. She pulled him inside the front door, pressed him up against the wall and hugged him. 'Shhh!' she said, finger at her lips. 'The boys are in the living room.'

He could hear them. They were laughing like two year olds. Allan wrapped his arms round Lorraine's waist and drew her in close. Her body was warm and cushioned and fitted in to his in all the right places. She breathed to him, 'I missed you last night,' and then kissed him, tongue pushing as they nestled in deep among the coats on the wall. Then Emma Gough spoiled it by phoning him. His phone was in his back pocket. It had one of these ring tones that grew louder and louder until you answered it, and by the time he'd disentangled himself from the jackets and Lorraine's arms and retrieved the phone from his tight pocket, the noise had ended the laughter coming from the living room, too.

'Hello,' Allan said, brusquely, pressing his hard-on with his other hand while Lorraine motioned she would go into the kitchen to carry on prepping dinner.

'Hi, Allan.' Emma Gough's voice sang out and he knew at once she hadn't stopped drinking.

'Emma. What is it?'

'I've thought of something,' she said, clearly trying to talk without

73

slurring. 'Can I see you?'

Khalil's head appeared at the living room door, unsmiling. Allan up-nodded to him, but the boy disappeared back into the room.

'I'm busy. Dial 111 and tell the office. Otherwise, you can tell the officer at school tomorrow.'

'Och, don't be like that,' she said. 'It's important. I've remembered seeing a man –' but he'd already decided to break off the call, talking over her with a quick, 'Bye.'

He tucked his phone back into his chinos' pocket. At the kitchen door, he watched Lorraine cooking. There was meat this time, and he wondered if that was a sign he was moving up in their relationship, given she was spending more money on him. He was glad he'd gone for a more expensive bottle of wine. 'That was just work, but I got rid of them. I'm all yours.'

She laughed and turned back to stirring the pan. 'This'll be ten minutes. That okay?'

'Brilliant. Smells good.'

She smiled.

'Want me to pour the wine?'

'Can we wait? It goes straight to my head if I drink it before I eat.'

'That's the plan,' he joked.

She'd moved to the sink to rinse her hands and aimed a splash of water in his direction. He was feet away, so it missed. 'Why don't you go and chat with the boys till dinner's ready?' she said. 'I'll give you a shout.'

He pulled a face. 'I don't know. That's scary. Two teenagers?'

'Away you go!' she said and he did.

The living room door was firmly closed. He opened it and went in in as friendly and unthreatening a manner as he could muster. The boys were sitting on the couch, or, rather, they'd slid down so their backs were on the seat and only their heads were against the back. Their legs were at all angles, and their controllers were zapping in between them in the direction of the TV.

Allan settled into the armchair and tried to be friendly. 'Who's winning?'

Khal drew a dour look but otherwise ignored him. Ahmed looked to Khal then followed his lead.

'Nobody? Okay.'

'Scores on the screen,' Khalil said and turned up the sound.

It was a racing game. Pretty innocuous. Well, totally innocuous. Khalil seemed to be marginally ahead. Allan decided to sound them out while most of their brains were focused on racing. 'Did either of you guys know that boy Jamie? Jamie Brooks?'

'Everybody at school knew him,' Khal said. 'And if they didn't, they do now.'

'He was on the news,' Ahmed said. 'But you know that. You were as well.'

'You mean I missed it?'

The two took their attention off the game long enough to stare at him, clearly not appreciating his sense of humour. His strategy worked, then. 'What did you think of the broadcast? Did it trigger any memories – anything that might help find who did it?'

A look passed between them, but before they could speak – assuming they even planned to speak – Lorraine opened the door and called them for dinner. 'Time for you to go home, Ahmed. Okay?'

The table was set with knives and forks, gleaming glasses and a jug of water. Allan screwed in the bottle opener and popped the cork then half-filled two glasses. He and Lorraine clinked and she clinked hers against the glass of water she'd already poured for Khalil. She sipped, said, 'Ooh, that's nice,' and put it down so she could serve up. There was a huge dish of lamb moussaka and another of salad. She gave Allan his first, then gave a bigger portion to Khalil, and in an attempt to score points Allan feigned outrage. It worked with Lorraine, but Khal remained poker-faced. The food was rich and tasty, especially when Allan added salt.

'That's not good for your heart,' Lorraine warned.

'I'm from Glasgow. Salt's the last thing to damage your heart where I come from.'

They were quiet for a while, eating, until Lorraine said, 'Oh, I saw that broadcast. That was awful. The school sent a letter round.'

'Yeah? Good. I was in with the headie this morning.'

She nudged his hand. 'Bad boy, were you?'

'Felt like it!' Their smiles flared and faded. 'I spoke to the second year assembly, too, but not to Khal's year. Did someone talk to you all, Khal?'

Khalil said nothing but kept his eyes on Allan and chewed dolefully.

'Khal!' his mother chided.

He swallowed. 'I was eating!' To Allan, he said, 'Yeah, some PC Plod spoke to us.'

Lorraine mouthed Allan an apology.

'Right. What about Jamie? Were you and he close?'

Khal shook his head. 'Nope.'

'That's good,' Lorraine said. She reached to stroke Khalil's black hair. He shrugged her off, but she persisted. 'Horrible thing to happen to that wee boy,' she said.

'He was a wee dick, anyway.'

'Khal!' Lorraine's hands fluttered to her napkin. She scrunched it up in her hands. 'The boy's dead!'

'Well, he was.' He glared at Allan. 'Always bragging.'

'What about?'

Khal squirmed. 'About the new games he was playing. Thought he was somebody.' He sneered at his mum again. 'When he was just a prick-teasing wee dick.'

Lorraine was flustered. 'Watch your language!'

Allan kept eating. He knew the boy was trying to provoke him, and that wasn't going to work. He did file the information away in case there was truth in the animosity between the boys. 'Just ignore him,' he said to Lorraine. 'He's a teenager. It's his job to wind you up.' He pinned Khalil with a look. 'Isn't that right, Khal?'

76

Khalil chewed.

'But while we're at it, maybe I could ask your opinion on something else,' Allan said. He put his knife down. 'Do you and your friend Ahmed happen to know anyone who might hang around the bins at the Inchmarsh Industrial Estate?'

Khalil dropped his cutlery on his plate. 'Can I go now?'

Lorraine frowned. 'Allan asked you a question. Are you not going to answer him?'

'No.' The boy began to kick against the table leg. Each kick became a bit stronger, till the table jolted, Allan's wine glass clinked against his knife, and the table inched forward towards Allan.

Lorraine was angry. Confused and angry. 'Behave yourself! Look what you're doing!'

Allan took it all in. 'Are you sure about that?' he said, keeping his eyes on the boy. 'Maybe you and Ahmed hang about Inchmarsh?'

Lorraine looked from one to the other. 'Wait a minute,' she said. 'What is this? An interrogation? I invited you here for dinner, not to bully my son.' She pushed up from the table. 'As for you,' she said to Khalil, 'Don't be so blooming rude, and get up to your room. And you,' she turned her attention to Allan. 'If you want to speak to my son like that, you can handcuff him and drag him away in a black mariah. Otherwise, I think it's time you were leaving.'

'Hold on,' he said, taking her wrist in appeasement, but she shrugged him off angrily. So he scraped back his chair. Still chewing, he nodded to Lorraine and went into the dim hall, where he lifted his jacket from the collection behind the door. It wasn't even an hour since he'd been there, kissing.

'I didn't mean it to go like this,' he said.

Lorraine was standing lit up in the kitchen doorway, her arms folded, hugging herself. 'I'll bet you didn't,' she said. 'Hell mend you.' From upstairs came the sound of loud rap music.

Allan weighed up whether there was any chance of her changing her mind. Then he slid his arms into his leather jacket. 'I'll call you.' She didn't reply, so he let himself out and let the door bang behind him. It had started to rain. Just a smir, but it was chilly, too, after the warmth of the house. He stood on the path outside the house and heard the key turn to double lock the door behind him. He fastened his jacket and walked to the car.

In the driver's seat, he rested his head on the headrest and scolded himself for being so stupid. Fine rain drops drizzled against the windscreen and blotted out the world outside. Funny the boy had called Jamie a prick-teasing wee dick. That was something he ought to check out. Allan rubbed his hand on his stomach, feeling utterly wiped out. His breath steamed up the inside of the glass but he still sat there. Eventually, he switched on the ignition and set the wipers to clear away the rain, and the heater and fan to make a thorough job of it. He took out his phone, selected a contact and keyed in a message.

That done, he switched the engine on, checked his mirrors, and put his foot down.

Chapter 17

Allan reversed his Alfa into one of the few remaining parking spaces outside Emma Gough's. Roaring the beast from a standing start away from Lorraine's house was childish, but it got rid of his irritation and part of him hoped she'd heard it. But how sensible was it to turn up here, now?

He strolled across the car park towards the low-rise flats where Emma Gough had lived for the past seven or eight years. As he tucked his keys into his pocket, his eyes roved towards her third floor windows. Light glowed through the living room curtains and as he pressed the button beside her name on the entry phone, he wondered what he was letting himself in for. Did she have information, or was she just being Emma?

'Who is it?'

'Allan,' he said.

She buzzed, and he pushed through the glass door. The flats were chic, expensive, bourgeois homes to lawyers, accountants and childless professional women. Light gleamed on the entrance's marble veneer wall panels. From habit, he took the stairs, but quickly regretted it, feeling his heart race after the first flight. Then, there she was, looking down over the banister at him and calling a greeting. By the time he reached her landing he was sucking air in and out like a bellows.

'You didn't need to run!' she teased, stretching to air kiss him, though taking that moment to hug him, too.

He held his hand up. 'Give me a minute. I should've taken the lift. Forgot you were so high up.'

She slipped an arm through his, pressing herself against his leather sleeve, and drew him towards the glow coming through her open door. He felt he was prey to a black widow spider. Yet she was acting girlish, coquettish, and he remembered when she could be light-hearted and fun. Not that he was going to fall for that. Tonight, he was going to be professional.

'They suit you,' he said, nodding to her lilac fluffy slippers.

She'd changed out of the clinging woollen dress she'd worn at school, into soft cord leggings and a long, fitted tee-shirt. She knelt on the leather sofa and grinned at him. 'My niece bought me them for my birthday. Cute, aren't they?'

'So "you".'

'She clearly thought so.'

'What age is she?'

'Nine! She's yet to meet the real me. Anyway, what can I get you?'

He stood, hands in his jacket pockets, and said nothing.

'Wine? I opened a bottle of Carmenere half an hour ago.'

'And you've still some left?'

Ouch. That made her frown. 'Most of it. I was just letting it breathe. Or you can have tea.'

He was driving, but the Carmenere was tempting. 'Ach, shame to let the wine go to waste. A small glass would be great.' He shrugged off his jacket and draped it over one of the chairs at her dining table. The room was open plan – high gloss aubergine-coloured kitchen lit up at one end, solid wooden dining suite with brown leather chairs in the middle, and lounge area at the front. The navy leggings and fitting tee-shirt emphasised how lean and supple she was, and as he watched her move round her kitchen, he tried to mentally double-lock any doors that were easing open.

'Here you go.' She walked towards him with two brim-full glasses of deep red wine, handed one over to him and chinked her glass off his.

He raised an eyebrow. 'I asked for a small one.'

'Yeah, yeah,' she said. 'I'd rather be remembered for being generous than a mean cunt.' She flashed her eyes at him, as if to see if he was shocked. He wasn't. 'You don't need to drink it all.' She sipped then set hers down on the coffee table. Hands on hips, she asked, 'Hungry? Or have you eaten?'

'No, I'm okay, thanks. Can we talk about what you said on the phone?'

'Sure.' She picked up her glass again and sat on the other end of the couch from him. 'What do you want to know?'

'You tell me. You said you'd seen a guy – somewhere at the school?'

'Yeah.' Her expression grew more serious. 'It was on Monday. I was leaving to go to a funeral – it's murder to get time off for that normally, but I didn't have class in the afternoon. So I know it was Monday.'

Allan nodded and tasted his wine.

'You get the usual mass grouping of cars, right up to the yellow zigzags, but I noticed this guy was actually on the zig-zags. He was in the cab of his delivery van, right across from the school gates on the other side of the street. He – well, the cab of his van – was half hidden under the overhanging branches of the big trees.' She shuddered. 'He was a big guy, heavy jowled kind of like a bloodhound, if you know what I mean, and he just stared, not blinking. A bit of a creep. Gave me the heebies, to be honest.'

Allan couldn't resist. 'What, because he didn't roll over for you, you think he's a creep?' That wine must be good.

She leaned over and slapped at his arm. 'What do you take me for? Don't answer that. No, I just felt – there was something wrong.' She reached forward and put her glass on the table. 'Well, to be fair, he shouldn't have been on the zig-zags, but it was the way he stared at me that was scary. He wasn't going to let me or anyone tell him off for breaking the school rules.'

'Had you seen him before?'

'Nope. But I was early. If he's parking on the zig-zags, he'll pick up his kid and make a fast getaway.'

'Does no one patrol them?'

'Well, at home-time, but this was nearer lunch time. So he might be there every day for all I know.'

'Right.' Allan put down his glass, conscious he was drinking it too fast. He reached for his jacket and slid his notebook from his pocket. He flipped it open and jotted down a few notes, leaning his forearms on his knees. 'We can check CCTV. Did you mention to anyone at school? He's probably a parent.'

'No, it was only when I was driving home today that I remembered him.'

'What did he look like? Other than a bloodhound.'

She grinned wryly. 'Mid thirties? Asian.'

'Chinese?'

'Sorry – geography's not my strong point. Pakistani or Indian.'

'Short hair? Beard? Turban, anything like that?'

She gazed into mid-air. 'Er – I had a definite impression of hairiness. I'd say he probably had a full head of hair and a bit of a beard. But I couldn't swear to it. I don't remember seeing, like, a turban and a massive heavy beard. But dark and hairy. That was my impression.' She wrinkled her nose. 'Is everyone so duff at describing people?'

'Yep.'

'But there were overhanging branches!'

'What kind of van did you say it was?'

She rolled her eyes. 'A delivery van. Not the size of a truck. Not the size of a car. A white-van-driver kind of van, only not white. A van you could stand up in. Know what I mean?'

'You don't remember the livery?'

'What, like, the name of the company?'

Pen poised, he nodded.

'Well, it wasn't Tesco.' She chewed the inside of her lip. 'That's a hard one. Oops.' Eyes wide, she reached over and slapped his arm again.

'Don't even think it,' Allan said.

'No, honestly, remembering that's beyond me. I had a funeral to go to, so I probably wasn't thinking at my best.'

'Somebody close?' Quieter, he said, 'Anyone I met?'

She shrugged. 'An elderly aunt. I mean, she was sweet and I loved her, but she'd lived a long time.'

'Okay.' He nodded. 'If you remember anything else, can you let me know? Or the boys in the school. The PC boys, I mean.' Allan stifled a yawn.

'I never used to bore you.' She leaned back on the sofa, head tilted, the overhead light coating her throat with a peachy luminescence. Her tee-shirt neckline wasn't low-cut, but it was low enough.

He squeezed his eyes. It was only 9.30pm, but he felt tired. He hadn't even emptied his glass. He shook his head slowly and folded up his notebook. 'I don't know what's wrong with me these days,' he said.

She sat up again. 'Are you alright?'

He tucked his notebook in his jacket. 'Yeah, I'm just always knackered.'

She rested a hand on his arm. 'Well, there's no need to rush off. Sit for a minute. A half an hour. Relax!' She slid over the sofa towards him and started to massage his temples. He didn't resist. In fact, he angled his head to make it easier for her.

'You always loved this, like a cat.'

He lifted her wrists and moved her hands away from him then reached for his glass and took a sip. 'What about you? How have you been?'

She toyed with her rings. 'Okay,' she said. 'But not as good as when I was with you.'

A moment passed. And a look. Then she took his glass and put it on the coffee table.

Chapter 18

It had been such a stupid thing to do, lose his cool with the kid. All he had to do was show an interest in his computer game, and he might have spent the night with Lorraine. And he might have got some information about the bin fire. Dour bloody teenager!

Allan slid open the shower door and punched the 'on' button. The water was scaldingly hot, the way he liked it, and he turned his face up into the hot surge. He was pretty sure Khalil and Ahmed were harmless, but there was something going on. For a start, they knew Jamie. Okay, they were a year or two older, which was a lifetime at that age, and they probably had no time for the kid. What was all that stuff about the boy being a prick tease? That was worth remembering.

Allan turned the dial to increase the water temperature, hoping it could scorch the image of the dead boy from his memory. It wasn't working. As for Khal and Ahmed, he'd seen them idling on their own at the fence when he'd gone up to talk to the head teacher the day before. There weren't many Asian kids at the school, and he supposed it was understandable that they hung about together. Jamie wasn't Asian, though. Not with that ginger hair. Having said that, Khalil was only half Asian. He thought about Lorraine's blonde hair. Nah, but surely Jamie was too fair to have an Asian dad? Well, of course, Michael Brooks had come in for the media briefing, and his was Scots-Irish heritage through and through, so that ruled that out.

He rubbed his eyes, still letting the water stream over his face, then reached for the body wash. Bergamot and a touch of pistachio oil? He sniffed at it and squeezed some on the cloth then rubbed it under his arms and round his neck. What did the boys know about the bin fire at the industrial estate? The shadowy figures on Ross's CCTV footage hinted at their body language, but it was dark, and grainy, and even blown up it would probably be inconclusive. Anyway, he'd keep an eye on the boy. There was nothing he could pull him in for, so the best way to do that was to keep in with his mother, which wouldn't be an issue, except for the way he'd blown it yesterday evening. He'd need to put that right.

He heard the perspex panel slide open. Emma stepped in against him, the water cascading down her body, over the crests of her breasts as she pressed herself against him and pushed her soft lips against his mouth.

'Let me do that,' she whispered. She took the soapy cloth from his hands and rubbed it over his shoulders and chest, and down the line of hair below his navel, while he looked down at his dick standing ruddy and waiting, water and froth flowing over it.

~~~

Such a stupid thing to do.

She'd gone into the kitchen in her towelling wrap to start the coffee and toast, her hair gleaming black and still dripping. He rubbed himself dry with the towel and sat on the bed. He dabbed his shoulders, tender where she'd scratched him, and cursed himself all over again. But what was done was done.

When they separated to go to work, she asked about seeing him again, that look of hope in her eyes. It was the closest she really came to naked. But he left it hanging. Hadn't they been here before?

He thought she might cry. Just for a moment, that despair in her eyes. A depth she couldn't come up from. Please, no, he thought. Not now. Not again. He didn't have the guts to go through it.

Then the hard edge reappeared, her voice curt. 'Who's Lorraine?'

By now, they were waiting for the lift down. How did she know about Lorraine? 'Have you been looking at my phone?' The doors opened with a ping and they went in without speaking. He repeated his question. 'Have you been looking though my phone? I'm a policeman, Emma.'

'Well, you shouldn't leave it lying about,' she snapped. 'With the same old password.'

The lift stopped a floor down and a younger couple got in. Allan seethed at the back, conscious of his rib cage expanding and contracting in fury. At ground level they all got out and as soon as they left the building, Allan let the younger couple walk a few steps ahead of them into the car park before he caught Emma by the arm and forced her to look at him. 'I'm a policeman. Don't look at my phone. Don't stalk me.'

Emma glared, defiant. 'Who is she?'

He shook his head. 'She's a friend. A girl friend. We're not together anymore, you and me. You need to get used to that.'

She looked down at his hand clutched on her sleeve. 'Then get your hand off me.'

He withdrew it angrily and walked to his car.

Chapter 19

This time, driving the red Alfa couldn't soothe him. The roads were snagged all the way into town and out the other side to the police HQ in the business park, and the stop-start on the pedals provoked Allan so the sweat stung under his arms and on the backs on his hands. He bellowed in fury at a cyclist who cut in front of him on the inside. Up ahead, at the roundabout, the boy tried to overtake on the inside of a blue van waiting to turn left. The van hit him. It outraged Allan all the more, but he threw off his seat belt and dashed out of his car to see what he could do. The boy seemed fine, even if his bike's front wheel was mangled. But Allan's heart rattled in his chest.

The last thing he needed when he finally made it to work was to see the media staking out the entrance. If ever he wished he'd a key to the back door, this was it. There must have been a dozen of them with stills cameras, TV cameras and boom mikes, and as soon as one of them identified Allan they crowded round him, impeding his path to the front door of the building, where the concierge could do nothing to stop them.

'DI MacIntyre? I'm from BBC Highlands. Can you tell us what progress you've made in the Jamie Brooks murder case? Are our children safe? The murderer's still at loose. Who are your suspects?'

'No comment, guys.'

'DI MacIntyre? Press and Gazette. Should we keep our kids off school? Is there a paedophile on the loose in the streets of Inverness?'

'No comment.' Shaking with rage, Allan pushed his way through and climbed the three steps to the front doors. Then he turned and said, 'Look – it's early days. My team's working flat out. We've got extra officers at the schools for protection and to gather information. The media department will give you updates as soon as we have them, but be assured, we'll get who did this, and we'll get him quick.' Cameras flashed and he pushed his way into the building.

In his office, he swallowed paracetamol with coffee held in trembling hands.

'Oh – hitting the sauce too hard, Sir?' Jane said, grinning, as she put her latest report on his desk.

'Call a team meeting for 9.30. I want everyone there.' He didn't even meet her eyes.

'Yes, Sir.'

Allan stood in a toilet cubicle, leaning against the partition wall, and tried to calm down. What enraged him was that it was his social life – his private life – that was messing him up, when he should've been focused on the case. It was a big case. Here he was with the press on his back and no progress to show. Those guys were right. There could be a paedo on the loose and kids could be in danger. And all he could do was screw things up with women. Screw things up full stop. And there was this feeling that his body was letting him down. This feeling he couldn't control. What the fuck was going on with him?

Someone else came into the toilets, so he flushed and went out to splash cool water on his face and hands.

At 9.30, half of the team were in the incident room already when he arrived, chatting languidly among themselves. Only half. He checked his watch. 'Did you tell them half past?' he asked Jane, who said she did. He drummed his fingers on the desk, jiggled papers. Walked to the door and looked outside. Called to the others who were straggling along the corridor that they were late and should get a move on.

In the incident room, Jane and Ross exchanged looks.

'When I say 9.30, I mean 9.30.'

There were mumbles. Apologies.

'Right. Let's take stock. Jamie Brooks' body was found three days ago. Three days ago. What progress have we made to catching – let's take this back a step – how close are we to actually identifying his killer? Jane?'

'Well, we've talked to the staff and kids at the two schools Jamie didn't go to, given them advice about protecting themselves and what to look out for.' She shook her head. 'Not surprisingly, we've turned up no leads. They didn't know Jamie.' She broke off.

'Okay. Both schools?' Allan said, and she nodded. He looked at his notes. 'Well, I did Jamie's Thistlebank Academy and a team's going to be based there for the next few days at least. He turned to the board. 'An early lead has suggested a man in a delivery van was seen hanging about at lunchtime on Monday – the day of the murder.' He turned back round to face the room but kept his eyes on his notes and the other pieces of paper he was sifting through on the desk in front of him. Eyes up. 'A man in his thirties, dark hair and could be bearded, possibly Indian or Pakistani origin. Probably a parent, but we should check it out. The guy was dour, and unsettled the teacher who reported it, not just because his van was parked on the zig-zag lines where he shouldn't have been. Ross – can you call that up on the CCTV? See if we can get a clear shot of him, or the van at least.'

'On Monday?'

'Yep – just about lunchtime. The teacher thought it was a bit suspicious. Not at the time, but worth checking out in the circumstances.'

'Right, Sir.' Ross's voice took on a desperate note. 'Any chance of help going through the CCTV, Sir?'

Allan stabbed him with a look but said nothing for a moment. Eventually, he said, 'Sure. That PC Welsh – what's her name? Anna? – she'd be good at that, wouldn't she?'

Ross's cheeks coloured deep red and everyone in the room fidgeted, pretending they weren't grinning.

'Right, that's enough. Back to business. Sam – you were checking for known paedophiles. In the community or recently released. Any word?'

Sam opened a thin folder, licked his fingertip and selected an A4 sheet. 'These are the names of those at large. I've been to speak with most of them and they all have alibis. Still got...' , he ran his finger down the list, '...three more to reach. I'll get those done this morning.'

'Cool. What about forensics? Jamie's clothes? The phone? Who's looking into that? Jane?'

Jane looked shocked. She shook her head. 'Not me. You said me, and then you told Ross to do it.'

'Me? I've been stuck with my head in CCTV footage!'

'From that bloody bin fire? Did you at least get me the print of that footage from the garage?'

Ross shuffled in his seat. 'The printer's broken. The engineers are supposed to be fixing it today.'

Allan stared in disbelief. 'Are you trying to tell me every printer in the building's broken?'

Ross cringed. 'Well, no.'

'Take the bloody file next door and get the stuff printed. Take it to bloody Asda if you have to. Get it done!' Allan looked from one to the other. 'So who's looking into the phone and the forensics? Who's chasing that up?'

There was silence.

'Fucking hell! Why isn't anyone doing it?'

The team went from drowsy to caffeine-hit in a second, glancing sideways at each other. Eventually Jane said, 'Well, Sir, if Forensics had got back to us, we'd be doing it. We'd know about it.'

Allan blew out cool air over his lips. He could feel sweat patches on his shirt and yet again his heart was racing. Hands on his hips, he stalked to the door to open it, and back again.

'Are you okay, Sir?' Jane said. 'D'you want me to get you a coffee? Or a glass of water?'

'I'm fine,' he barked. He looked round the room. 'Ross – get in touch with Forensics and see if you can persuade them to send you Jamie's phone's call logs and address book – and anything off the memory card. Okay? Actually do it this time. Everyone else – keep at it. Keep taking statements. Keep your eyes opened. I need to take some time to think. We can do this, and the sooner we get it done, the better. We've got the media camped at the doors, and parents out there getting agitated. Any kind of information – any information at all – feed it back. Let's keep each other in the loop so there's none of this not knowing who's doing what.' He shuffled his papers again, looked at the white board with Jamie's photo on it and the big question marks in red, then dismissed the team with, 'Get to work.'

Chapter 20

Allan got back in the car and drove out of the business park. He took the road along the river Ness, tilting his visor when the low sun burnished the water. Soon there were low lying fields to one side of the road and the hills rose, dark green with conifer plantation, on the other. He indicated to turn off the main road and the car responded to the shift of gears and his pressure on the accelerator, eager for the climb. The road twisted past solitary homes tucked into corners, and skirted fields where small groups of brown and black highland cattle glanced laconically up as they tugged and chewed at bales of hay.

At length, he pulled off the road where he'd stopped a few days earlier, got out the car and stretched his back. The road was quiet. Deserted. Just normal. On one side was the mixed woodland, red with rowan berries, and on the other the hill fell away at a sharp angle, the field a scrubby grassland for grazing sheep. He walked the few steps back to where he, PC Smith and Jane Coburn had gone off-road, climbing uphill towards the crime scene through the trees, moss and brown bracken.

Once again, he entered the woodland and started to climb. As he went, he took his time, heaving himself up when he needed to with a hand on the rough grey and white trunks of the birch trees, securing his footing on the slippery moss-covered boulders, and all the time fighting to keep his breathing even. The weather hadn't changed, and the earth was still dry. At length, he reached the place where the blue and white tape had fluttered, tied between trees. It was gone now. Forensics had done their job. He stood for minutes, letting his breathing settle after the trudge uphill, and mulling over what he knew, and what he'd seen. Still, the sunlight dappled through yellow leaves to where the boy's body had lain, pink and vulnerable.

He took a few steps to the scene itself: kicked at a few crisp leaves, crouched to toss aside some broken twigs. What was the motive? Purely sexual? Where was the DNA? The killer had cleared up thoroughly. Allan scoured the fallen leaves, but there wasn't a trace. There was nothing caught on the trees. Nothing. Only the peace. He breathed deeply. He'd been harsh with the team. Jane especially. Ach, he thought. Shit happens. Fuck knew what was wrong with him but he needed this mini-escape to restore his balance, even if it was the scene of a boy being raped and killed. He breathed deeply. Squinted over towards the sun. There wasn't even any reception on his phone.

He took the other route downhill to the road and walked back towards his car, checking his mobile. There was reception here, since this was where Irma Russell had phoned from when she found the body. None of Allan's team had tried to contact him, nor had anyone from Forensics. As he slipped his phone into his pocket, he noticed tyre tracks half smudged in leaf mould. It might be nothing, but experience had taught him the most commonplace thing could be meaningful if it was found near a crime scene, so he took his phone out again and photographed them. They were broad tracks – broader than a car, or a jeep. He looked around. His car was parked in the nearest passing place. This was probably just someone impatient to get by some slower, older driver – there were plenty of them peering over their steering wheels on the roads round Inverness – but he'd log it for Forensics.

He heard an engine in the distance but there was no sign of anything yet. So he dialled Forensics' number, and held the phone to his ear as he walked back to the car. The engine noise increased. Allan whipped his head round to see a blue van storm down the centre of the single track road, accelerating towards him. In his ear, the man from Forensics said, 'Hello? Hello?' Still, the van accelerated. Surely he must see him? The van bore down. Allan leaped out of the way, stopping short of sliding down the steep embankment.

'I'll get back to you,' he said into his phone.

There was a house at the bend of the road. A man in his seventies came out and began walking up the hill towards Allan. 'Are you okay?' he shouted. 'That was some speed that guy was doing!'

Allan's heart was rattling again, and – stupid bastard – he had to put his hands on his knees to catch his breath and lose the twinkly stars he was seeing.

The man put his hand on Allan's shoulder. 'Want to come in for a minute?'

Allan squinted up and nodded.

The man's house was in a bend in the road, and as they walked towards it – Allan's legs shaking now, too – he couldn't help notice the mush of brown leaves that had dropped from the overhanging branches. Then he noticed a fresh impression. 'Hold on,' he said, and took his phone out to photograph it and compare it with the picture he'd just taken. The local man was still standing there. Allan looked at him. 'Have you seen that van before?'

The man shrugged. 'Once or twice.'

'And does he drive like that all the time?'

He rubbed the stubble on his chin and grinned. 'I think he must be in a hurry to knock off.'

'When did you last see him?'

'The van? The Q-buster van?' he frowned. 'Well, it's the highlands.' He looked at Allan, obviously alert to his lowland accent. 'We get a lot of things delivered, here.'

'Yeah, I get that,' Allan said. 'But can you remember when you last saw that particular van?'

'Well, I never saw the guy behind the wheel, but the van – a Q-buster van – comes up here a couple of times a week, probably.'

Allan got through to Forensics and asked them to come up to check it out. Then he turned back to the older man. 'So, was it up here earlier this week?'

The man thought about it. 'I expect so. What about it?'

'Did you tell the investigating officer about it, on Tuesday, when we found that boy's body?'

The man almost laughed. 'No, it never crossed my mind! The van's up here all the time! Are you trying to say he's responsible? Just because he nearly ran into you?'

Allan felt the surge of frustration but held it in check. 'Just so we can rule it out.'

The man's face lit up in a lightbulb moment. 'No, wait – I saw him on Monday. I know, because this is a bad bend, and I was backing the car out to take my wife down to the GP for an appointment. Late afternoon – just about dusk – and I almost didn't see him because it's blue and the light was poor,' he indicated upwards. 'We're a bit overhung with these trees.'

'Monday?' Allan said. The afternoon before the boy's body was found.

Chapter 21

'Hello, Emma?'

A woman in a blue tunic top squeaked along the corridor towards Allan, her mouth and eyes a mix of humour and disapproval. She gave two little taps with her pen against a poster next to where he was standing and walked on without missing a beat. Allan checked the poster. Please switch off your mobile phone, it said.

He'd reached Emma's voicemail. It was morning and she'd be teaching class, of course. He left her a message, asking if she could remember the colour of the delivery van she'd seen outside the school, then he hung up. He flicked through his notebook. She'd described it as a white-van-style van, that you could stand up in, only not white. Maybe she'd just text him the answer, save any further complications. Knowing Emma, she wouldn't respond. She always had loved a power struggle, and if she knew something Allan wanted to know, that gave her power and she'd dangle it. She would dangle it.

He hated hospital corridors. Too much bad history. Double doors, light panels gleaming on polished vinyl flooring, anti-bacterial hand-wash and the chink of cups on a passing tea-trolley... he made a deliberate effort to push his shoulders down. This wasn't even a hospital – just the new clinic his GP had moved into. It was so big it felt like a hospital.

Allan pushed through a door into a waiting room and sat down in one of four rows of turquoise padded seats. There were three people in front of him, sitting singly. And two beside him, sitting together. They were all older than him except a mother whose drippy nosed toddler was sitting directly behind him and kept clinging to the back of his chair and dragging his hands over Allan's suit jacket. Allan peeled his back away and sat forward, skimming through his phone. The woman in front of him stank of stale tobacco and had a hacking cough that sounded as if it had lumps in it.

See this, he said to himself, this is why you don't come to places like this. He checked the time. It might be Emma's tea-break, so he went back to the corridor, pointing out where he'd be to the reception staff, though they were too busy to notice.

Out in the corridor, with no sign of the mobile phone police, he redialled Emma's number but was put through to voicemail again. He sighed, convinced she was playing him. Then he phoned Jane.

'Yes, Sir?' she said.

Her tone confused him. It was clipped and formal. Then he remembered he'd been short with her, which was something else he'd have to smooth over. 'Jane. Can you phone the Head at Thistlebank to ask if one of the kids in the school has a dad who drives a Q-busters delivery van? Or a blue delivery van?' Remembering Emma's description of the driver at the school, he added, 'He might be South Asian – Indian, Pakistani, Bangladeshi, whatever.'

'Right, Sir.'

'Keep it low key. No point in stirring anything up for a hunch.'

'No, Sir.'

Allan said nothing for a few seconds. Then, 'Any news?'

'Still waiting for Forensics; still analysing data; still going through witness statements. And Ross has put a file on your desk. A picture you'd asked for, from CCTV.'

'About time!' he closed his eyes and breathed. 'Good work, Jane. Thanks.'

Was that a catch in her breath? Shit, what was it like to work with women sometimes? He closed the flap on his phone cover and tucked it back in his pocket. He probably wasn't allowed to think that these days.

Back in the waiting room, the receptionist peered over half-glasses at him. 'Mr MacIntyre?'

'That's me,' he said, resting his hands on her counter.

'We've been calling you for ages! Room 6, on the left, please.'

Chapter 22

Khalil was aware of a kind of Doppler effect as the cars went by, not only in terms of the engine noise, but the white and red lights streaming past in the gloaming, too. There was a tang of November, but that was an illusion. They were still a couple of days away even from Hallowe'en guising before they got to Guy Fawkes Night. There was something in the air that made him think about it, though. Something in the early dark, and the coming on of the street and car lights, and something wispy, like a trace of woodsmoke, and a mist of exploded fireworks.

Khal's house had a low wall outside it, edging the pavement. It was an old brick wall topped with what had been a pale grey, almost white cement cap. It had been there as long as Khal had lived there, though now the red bricks had started to chip and crumble, and the cement cap was often charcoal grey with the rain. Khal perched on the wall, on the pavement side, hidden from the house by the hedge that grew above the wall. The rain had stopped, but little pools of it were held in the privet leaves and it felt like the wall caps themselves held a reservoir of it, slowly seeping into his jacket and trousers.

Khal's backpack was heavy over one shoulder. Hearing a jingling sound, he glanced up from his phone and identified it as coming from the collar worn by a black dog that lived a hundred metres along the street. Out of the dark, the dog trotted, tail up. His owner was with him at the other end of the lead. Khal slipped his phone inside his jacket pocket till the man had passed. He dropped the backpack from his shoulder on to the pavement between his feet, the bag's weight taking him by surprise, even though he knew what was inside.

The boy looked up at the sky as a plane passed, low, making its final approach. He dug his phone out of his pocket again, drew in his passcode and sought out the page he'd been on before. He looked from the phone to the sky; from the plane on its approach to an area over to the east where the app told him a freight plane was passing, high beyond the clouds. DG541, heading for Turkey, out of sight and out of mind.

The phone rang, making Khalil jump. 'Hey,' he said, scanning the street to ensure he wouldn't be overheard.

'Hey. What's happening?'

'Nothing. Just waiting. My mum's out and I forgot my key. You?'

'Just wondering what you were doing.' It was Ahmed. 'Are you coming to the centre?'

Khal sniffed. 'Nah. Not tonight. Too much to do. Are you?' Without waiting for an answer, he added, 'Will he be there? Are you going to see him? We need to challenge him, man.'

'I know we do.' Ahmed's voice was clipped. 'You don't need to tell me that.'

'We have to stop this, man.' Khalil stirred on the damp wall. 'I can't believe he got us into this. We have to stop him.' A car went by. When Ahmed didn't say anything, Khalil repeated, 'We have to.'

'Yeah, yeah – I know. I know, man. But we have to stop him our way. Give him a fright so he won't do it again. You got me?'

Khal clenched his teeth. 'But it's not good, man. I'm not comfortable.' He cut himself off short, emotion making his voice rise. 'Are you going there tonight – to the centre?'

Again, there was a time delay, before Ahmed spoke. 'I might be, but with my dad. Listen – did you get the stuff?'

'Yeah,' Khal said, looking around himself again, even though the pavement was empty. A few cars went by, slowing to go over the uneven speed bumps ten metres from his garden path. One slowed completely, its indicator flashing. The rear passenger doors opened and two boys got out then the car drove away.

'How you doing, Khal?' A voice asked.

'Shit,' Khal said into the phone. 'I'll call you later.'

Chapter 23

The CID office was ablaze with light even though it was just after five in the afternoon. That footage Ross had printed was inconclusive. It showed only two young male figures of indeterminate age, hanging about the petrol-station shop in the small hours of the night. The close-up of the face was too indistinct to prove anything, even if it did bear a vague resemblance to a young lad who might or might not have black hair and a Middle Eastern or South Asian appearance. All boys looked the same at that age, anyway, didn't they? Dour and lanky.

Allan squeezed the corners of his eyes. Glare from the lights and the screens was getting to him, and if this was the future of police work, he thought he might just apply for a job as a postman. He was taking a turn of looking through CCTV footage, hoping to catch sight of the van he'd seen being driven at him at deliberate speed this morning. So far, all he'd seen was taxis cutting people up on the inside lane.

'Sam,' he called across the office, 'what was the name of that company that reported the bin fire at Inchmarsh Industrial Estate? It was Q-busters, wasn't it?'

His mobile rang before Sam could answer, and he stretched his back and shoulders while he looked to see who was calling.

'Emma,' he said. 'Thanks for getting back to me.' Businesslike. He'd learned his lesson.

She breathed out into the phone. 'Hi, Allan.' Kittenish. Clearly, she hadn't been at the same lesson. 'I'm not good in the morning. Can we – erm – can we rewind?'

He gazed out of the huge windows, seeing his team-mates' reflections, and beyond that, the line of red brake-lights as people queued to leave the business park. 'Did you get my message? About the colour of the van, or anything?'

'Mm-huh.' She was probably fingering her hair or touching her earring. 'Will we meet? I'm free. Anytime. Now, if you like.'

He looked at his watch. 'I just need to know if you remember the colour of the van, Emma. You've had time to think about it. Thought of anything else? A name, or anything?'

Her voice came in a single laugh, quiet, maybe contrite? 'Okay, okay – you've got me. It's just, if I tell you, that'll be it, won't it? You won't want to see me.'

'I'm pretty busy with this investigation.' He swivelled on his chair, the cellophane wrapper making its regular crinkling sound. 'You understand that?'

'Of course.'

Well, well, he thought. Goodbye Miss Kitten. 'So, the colour of the van?'

She sighed. 'It was blue. Deep blue. Close to royal.'

The phone on his desk buzzed. 'Great. Any thoughts on a name?'

She hesitated. 'I'm not sure.'

He sat forward. 'Look, Emma. I've got to go. Someone on the other line.'

'I might recognise it if I saw some pictures!' she said, eager.

'I'll get back to you.' He cut the call and picked up the desk-phone handset. 'DI MacIntyre?'

It was the sergeant downstairs. 'We've a young man in custody, Sir, asking for you.'

Allan gingerly inspected the inside of his elbow where the nurse had taken blood. He peeled the plaster off. 'Oh, yeah? Who is it and what's he in for?'

'Well, we're holding him on terror-related charges.' There was a pause and a sound of paper sliding on a desk. 'Khalil Buchanan?'

Allan was stunned. Khal? Terror charges? 'Are you sure?'

103

He could almost hear the man on the other end of the phone shrug. 'That's what I'm told.'

Allan reached behind him for his jacket off the chair. 'I'll be right there.'

As he put the phone back in its rest, his mobile rang again.

'Lorraine. What's going on with Khalil? They've just got in touch with me.'

'They're harassing him, that's what. Because his name is Khalil and his dad's a Muslim. They've taken him into custody. He's fifteen! It's a total disgrace. He was just doing a bit of shopping and now they're calling him a terrorist! How could my Khal be a terrorist?'

Allan thought about the truculent teenager he'd caught looking up flight paths of planes flying over Britain, but he didn't mention that.

'It's ludicrous. He's just an easy target, so they're harassing him. Have your lot nothing better to do with their time?' Even Jane Coburn and Sam Abouwaye looked up, hearing her tinny tirade coming out of the mobile Allan was holding six inches away from his ear.

'What was he buying, any idea?'

'Stuff for Bob. Gardening stuff. Fertiliser.'

'Fertiliser?'

'I think so. And other stuff. Nails. Things like that. White spirit.'

'White spirit? Fertiliser, nails and white spirit?'

'He was going to help Bob with a bit of decorating.'

'Okay. So, listen – are you in the building? Wait there and I'll come and get you.' He signalled to Jane and Sam that he was leaving.

'Wait!' Sam said, standing up. He gathered papers into a folder and held it up – something Allan needed to see before leaving.

'What is it?'

'Forensics about the bin fire.'

Allan frowned. 'No time for that. Leave it on my desk. I'll get it in the morning.'

'No, Sir,' Sam insisted, holding out the paperwork. 'If body language was anything to go by, contradicting his senior officer was taking him out of his comfort zone. 'You'll want to see this. Especially if that boy's being interviewed on terror charges. And the company that phoned in about it is called Q-busters.'

Allan took the folder and flicked through it. 'Shit. Right.' He looked up from the photos and forensic reports to meet the young man's eyes. 'Shit. Good timing, Sam. You'd better come with me.'

Chapter 24

Khalil Buchanan was in one of the friendlier holding cells. The walls were a sickly shade of pale green, still too new to have graffiti and gouge marks, and the long low shelf which served as seat and bed was covered in functional, practical – wipe-down – navy PVC. Though the window was high, small and barred, the room was brighter than most cells Allan had been in. At this time of day, and this time of year, it was bright only because of the strip light in the ceiling.

The duty PC unlocked the heavy door and let them in. The boy was sitting on the bench, head down, and when he lifted his face to look at them, Allan froze with shock. No one had warned him the boy had been beaten. His left eye was swollen and closed shut; his nose had been bleeding and a folded square of white gauze was taped to his right cheek just above the jaw line. There were blood stains down the front of the sports top he was wearing.

'Thanks, PC Macready,' Allan said, recovering himself. 'Get us in a couple of chairs, will you?' He waited till the PC brought in two folding chairs then left, closing the door behind him, before he said, 'Khalil, this is Sam – Detective Constable Sam Abouwaye.'

'Hey, Khalil,' Sam said. He held out his hand to the boy, turning it knuckles-forward, and to Allan's surprise the boy knuckled him back.

Allan sat down and put the folder on the floor under his seat. 'Those are some bad knocks. I take it you've had someone look at them? Did they check for breaks?'

Khalil nodded and rubbed his hand up the point of his nose.

106

'Okay, so what happened to you?'

'I just got jumped.'

'Yeah? So why are you in here and not the guy who jumped you?'

Khalil raised and slumped his shoulders. A wince suggested the beating had affected more than his face.

Allan stretched one leg towards the boy. 'This is just a chat. Sam and I are working on a case, but I heard you'd been lifted and were asking for me, so we stopped in to see what's happening, okay? The duty sergeant told me you've been detained on some pretty serious charges.' He tapped his foot against Khal's to get him to look up and meet his eyes. 'So, you will be interviewed. He's arranging for a responsible adult to be in here with you. But as I say,' he looked at Sam, 'Sam and I thought we'd see how you're doing, off the record.'

'That looks a sore one – your eye,' Sam said. 'Who did that to you?'

Khalil wiped his nose again, saw the watery blood on his hand and rubbed it off on his trousers. Again, he shrugged.

'Okay, Khal,' Allan said. 'You asked for me, but now I'm here, you're not talking? How about you tell us in your own words what you were doing today that meant you ended up here?'

The teenager said nothing for a minute till Allan was almost ready to get up and leave. Then, still looking at his bloodied hands, he started to talk. 'I went to the shops for the old guy next door. Bob. I go quite often. Usually I get him bread, or pick up a balti or fish and chips, but sometimes other stuff.' He glanced up at Allan.

'Uh-huh? And today it was something else?'

'Yep.'

Allan flicked his eyes sideways to Sam, who'd started taking notes. 'So, what was it?'

Khalil sighed and sat back against the wall. He looked up at the ceiling. 'You've got my bag. You know what it was.'

Allan mock-looked round. 'I've not got your bag. You, DC Abouwaye?'

'Nope.'

'Come on, Khal. Just say it. Your mother's out there, frantic. Just put your side of the story and we'll try and get you out of here.' He let that sink in. 'Trust me. You know me. It doesn't do me any good having you locked up in here.'

The boy glowered at that bit of code between them, but then he started talking again. 'Bob likes gardening. And he likes doing things in the house, like putting up shelves.' He dabbed gingerly at his sore eye. 'See, you'll not get it.' He shook his head.

'Try me.'

Khalil sighed and kicked one foot against the sole of the other. 'It's just – Bob's there for me. D'you get it?' He looked to Sam.

'What do you mean, Khal?' Sam asked, leaving his pen aside for now.

'Like, I've not got my dad around much, but Bob – Bob shows me stuff. Like how to put up shelves; how to do electrics. He likes his garden. I mean, he really likes his garden, but he's not been able to do it since he had his stroke.'

'Go on,' Allan said.

'So, like, he was going on about how it was time to sort it for the winter and, like, mulch bits and feed bits and stuff. And I just thought...' Once again he ran his knuckles over the tip of his nose and it came away bloody. For a minute, Allan thought he was going to lose the dour, hard teenager act and start to cry.

'Use the cloth, son,' Allan said, nodding to the wipes the duty doctor had left on the bench. Khalil grabbed them and plugged his nostril. 'Better?'

The boy unplugged the wipes, examined them, sniffed and then nodded.

'So – you just thought...?'

He shrugged. 'I thought I could get him some stuff and he could tell me what to do.'

Allan shifted in his chair and checked that Sam was getting this down in his notebook. 'So that's why you bought fertiliser?'

'Uh-huh.'

'And what about the rest – the nails and the white spirit? Was that to put up shelves?' It was hard to keep the irony out of his voice.

'Yeah. Something like that.'

'Right – moving on. Who beat you up?'

'Two guys from school.'

Allan had a memory of something. 'Those same two I saw harassing you the other day?'

Khalil's good eye lit up. 'Yeah!' His face turned sour. 'They say I'm a terrorist. Well, they usually say something else, but they went through my bag and said I was a terrorist. And somebody heard them and that's how the police got involved.'

Allan checked his watch. He reached down to pick the folder off the floor and looked through it, isolating three pictures. He held one out for Khalil to see. 'Do you know anything about this?' It was a picture of a burned-out bin.

Khalil shook his head.

'And what about this?' Allan held up a picture of some of the contents found at the bottom of the bin. There was something metallic and charred plastic, which could be a bit of broken phone, some remnants of clothing, and a bit of scorched rubber, possibly from the sole of a trainer. 'No? You don't recognise it?' When Khalil shook his head, Allan looked once again at Sam then back to Khalil again. 'Do you know anything about a fire in a bin at Inchmarsh Industrial Estate on Tuesday morning?' He paused, waiting. Then he took out the blurry, impressionistic photo of two boys at the service station and added, 'Do you know anything about a company called Q-busters?'

Khal's mouth was pinched. He held Allan's gaze with his good eye. Then he said, 'No.'

~~~

Lorraine was pacing the area to the right of the police desk in the entrance hall of the police station when he and Sam left the cells. A bundle of fizzing energy, she was bound up for now in her mustard-coloured coat that she'd cinched in tightly at the waist. Her cheeks were flushed and with the lights accentuating the red in her strawberry blonde hair she looked like a match ready to ignite. She may have been annoyed at Allan when he left her house last time, but it didn't compare to this. He could see she was fit to bursting as he said a few words to Sam about what work to do in the morning. Finally, 'He's only fifteen!' she said, as soon as he crossed from the police side to the public side of the high desk. 'How can anybody think he could be a terrorist?'

'Shhh,' he said, hand on her coat sleeve as he steered her towards some quiet seating.

'Did he say anything? He's innocent, isn't he? What did you think?' She scanned his face. 'I mean, he can be nippy – sullen – but what teenager isn't?' She broke away and blew her nose. 'He likes you, so I think he'll trust you.' She blinked a few times, droplets of water glistening on her lashes. 'He'd better trust you! If he knows what's good for him. What did he say to you?'

'That he bought stuff to do a job for your neighbour?'

'That's right!' Lorraine said. 'For Old Bob! He loves Bob. Bob's good to him. He's like a father to him. Well, a grandfather. They do man-things together. Bob's a good role-model for him.'

Allan weighed it up. What mother wouldn't believe her son? But she didn't know about the bin fire. The bin explosion, which is what the forensics were suggesting. Something was going on that Allan needed time and space to think about.

'Look,' he said. 'We're going to have to keep him in overnight.'

'No!'

'He'll be fine. Trust me. D'you want in to see him again? Then I'll take you home?'

The flame had gone out. Too much water coming from her eyes for her to be able to sustain it. She nodded.

Allan drove her home after she'd seen the boy again, but this time he didn't go in her house.

Chapter 25

The report on the bin fire elevated a random prank into something serious. Allan mulled over the forensics while he drove home on automatic pilot. The dead boy's mother said the only phone Jamie had was her old one, and she'd been planning on buying him a new one for Christmas, yet they'd found that expensive, up-market one under his pillow. Hopefully, Ross would've got his arse in gear by now and got hold of the call logs from it. And now Forensics had found something metallic and plastic at the bottom of that bin in the Inchmarsh Industrial Estate, along with fibres and rubber which could be the missing boy's clothes. If the kid had come by the phone illegally (or at least was keeping it quiet from his mother) he could've kept it in his room and was taking the one she'd given him to school and back. There was a strong possibility the boy was murdered on the Monday after lunch and everything he had on him – clothes, shoes, the duff phone – were dumped in the bin and burned. That hypothesis was straightforward. It fitted the profile of a paedophile rapist and murderer obliterating any evidence against him. Or trying to. Though why he'd chosen a bin in Inchmarsh Industrial Estate was anybody's guess. That was a link that needed evidence.

The other scenario was altogether dodgier. Allan swung the Alfa into his street and parked up. He sat for a minute, while the engine ticked as it cooled, thinking about Khalil. Could Lorraine's boy really be involved in terrorism? He was fifteen, for god's sake. Just because he was mixed heritage and had tangential links to Islam – and mainstream Islam at that – didn't mean he was programmed to be a murderer. Okay, there was the white spirit and fertiliser. And the nails. He forgot about the nails. And the obsessive way Khal checked those aeroplane travel screens. And the collusion between him and Ahmed. Christ. There was even that grainy CCTV footage Ross had shown him from the garage on the night after Jamie's murder and before the bin fire. The more Allan fought to damp down the notion, the more it sprang back alight.

Then there was that deep blue Q-busters delivery van that might connect both crimes. He saw, again, the van accelerate towards him on the hillside that morning.

His hand went to the inside of his left arm and he tentatively pressed the tiny point where the needle had been inserted to draw blood today. That had been a surprise. That had been a lot of bullshit. Whatever it was they were testing him for. It was bullshit. He was fit as a dog. He tugged the keys from the ignition, got out and slammed the car door and headed for his house. Tomorrow, he and Jane would take a trip to Q-busters to speak with the woman who phoned them about the fire.

~~~

Inchmarsh Industrial Estate was on the periphery of the city. Its featureless metal and brick warehouses sat in acres of tarmac on flat land that had probably been the flood plain for the river or had been home to grazing sheep. The directory signing had faded and not been replaced, so Allan had to drive round each section of the site until he found the deep blue-painted Q-busters signage. There were a couple of vans in the yard, but Allan drove past and pulled over beside other cars in front of the two storey brick building he presumed was the office accommodation.

Jane had been reading the bin fire forensics report while Allan drove. When he put on the hand brake, she closed the file. 'Are they doing further tests on the fibres? To see if there's a link to Jamie?'

'That's the plan. Sam's on it.'

She nodded and looked out of the window. 'So, the bin was found – where?'

112

'Probably over there.' Allan pointed to a bright new bin beside a few older ones. 'But let's go and find out.'

A buzzer sounded as they opened the heavy door into the office block, and soon a woman in her late fifties or early sixties slid open the window in the partition wall that separated the office from the entrance hall.

'Cathy – ,' Allan said, floundering in his search for the woman's surname. Ross still hadn't noted it down. 'DI MacIntyre and DS Coburn.' They showed their ID. 'We'd like a word about the fire you reported a few days ago?'

'Coates,' the woman said, and held a rather thin hand out through the window towards them.

Allan was tucking his badge back in the inside pocket of his jacket. 'No, it's fine,' he said. Jane had already begun slipping her arms out of her sleeves. The woman shook her head.

'No, no – I mean my name is "Coates". Cathy Coates.'

There was a pause. 'Sorry!' Jane said and struggled to re-insert her arms into her jacket in time to shake the hand before it became too awkward and was withdrawn.

'Don't worry about it,' Cathy said, squeezing Allan's hand firmly and tossing her rather tousy hair as she laughed. 'It always happens! Come in! The door's there.' She pointed and scurried over to open it to let them through, then pulled out seats for them and cleared some papers off one on to a desk.

Thin-limbed and featured, with hair that was still mostly brown but threaded with grey, Cathy Coates looked physically brittle and Allan wondered if she'd always been powered by nervous anxiety or if this was something special. She had one pair of glasses on her nose and another hanging from a pin on her homespun cardigan.

'Thank you,' Jane said, and smiled.

'Mrs Coates,' Allan began.

'*Cathy* is fine.'

'Cathy.' Allan looked around the small office. 'Do you work here on your own?'

'It looks that way, doesn't it?' she said, brushing her hair back from her forehead with two hands. 'But no, we've a few others. The one that's usually sitting at your desk is at a dental appointment. Again, poor soul. And Jess mans – womans! – the phones but this is her Saturday off.'

'And the MD?' Allan checked the folder of notes. 'Hugo Thompson?'

'He's in his office.' Cathy nodded behind her. She leaned towards them a bit and mock-whispered, 'He owns the company.'

'We'd like to speak with him, today, too, if that's possible.'

The phone rang and she broke off to answer it and transfer a call. 'What were we saying? Mr Thompson? Och, he'll not know anything about the fire, other than what I told him. And I told the other police officer everything. He wrote it all down,' she said, pushing her glasses up to the top of her nose and eyeing the folder Allan had put on the desk in front of him.

'Nothing else has come back to you?'

'No. It was all straightforward. I didn't notice anything when I arrived, but then the smoke got to me, and I dialled 999. That was all.'

The phone rang again and Cathy answered it. She called up a screen on the PC in front of her and Allan could see it was some kind of rota or personnel file. He signalled to Jane, who edged forward in her seat to peer at it. She moved back when Cathy ended the call.

'Could you check if Mr Thompson's free just now?' Allan asked.

'Of course.' Rather than phone him, she got up and tapped at the door to his office. When she disappeared inside, Jane slipped closer to the PC.

'It's the rota,' she said to Allan. 'The drivers.'

He glanced at the office door. 'Does it give dates and times, and names?'

'Yep. But we'd need to go back through it.' She sat down quickly when she heard the door open.

'You can go in right now, he says.' Cathy smiled at them then frowned and made a dash to answer the phone when it rang again.

Hugo Thompson rose to meet Allan and Jane when they entered. Tall and suave in a well-cut navy-coloured suit, he held out a manicured hand. 'DI MacIntyre, pleased to meet you. Take a seat, please. DS Coburn. How can I help you?' He blinked lashes so pale they were almost white, like his white-blond hair, which was swept back over his head.

Allan explained they were carrying out routine enquiries in the area and had stopped here in particular because of the bin fire.

'Yes – strange thing. Boys, I expect. Still, no damage done. It could have been worse, of course.'

Allan studied the man in front of him. Thirty-five to forty, he was well spoken with what Allan thought of as a sanded-down Inverness accent – the rough edges filed off. It was the accent of someone who thought he'd moved up in the world.

'Probably teenagers, as you say, but we're carrying out tests.'

'I'd like to see the report on that. Just in case. We can be carrying a lot of expensive goods at any one time on site, and I don't want them going up in smoke.'

'You're insured, yes?' Jane asked.

'Of course,' he said, smiling to her. He put his fingertips together, elbows on the arms of his chair, and gave her his full attention. 'Comprehensively.' Then he turned to Allan. 'And before you ask, business is good and we've no inclination to make any claims on it.'

Allan nodded. He finished scanning through the files in his folder then closed it and put it on the floor under his seat. 'Mr Thompson,' he said. 'As I mentioned, this is a routine enquiry. You'll know there was a young teenager found dead in the woods at Abriachan.'

Thompson's white brows pushed together. 'Yes. Sad business. Not what you associate with Inverness area.'

'Quite. We're pursuing several lines of enquiry. Several. And we're in the process of checking to rule out some of the information that's come in from the public. You might have seen the TV appeal?

It's thrown up a lot of leads, some of which might come to absolutely nothing, but we have to investigate them.'

'Of course. But I don't see how we can be connected with that.'

'One of the leads puts a Q-busters van in the vicinity.'

'Right.' Thompson leaned back in his chair. 'Wow. In the vicinity?'

'Yes.'

The MD rubbed his jaw. 'Mind you, we have almost a dozen vans out delivering every day, so there's bound to be one in the vicinity of every crime, when you think about it. Depends how much "in the vicinity" you mean.'

'Absolutely. And as I said, there are a lot of leads and it would be remiss of us not to follow them up.'

'Of course.'

'So, you won't mind if I send one of my team to check out your rotas and speak to the drivers?'

Thompson pushed up from the desk. 'Do you want to look now? Cathy has the rotas.' He walked towards the door and waved his hand for them to follow. As they got up, Jane hesitated but Allan couldn't see why. As he lifted his folder, she set her bag down under her chair.

'Good timing!' Cathy said and held out the phone for her boss.

He took the receiver and covered the mouthpiece. 'Cathy,' he said. 'Can you show the officers the drivers' rota? They'll probably need it for – what date?'

'Monday just gone,' Allan said.

Cathy changed glasses and scrolled back through the screen till she found it. 'There are quite a few pages,' she said. 'It's kind of convoluted, the way the info's input for each driver, each van, and each geographical area.'

Allan was leaning over, trying to make sense of what he saw. 'Yeah – I'll send an officer over to go through it.'

'Look, Sir,' Jane said, and pointed at a small area of the screen, trying not to isolate one name in particular in front of Cathy.

'Any chance you can print that one screen?' Allan said.

While Cathy did a screen grab and sent the page to the printer, Jane said she'd left her bag in Thompson's office. He was still on the phone beside them and waved her through.

The office had a generous window on one wall that overlooked the car park, the bins, and the old trees beyond and filled the room with light. Thompson's desk was a big and solid modern one, whose top was mostly clear. There were filing cabinets and a large bookcase with just a few box files on one wall, yet despite all that space, there was a small pile of catalogues and papers on the floor. On top of the pile was a cutting from a newspaper article. Jane spun it so the writing was the right way up for reading. 'What does someone like you want with something like that?' she muttered. She retrieved her bag from under her chair, pulled out her phone and snapped a photo.

Chapter 26

Back at HQ, Allan and Jane were going over the interview they'd had with both Cathy Coates and Hugo Thompson. The screengrab they'd had Cathy print because Jane had spotted a Muslim name led them nowhere, because 'Mohammed Khan' was recorded as being fully occupied and some distance away the afternoon Jamie went missing.

'Anyway, we can't – mustn't – assume the man the witness saw was Muslim or Middle-Eastern. That was just an impression she got,' Allan said. 'But I trust the witness, so it's a good place to start.'

'There's plenty of dark-haired, brown-eyed east-coasters,' Jane said. 'Not a lot of cultural diversity here unless you count white settlers, and Weegies like yourself.' She wrinkled her nose at Allan.

'And we can't assume there's only one Muslim driver, either.' Allan got up and left the screengrab on Ross's desk. 'I'll get Ross to go up and sift through the full rota. Do a profile of all the employees. Where is Ross, by the way? And Sam?' Apart from themselves, the office was empty.

Jane shrugged. 'I meant to ask – did you notice Hugo Thompson actually had a press cutting about the bin fire?'

'Did he?' Allan came back and sat at his desk again.

'That's what I went back into his office for. It seemed a strange thing to keep a press cutting of.'

'Why? Why strange? It was outside his office. If the place had caught light he'd have lost a lot of stock and money.'

Jane rocked her head from side to side. 'But to keep a press cutting?'

'I don't see why it's such a big issue.'

'Well, it's a bit old fashioned. I can understand him reading about it and being curious. Interested. I get all that. But to cut it out? What's he going to do with the cutting?'

'Send it to someone?' Allan mused.

'Wouldn't he do that by email or share the link online?'

'What, d'you think he's got some kind of shrine to his work, somewhere?'

Jane looked at the picture she'd taken on her phone. 'It's maybe something worth remembering.'

Just then Ross came in with a disposable cup of coffee in his hand. Allan shared a smile with Jane.

'Thanks for those pictures of the two boys from the CCTV at the service station, Ross.'

'No problem, Sir.'

'Inconclusive, more's the pity, but we'll keep hold of them anyway.'

Allan went over to sit beside Ross to explain about the screengrab and to arrange for him to go through the full files at the Q-busters office. 'And while you're looking at the rotas, see if you can find out who was up at Abriachan when I was there yesterday.' He told him how the van had borne down on him. 'Most important, check to confirm there was a delivery in the area on the afternoon of the Monday Jamie died, and find out who the driver was. And if there's a match with the van that was spotted at the school at lunchtime on the same day.'

'Okay.'

'Where's Sam?'

'Up seeing Forensics about the fibres and stuff found in the bin fire. He picked up some stuff from Jamie's house for them to compare it with.'

'Good.' Allan spun round to Jane. 'Did you get in touch with Jamie's head teacher to ask if she recognised the delivery van driver as one of the parents?'

119

'I phoned up yesterday, Sir. Without a name... There are a thousand kids at that school.'

'Okay. Did she say she'll look into it?'

Jane nodded. 'Yeah, but I won't be holding my breath.'

'Ross – make that trip to Q-busters a priority. First thing on Monday. The sooner we get some names we can look into, the better.' He tapped his pen against his lips. 'While you're at it – see if there were any deliveries recently to the dead boy's street.'

'What about the CCTV, Sir?' Ross asked. 'There's still loads to go through.'

Allan frowned. 'I thought PC Welsh was going to help you?'

Ross blushed again and fumbled with his coffee cup. 'I haven't asked her yet.'

Allan turned to Jane and exchanged a look, tinged with amusement. 'You're not asking her on a date, Son. Business, not pleasure. Get to it.'

Back at his own desk, Allan checked through the notes he'd made. He'd lost track of who on the team was doing what and he wasn't prepared to let that happen again. As for this one name they'd already got – Mohammed Khan – he'd make a start on that. There was a partial address on the screengrab, which Allan had noted before passing it to Ross. He looked it up on the voter's roll, but there was no Mohammed Khan registered there. The phone book was no use either. A thought occurred to him, and he crossed to Sam's desk. Sam had been working his way through the list, interviewing known paedophiles and those recently released from jail. Allan flicked through the list on his desk, but Khan's name wasn't on it.

Chapter 27

The mosque was a new-build on the outskirts of town. It was constructed of yellow and orange-coloured bricks with arched windows and elegant cupolas, and the minaret to the side of the building was as slim as a Cleopatra's Needle.

'Nice!' Allan said, pulling on the hand-brake. 'You been here before?'

'Nope.' Jane craned her neck to be able to see to the top of the building through the car windscreen. 'Busy place.'

The car park was half-full and there were groups of men, and some families, heading towards the entrance or standing, talking.

As they approached the door, two men in their mid-fifties, wearing skull caps, and traditional knee length shirts over their trousers, broke off their conversation and waited for Allan and Jane to draw closer. Allan drew out his badge.

'Salaam alaikum! Good morning,' one of the men said. His attention was focused exclusively on Allan. 'Can we help you?'

'Good morning! I'm DI MacIntyre and this is DS Coburn. We're trying to trace someone and we were told he might be available to talk to us here.'

'Who is it you're looking for?'

'His name's Mohammed Khan.' Allan observed the men keenly to gauge their reaction. There was one. The man who'd been speaking to them shot a very quick glance at his companion.

'It's not an unusual name,' the second man said.

Allan smiled. 'A bit like John Smith?' He nodded to the two, trying to keep the atmosphere relaxed. The two men's faces stayed serious. 'This Mr Khan is probably about ages with me – late thirties or thereabouts. He drives a delivery van for a local firm. We're just looking for a quick word with him. And if we need to talk to him again, I'm sure he'll be happy to give us his full address and cooperation.'

The two took their time to process this information, breaking off now and then to acknowledge men entering the building. Then one said, 'Excuse us a moment,' and the two stepped aside to confer. One took out his phone and made a call.

Allan glanced at Jane. She was dressed in her usual work outfit of a brown trouser suit. He did wonder if she had a wardrobe full of them. Anyway, he imagined it was demure enough for a visit to the mosque, in that her limbs were covered and her blouse was fastened right up to the neck. Her brown hair was tied back as usual, too. Scraped back, the way she liked it. It seemed strange to be evaluating her like this, imagining how people – men – might see her. Allan saw her only as Jane, the sturdy, dependable, five-foot-nothing, opinionated womens' football coach DC. He supposed she was a woman, too. He noticed it was only men going into the mosque, and he was just beginning to wonder if he should have brought Sam instead, when the first man addressed him again.

'Mo's in the food hall. He says he's happy to talk with you.' He'd shed the guarded look from his face. Then he turned briefly towards Jane and in a softer tone, said, 'I'm sorry, but only the gentleman can come in the main area, but you are very welcome to visit the women's rooms,' and he pointed towards a smaller entrance further on, where women and children were going in.

'Fine. That's absolutely fine,' Allan said. To Jane, he added, 'I'll come for you – or send a message for you – in fifteen or whatever.' He looked down into her eyes, which he could see were stinging with annoyance. 'Diversity training. Remember? It's important and you know it. And this way, you can sound out the women. Don't be crabbit,' he said. 'Use your charms.'

Inside the mosque, one of the men accompanied Allan as he removed his shoes and took him part-way along the corridor to the food hall. The smells alone could have led him. The hall itself was smaller than the light and spacious prayer room he'd glimpsed on arrival. A big rectangular room, it, too, had high arching windows filling the room with light. Allan didn't have much experience of religious buildings of any description, but the white walls, accented here and there by framed geometric designs and the sweeps of blue and green calligraphy, struck him as far more welcoming than the dour grey stone inside the Presbyterian church where his old school held their end-of-term services.

'This is amazing,' Allan said.

His guide's face lit up. 'You like it? We're very proud of it. Took us a long time to get this!'

Allan put his hands on his hips and looked around him, nodding. 'Yeah – I've never been in a mosque before. Been to all sorts of Cathedrals and so on, on holiday, and I've seen the Alhambra from the outside, but this is a first.'

'Well, if you've any questions – just ask! I'll leave you here?'

Allan quickly held his hand out. 'Absolutely. Thanks.' The two men shook hands warmly and his guide left.

There were several men serving food at the far end of the room. Allan scanned their faces. Two were older, and there were two teenagers, but there was one man who fitted the description Emma had given: heavy-jowled, bearded and with thick hair, and probably in his mid-thirties. He was serving portions of food and handing them over, while one of the teenage boys added some kind of flatbread to each plate. As Allan watched, the man's doleful eyes lifted to meet his, and Allan knew straight away this was Mohammed Khan. He could tell by his sweating anxiety: the look of unease that crossed his face.

Allan approached but waited while his suspect completed the dish he was serving.

'Mohammed Khan?' he asked.

The boy beside him glowered. 'He should leave you alone!' he said. 'You've not done anything wrong.'

'Shh,' Khan said, and clapped the boy on the forearm.

'But you've not! This is harassment.'

Khan exhaled a shaky breath, took off his apron and passed it to the boy. The boy himself looked familiar, but Allan couldn't place him. Khan came round from behind the bank of tables and together, they walked to the side of the hall, to where there was a small square table with two empty seats.

'Sorry about that. He gets quite heated.'

'Ah, that's okay. Typical teen! Sit down, please. Be comfortable. I'm DI MacIntyre.' Allan showed his badge. 'Thanks for agreeing to see me. I'm doing some routine enquiries.'

'Okay.'

Khan sat back with his legs slack and his hands palms up on his lap. The skin round his eyes was flushed and puffy. His breathing was still fast, but Allan knew people could be like that from anxiety even when they were completely innocent.

'What is it you want to know?'

'I understand you work as a delivery driver for Q-busters over on the Inchmarsh Industrial Estate.'

'I do, yes.'

'So, you'll be familiar with the recent incident there.'

Khan's bloodshot eyes had been shifting from point to point, from Allan's face to some movement in the room, to the windows and back again, but at this statement, he glued them to Allan's. 'What incident?'

Allan shifted in his seat. 'Well, the bin fire, for one.'

Khan frowned. 'Oh yeah, that.' He braced his hands against the table. 'Yeah – kids, probably. You know what they're like. No damage done, Mr Thompson said. Except to the bin itself, of course. Nobody hurt.'

'Indeed. So – you don't have any idea who might have set light to that bin, or why?'

Khan shook his head. 'Phh. No – not me. No idea. CCTV not pick anything up? They've always got that on.'

Allan stifled a grin. 'We're checking that.'

Khan squeezed the corners of his eyes between finger and thumb. 'Okay. And is it just me you're interviewing?'

'We'll be interviewing most of the drivers. We've already spoken to the office staff.' Allan was silent for a moment. He thought about the bin fire. The flash if it had been some kind of explosion. 'Something wrong with your eyes, Mr Khan?'

Khan was rocking slightly, back and forward. He shrugged. 'Conjunctivitis.' He braced himself against the table. 'Seems a lot of work for a bin fire.'

Allan agreed. 'Well, we think it might be connected with something else.'

'Oh?'

'Another incident. Can you tell me, Mr Khan, where you were on Monday last week? Round about lunchtime?'

Mo Khan went back to his slack position. 'I was at work. I'm not sure where I'd have been driving. You'd need to check the rota.'

'We will. Can I ask you – do you have a connection with anyone at Thistlebank Academy?'

Khan's eyes flicked up again, and his breathing grew faster. He ran his hand over his beard then gestured over his shoulder. 'The boy there. I sometimes pick him up.'

Allan looked back at the boy serving food. 'Is he your son?'

'Nephew.'

'Okay. Mr Khan, as I say, we'll be contacting quite a few people as we follow up some leads. You'll know that a young boy from that school was found murdered on Tuesday.'

'Nothing to do with me.' His voice was louder, now, and Allan sensed the general hubbub in the room dip.

'I've got nothing to do with that boy's murder.' Khan's voice was uneven.

Three men moved towards their table, hovering close by. 'Are you alright, Mo?' one of them said. 'Is it time for your visitor to go?'

Allan raised his hands to suggest he wasn't a threat then took his badge out to show his ID. Addressing them as much as Khan, he said, 'No one's accusing you, Mr Khan. We're having a wide sweep to build up as much of a picture as possible. I will ask you to stay local in case we want to speak with you again, and I'll need your address and phone number.' Allan took out his pen and clicked it on.

Khan ran his hand over his beard again. 'I wasn't anywhere near the boy. The signatures on my delivery schedule will prove it!'

The hall fell silent.

'It's time you left,' the spectator said and grasped Allan's shoulder. 'Mo Khan does good work in this community. He doesn't need you hassling him.'

'Don't do that, sir,' Allan said, holding up his hand. A second man mumbled to the first. Allan didn't catch the words, but the body language was clear. He was urging calm and telling him to take his hand off the policeman. Allan waited, pen poised over his notebook. When the hand was removed, Allan carried on, 'So, if you can just give me your full address and phone number.'

Khan grabbed the pen and wrote it almost illegibly, hands shaking. He slammed the pen down and stood up. The teenager had approached now.

Allan stood, too. 'Thanks for your time.' He didn't offer a hand, choosing to use his to return the notebook and pen to his inside pocket. He turned to the boy. 'Aren't you a pal of Khalil Buchanan?'

'What if I am?' the boy said.

'Ahmed? And this is your uncle?'

The more aggressive man once again put his hand on Allan, but this time, he took him by the elbow, in much the same way that Allan himself had shepherded Jane earlier.

'Fucking ridiculous, how you treated Khal,' the boy spat from behind him.

Allan shrugged the hand off and turned to Ahmed. 'What d'you mean?'

'You know what I mean! You arrested him!'

Khal? 'Is he still in custody?' He was sure he'd be released that morning.

'Transferred him to a fucking secure unit, didn't they?'

'Watch your language in the mosque, Ahmed,' the man who'd spoken earlier said.

Allan took his phone out. How could he have forgotten to follow up what happened to the boy? Lorraine's boy? He fixed his eyes on Ahmed. 'I'll look into it. Trust me.'

Chapter 28

Allan dropped Jane off and headed back to the office, even though it was Saturday. He picked up a bacon panini for a late lunch and a cafe grande on the way in. The whole floor his office was on was quiet and there was enough natural daylight coming through the floor to ceiling windows for him to be able to work inconspicuously in comfort.

He and Jane had talked about the case during the car journey. They'd talked about motives. There didn't seem to be one for Khan, especially given he wasn't listed on the paedophile register, according to the list Sam had obtained, anyway. Not only that, but Khan had been pretty convincing when he said the signatures on his electronic delivery pad would prove he was fully occupied at the likely time of the murder. He could be lying, but to raise the subject himself suggested otherwise. As for where and when the boy was murdered – the preliminary report from the post mortem had given them an approximate time, but Jane was right – they still didn't have a location. Allan spent most of the afternoon going over the files but it was still as much of a puzzle as before. Despite Mo Khan's confident avowal that he had nothing to do with Jamie's murder, he remained the one Allan had the strongest hunch about. There was definitely something the man was hiding. Allan flicked the paperwork; flicked through screens of information. Could he be illegal? Acting shifty for that reason? Now Allan had his full name and address it was easy to find out one way or the other. But there was nothing in the records to suggest any wrongdoing.

The light through the windows dimmed. Allan sat back in his

chair and pressed his finger and thumb in the corners of his eyes. He checked his watch. Four-thirty. The office was warm and the cushioned back and sides of his new chair were very comfortable now he'd finally ripped the cellophane off. He swivelled slightly to left and right while he mused out of the window, lulled by the slanting sun.

He woke in darkness with his chair still facing the road, now lit by red brake lights and white side lights as the cars went by. Five-thirty! He was turning into his father. So much for the café grande. He sat forward and supped the dregs, then noticed an unused salt sachet that must have come with his panini. That would tide him over till he next ate. He tore the corner off it and poured the salt into his palm, then licked the tip of his middle finger and dabbed it in it. He just hoped no cameras were picking up this image of the DI licking white powder in the faint light coming into the office from the corridor.

Shit. Lorraine's boy. He couldn't believe he'd not followed through on that. He scrunched up the food wrappers and tossed them in his bin. Nothing else for it but to confess. Would he phone first? No. She'd only give him a hard time. He lifted his jacket from the back of his chair.

Lorraine opened the door, realised it was him, and would have closed it if he hadn't caught it.

'Hey, let me in?' he said, holding the door and talking through a gap of about six inches. She looked rough. Dishevelled and miserable. And maybe slightly drunk? 'Come on, eh?'

He saw the 'caving in' expression on her face and the door went slack. She turned away into the hall and he followed her, closing the door behind him. The hall was in darkness but there was a light in the living room, and he followed her into it. He was right: there were two bottles of wine on the coffee table – one empty and one with a couple of glassfuls left in it. There was only one glass on the table.

'Saving some for me, were you?' He nodded to the wine.

'Fuck off, Allan,' she said and sat on the sofa, one leg tucked up under her.

He stood and stared down at her. Where to start? 'D'you want coffee?' She looked as if she hadn't slept. 'When did you last eat?'

She shrugged. Sniffed. 'Don't be nice to me. I'm annoyed at you and I want to stay annoyed at you.' She wiped her nose on her hand and glared at him. 'I should be annoyed at you.'

'You certainly should. But let me get you a coffee and something to eat first.'

He went into the kitchen to pull together food and coffee. There was left-over cooked chicken in the fridge, which smelled alright, and avocado and tomato. He microwaved a couple of big potatoes, cut them and filled their insides with butter, plenty of salt and black pepper, and brought the whole lot on a tray with plates and cutlery into the living room. He set it down at one edge of the coffee table while he made space by clearing magazines, crisp wrappers and the wine on to the floor underneath.

After they'd eaten, they lay back, satisfied. Allan gestured to the wine and when Lorraine shook her head, he poured some into the glass she'd used and drank it himself. It was red. It tasted cheap but he gulped it for the hit and topped it up with what was left in the bottle.

'So – they kept Khal in?'

She was still leaning back on the sofa with her belly up and her legs, extended, crossed at the ankles. She'd been flicking through the TV channels, but when Allan spoke to her she shook her head. 'I can't talk about it. I fill up.' She covered her face with her hand.

'Did they charge him?'

She nodded.

'I'll look into it.'

She raised her eyebrows, sceptical.

'I will.'

A loud hiccup. 'You could've done that already.' She flicked through the TV channels again.

It was true. Inside, he cringed. He reached across to take the TV remote, switched the TV off and put the remote beyond her arm's length. 'I'm sorry. I've just been so busy. I didn't think for a minute they'd have kept him in.'

'They sent him to a secure unit.'

Allan nodded. 'I'll look into it. Into getting him out.'

Lorraine fished a paper hankie from her pocket and blew her nose. She sat up. 'He really was doing old Bob next door's shopping.' She glued her eyes to his to watch for signs he believed her. 'He really was!'

For a while, neither of them talked. Allan drank the wine and she was clearly going over everything in her head.

'It's not easy,' she said, and almost broke down in tears again. 'Bob next door is a lovely old guy. He looks after Khal. Not officially, but he's always been there for him. With Khal's dad being a ...' Her voice tailed off and she waved a hand to suggest a long slow separation process.

'A bastard?'

'Away.'

'Right. What happened to his dad?'

She blinked a few times, looking at him as if she thought she'd already answered that. Maybe she had on one of the times he'd been over. But he didn't remember.

'His dad wasn't very – let's say he wasn't very stable.'

'Wasn't?'

'Isn't. He moved around a lot when he was younger. Didn't have a stable home life as a kid. Spent time in care. That kind of thing.'

'Right.'

'So even though he wanted to be a good dad, he didn't have it in him. Not for 24 hours a day parenthood, anyway. We still see him. Sometimes. When I can face him. When he's in the area. That's why Bob's so good – because he sticks around.'

Allan wondered what kind of thing the old man taught him.

'And then there's the race thing.' Lorraine sighed. 'The heritage thing. He holds that against me.'

'Eh?'

She sat up and lifted the wine bottle. It was empty. 'You know what kids are like. Well – you saw that the last time you were here. Remember?'

Allan thought back to the argument between him and Khal over whether he'd known Jamie, which had resulted in Allan being evicted before he'd even finished his moussaka. Ah, but then, he'd spent the night at Emma's instead. Not that he'd tell Lorraine that.

'They're always testing you,' she went on. 'Kids. You're the root of all their problems, one minute, and then the next you're too stupid and ignorant to even understand what it's like to have problems like the kind they have. Especially when you're a single parent.'

Allan thought of his own dad. With a pang, he remembered how he'd taken his rage out on him when his mother died. 'It's a hard age.'

'To be a parent?' Vitality had come back into Lorraine's eyes and her whole body language was different. The food had been a good idea. And the coffee. 'I think I've got another bottle of wine. Fancy?'

Allan tilted his glass. It was almost empty. He checked his watch. 'Sure.'

She cleared away the tray with all the dishes and came back with a full wine bottle and two clean glasses. She scrunched open the screwtop and poured. As she passed the fresh glass to him, he said, 'What about Ahmed? What's he like?'

'Brilliant,' Lorraine said, and it sounded like she really meant it.

Allan thought back to the angry young man defending Mo Khan in the mosque food hall. 'You don't think he's a bad influence on Khalil? You don't think he's got a temper?'

'Ahmed? No way.' She curled her leg up under her and sat down again on the sofa, holding her wine glass out for balance as she did. 'He's a great lad. Honest, smart – a bit of a brain box. Loves computer games but I mean he's the type that wants to write them. He won a prize in school last year. Some kind of national competition to encourage kids to go into coding or computing or whatever. And the sweetest, most polite and friendly nature, full of respect.' She paused while she thought about it. 'I encourage Khal to spend time with him. Apart from the contact it gives him with that half of his cultural heritage, he's exactly the kind of friend Khalil needs.'

Chapter 29

Lorraine might have been feeling anguish about her boy being taken away and locked up in the teenage secure unit, but after she and Allan had eaten, and chatted, and drunk another glass of wine, her old self resurfaced. It was obvious Allan had drunk too much wine to be able to drive home. He checked his watch and yawned, and she said, 'Oh well, I could do with the company, anyway.' Then, once she'd raised his expectations, she disappeared upstairs and came back armed with a duvet and pillow, which she dropped on his lap.

'What? You didn't think I'd forgive you that easily, did you?'

He shrugged, disappointed but not about to admit to it. He may have prided himself on his people skills – all those hunches he got about whether suspects were telling the truth or firing lies with their spittle – but Lorraine stood in the doorway with an expression he couldn't crack. Akin to what Pierrepoint the Executioner might have worn.

'I'll go and get the kitchen cleaned up,' she said, bending over in front of him to pick the crisp wrappers and wine bottles off the floor. 'Make yourself at home.'

She was away a full twenty minutes, and when she came back, he was sitting with his shoes off and his feet up on the coffee table. His arms were folded across his stomach and the bedding she'd brought had been dumped on the floor beside the couch. The TV was showing football.

She stood, arms akimbo.

'What?' he said.

'Are you not going to bed?'
He looked her down and up again. She was small and curvy.
'Well?' she asked again.
'I'd rather go to yours.'

~~~

In the middle of the night, Allan got up for a pee and then, taking stock of Lorraine's slow and deep breathing, he let himself into Khalil's room. He closed the door behind himself and put the light on, uneasy about being naked with the blind open, and relieved to see no lights in the houses opposite.

The bedroom looked and smelled like a teenage boy's. Five grubby shoes lay abandoned in front of the chest of drawers. There were socks and tee-shirts, and a pair of tracky bottoms with one leg inside out, on a chair, yet the bed was spread up neatly. No doubt his mother had done it. Allan thought of Jamie's bedroom, and others like it, on their way to becoming a shrine for grieving parents, and how mothers unintentionally damaged or destroyed evidence in their desire to put everything 'right'. Allan pulled back the duvet and checked under the pillow. Nothing. He spread it up again. He went through the chest of drawers, finding nothing significant, and then slid the door of the mirrored wardrobe open. It rumbled on its track and he hesitated, expecting a livid Lorraine to burst through the bedroom door to upbraid him once again for spying on her son. But the moments passed and there was nothing. She'd sunk enough wine to keep her sound. And there'd been the sex.

There were boxes on the top shelf, but Allan wouldn't have time to go through those. There were bags on the floor of the wardrobe. He put his hand inside one of them and brought out a handful of wires. Could be an old gaming handset from the pre-wireless days. He stuffed it back and rummaged for more. Behind the bag, behind the overhanging clothes, were three mobile phone boxes. He crouched and opened them, one after the other. Top of the range. And looking recent, too. What was going on? He was in the scud; didn't have his phone to take a photo of them or any way of taking a note of the serial numbers so Ross could check if they'd been registered missing. All he could do was make a mental note of the make and model number. Then he slid the door closed again, put out the bedroom light and crept back along the corridor into bed with Lorraine, who was still sound asleep and whose warm body he wrapped himself round.

In the morning, she woke before him, surprisingly good natured given the booze she'd drunk. As for him, he was increasingly grumpy in the morning, which he took as a sign he was getting old and crabbit like his father. Perhaps as a result of his night-time exertions, he woke up starving. Yet, Lorraine naked beside him with her leg over his, dispelled his grumpiness and he was happy to put off for a good half hour the time when the two of them were ready to go downstairs for breakfast.

'I want us to go and chap up Bob,' Lorraine said. 'So you'll believe me.' She'd already phoned the secure unit and spoken to Khalil, and apart from a tremble in her voice and an angry edge when she spoke to the duty manager, she seemed upbeat and eager to prove to Allan that Bob was who she claimed he was – that this elderly man really was keen to induct a truculent fifteen year old into the dark and manly arts of handling drill bits, dowels and self-tappers.

Bob, however, didn't answer his door, or his phone when Lorraine pulled out her mobile and dialled him up. His curtains were all open, even in the back, where Lorraine assured Allan he slept. Allan screened his eyes from the weak sun, holding them up against the window as he peered in when Lorraine pressed him to check in case Bob was lying, helpless and dying, on the living room or kitchen floor.

It was when Allan was straining to see in the front room window that the neighbour across the road opened his window and shouted. Lorraine was still round behind the house, checking to see if Bob might have hidden a key under plant pots or stones, and it was a curious feeling for Allan to be thought of as a potential villain, trying to break into an old man's house in a quiet street, early on a Sunday morning. The surge of adrenaline came with a panicky discomfort. He was out in his shirt-sleeves. He didn't have his badge with him. He needed a coffee. He should have had a second coffee and something else to eat. He put his hand against the roughcast wall under the window for balance.

By the time the neighbour had crossed the street to speak with Allan, Lorraine had reappeared.

'Oh, it's you,' the neighbour said. He was a man in his early fifties with a paunch that suggested he was used to labouring and eating to match. 'Did you not hear? Bob had another stroke. They've taken him to hospital.'

'No!' Lorraine said.

'Yep. Couple of days ago. Where have you been?' he said, laughing.

There was small talk, Lorraine evidently not keen to divulge what had happened to Khalil, or to introduce the man she'd clearly spent a Saturday night with at home. When finally the neighbour left, she prodded Allan back towards her front door. 'Shit,' she said. 'You and your lot will think I was lying about Bob.'

'What do you mean?' he said, eager to finally be able to sit.

She glared at him. Her hands were trembling as she ran the water into the kettle. 'Well, you're hardly likely to believe anything Bob says now, are you? For all we know, Bob might not even be able to talk, if he's had a stroke.' She turned the tap off to cut the flow of water. 'He might not even remember who Khalil is!'

Chapter 30

Helena Finlayson's full report was on his desk when he arrived at work armed with a double-shot latte, first thing on Monday morning. He skimmed it while he mainlined the coffee, prior to morning briefing. Her timing was good; he needed this new focus to mobilise his thoughts, and the troops. So far, it felt as if he was floundering in a swamp, trying to find solid footing.

As soon as the team gathered in the briefing room, Allan told them the new information.

'Helena Finlayson's report confirms the cause of death as strangulation, with associated bruising likely to have been caused by the perpetrator repeatedly hitting the victim's head against the ground.' He took a breath. 'Time of death is given as the Monday afternoon, sometime between 1 and 5pm; most likely between 2 and 4pm. The bruising to the boy's head was inflicted before death.' He looked up. 'Just before death. They found plant spores and cells that fit the profile of the geographical location where his body was found. So, Helena's confident he was killed in the woods at Abriachan, rather than being murdered elsewhere and dumped there.

'Other injuries as previously suspected. In other words, the boy was entered anally. No trace of semen, so there's no DNA from that source, which means we can assume his attacker "came prepared". Helena confirms that the bruising and swelling and other tissue damage around and inside the anus stem from sexual penetration. No sign of any violation or aggression with foreign objects.'

He skimmed down the remainder of the report, the room silent. He glanced up. 'Helena's team also found fibres under the victim's nails, as well as mixed with the hairs on the back of his head. She also found hairs, including some thick black ones – you'll remember the victim was a red-head – and she's got the DNA from these hairs, but it looks as if they're from different people.' He looked at Jane. 'Just to complicate things further.

'Anyway, it doesn't seem likely that he picked up these hairs while he was lying in the grass and moss at Abriachan Woods. Forensics from the area round his body don't support that there might have been a whole team of people up there, anyway. The ground was barely disturbed. So, we'll work on the assumption that Jamie was in close contact with people unknown, in a public area, before being moved to the woods prior to his death.'

'Well, he'd been at school,' Sam said. 'Could have been from P.E.'

There was a bit of a tumbleweed moment, and then Ross raised his hand. When Allan acknowledged him, he asked, 'You said there were fibres as well, in his hair and under his nails. Where does Finlayson reckon they come from?'

Allan flipped a page in the report then looked up at the young man. 'Carpet and other fibres. So, together with the hairs from different sources, it looks to me as if Jamie was held in a public place. Maybe roughed up on the floor. I don't think it's the school.' He looked around. 'Can any of you think if the school's carpeted? It's mostly all wooden floors, isn't it? Or lino?' There were nods. 'But Ross – arrange for Forensics to check his school specifically for samples of the carpeting and other fabrics to rule in or out.' Ross nodded and typed in his tablet. 'Jane. Thick, black hairs, and fibres from carpeting. Does that remind you of the mosque?'

'Did it say what colour the fibres were?'

Allan flicked back to the previous page of the report. 'Fibres – mixed wool and man made. Polypropylene. Colours – again, mixed. Blue, green, dark brown.' He looked at Jane. 'The ones at the mosque were blue or green, were they not? Or maybe they had different colours in the girls' bit. Pink, maybe.' He winked at Ross.

Jane leaned back and crossed her legs, balancing her ankle on

Carol McKay

the opposite knee. She told the others, 'DI MacIntyre and I visited the central mosque on Saturday morning to interview Mo Khan, a delivery driver from Q-busters whose delivery schedule may or may not have taken him to Thistlebank Academy and Abriachan on the day before the boy's body was found. I'm sure the DI will give us a full report on his visit. I was not allowed in the men's part of the mosque but was shown great courtesy and hospitality by the leaders of the women's and family part, which – I can assure you – did not have pink carpets.'

'You told me you got a nice cup of tea and two recipes for samosas,' Sam said, and he and Ross grinned to each other.

Allan went on to tell the others what happened in his part of the mosque, from the initial reservation on the part of the men at the door, to their willingness to allow him to speak with Khan once Khan himself had okayed it, to the anxiety Khan had shown increasingly and the outright hostility of the teenage boy, Ahmed. 'But we can probably discount that, putting it down to his age. It was more concerning that a couple of the men in the mosque food hall were prepared to respond aggressively to Khan's distress.' He met Sam's eyes. 'I actually got my collar felt. But others arrived to calm it down and I got Khan's address and phone number before I left. He was pretty confident the delivery receipt signatures will show him far away from the murder, by the way. Very confident. And convincing. Ross – will you check that as well?'

Ross nodded and entered another note in his tablet.

'Okay. Sam – you were checking the paedophile list. I know Khan didn't appear on it, but you were looking further afield?'

'I'll just call up my email?'

From Allan's pocket came the sound of his phone ringing. He fished it out and frowned when he saw the number. 'Yep, on you go,' he said to Sam. 'We'll take five if anyone wants to grab a coffee. Get me one?' he walked off into the corridor to take the call.

Everyone reconvened a few minutes later once Ross and Jane had fetched coffees and buns from the cafeteria. 'They actually were the best,' Jane was telling Ross. 'I'm going to try out the recipe if I ever get a proper day off this place. They'd a great wee kids' library, too.' By now, Sam had powered up his laptop and was checking his email.

'Just got one from the Met,' he said, before a note of excitement rose in his voice. 'Bingo! Mohammed Khan, aged 36, born Bolton.' He flicked a fingertip against the screen then shook his finger as if it hurt. 'Registered as a paedophile after serving a sentence for illicit sex with an underage boy.'

'Yes!'

Ross and Sam high-fived each other. Jane pressed her lips together and looked over at Allan, who was drinking deeply from his coffee.

'Pull him in,' Allan said. 'In fact – Jane and Ross can do it. I need you to stay with me.' He turned to Jane. 'You might be able to work out where he is from the schedule, but I'll give you all his mobile number in case you need it.' He thumbed through his phone's address book and copied Khan's number into a message which he sent to all three officers.

Ross had a 'eureka' look on his face. 'I'll check it against Jamie Brooks' call records.'

'Good!' Allan said. 'ASAP.'

Sam looked disappointed. 'What d'you want me to do, Boss?'

'You and I'll have a word with "Old Bob". The guy that lives next door to young Khalil Buchanan?' Sam looked blank. 'He's the boy that got pulled in at the end of last week on suspicion of terror-related offences.' Allan updated the others. 'I was sure he'd be released, but they held him. He's been in secure accommodation since Thursday. His mother's doing her nut.'

'His mother? Isn't she...?' Jane said and raised an eyebrow.

'Doing her nut. I said that.' Allan glared at her. There was no trace of gentle sparring this time.

'What was it he did?' Jane asked, echoing his seriousness.

'He was caught with a bag of nails, white spirit and fertiliser

– could be innocent, but could be the ingredients to cook up explosives. Old Bob is his alibi. His mother says the old guy takes an interest in him, teaches him woodwork, gardening, that kind of thing. But he's had a stroke and been taken into hospital.' He looked at Sam. 'So – Sam and I'll check him out.'

Sam nodded.

'Right,' Allan said and pulled together his papers. 'Good to know we've got movement on this case at last. Let's meet up back here later.'

Chapter 31

The two men didn't say much as they left the car and walked towards the hospital. Sam attempted conversation a couple of times, but Allan's responses were monosyllabic. They entered the lofty atrium, all too aware of the burble of voices and feet around them, and quickly ascertained from reception that 'Old Bob' was in a high dependency unit on the third floor. Sam, who was in his late twenties and had legs as skinny and long as a stork, headed for the wide staircase, but Allan leaned on his elbow and directed him towards the lift, instead.

'You must be getting too desk-bound, Boss,' Sam said. 'Bit of exercise would do you the world of good.'

Allan sighed and stabbed repeatedly at the call button. 'I hate these places.' When the lift finally arrived, its doors making them wait while they opened in hospital-time, he glanced at his reflection in the mirrored strip that ran vertically down the inner wall. Maybe it was the gloom in here, the artificial light – whatever – but his skin was uncharacteristically dark, even though it was now many weeks since his holiday, and it worried him. 'D'you think I'm looking a bit brown?' he said. He glanced at Sam's reflection for comparison and saw the incredulity on his depute's face.

'What, Boss?'

Allan laughed. 'Sorry. I'm miles away.' He clapped his hand on Sam's upper arm as the doors opened and they walked out on to the stripped-down decor of the third floor. 'Look – I might have to cut this short. I'm supposed to be somewhere. If they badger me, will you take over?'

'Of course.'

Allan felt the younger man's eyes on him, evaluating him, instinctively being a detective. 'Thanks,' he said, 'but it might not come to that.'

'Old Bob' was in his own room, right beside the nurses' station. A glance through the window partition showed them an old man surrounded by monitors and drips, and there was a younger man sitting between Bob and the outer window. He looked about fifty. He met their eyes through the glazed partition and signalled with a nod of his head as if he'd been expecting them.

'DI MacIntyre,' Allan said, introducing first himself then his depute, and shaking the man's hand.

'Rob Ferguson. The nurse told me you were on your way. I'm Bob's son. Is there a problem?'

'Not with your dad, no. Sorry – I didn't realise you knew we were coming. I didn't mean to worry you. Just thought I could catch your dad and have a word with him.' He looked at the old man, who was lying, motionless and with his eyes closed, between them. 'How's he doing?'

Rob Ferguson's face twisted. 'Not so good, you know?' He shook his head. 'Nah, not so good.'

'Is this his first stroke?'

'Nah, second.' Rob met Allan's eyes. 'Three strikes and you're out. They think he'll pull back from this one, but it might take a while.'

'Right. Tough.'

Allan wished he could take a seat, but the only one in the room was the one the son had been sitting on. He leaned his hand on the bed's foot-board. 'Look, do you mind if we ask you a few questions?'

'About my dad?'

Allan took a deep breath. 'Connected to your dad. We're wondering if – do you stay with your dad, by any chance?'

'No, I moved out years ago. I live nearby, though. With my wife and kids. Why?' He nodded to his father, whose white hair and white eyelashes gave him a Father Christmas joviality and innocence, even sleeping, with a cannula in the back of his hand. 'Can't imagine the old guy being in any kind of trouble with you lot.'

Allan's phone sounded. He took it out and inspected it. 'Sorry about that,' he said, cutting the noise without taking the call. His eyes met Sam's. 'Five minutes.' To Rob, he said, 'We're looking into a story that your dad plays a kind of mentoring role to the young lad next door. The lad Buchanan?'

Rob frowned. 'Khal, you mean?'

'Yeah, Khalil. The boy says he does a bit of shopping, a bit of work around the house, helping your dad – that kind of thing. That your dad takes a bit of interest in him.'

'Hold on a minute –'

'No, no – I don't mean anything like that,' Allan said. 'No – completely above board. As I said, like a mentor to him.'

'Is my dad in trouble?'

Allan's phone rang again and Allan swore under his breath and stepped to the side to answer it. Sam stepped in. 'No, Mr Ferguson. Your dad's in no trouble at all. But the Buchanan lad has been taken in for questioning and we're checking out his story.'

'Right. What's the boy in for?'

Sam looked at Allan, who was talking quietly on the phone and shook his head. 'Well, I can't give the details on that just now, but it would be helpful if you could describe the kind of thing Khal and your dad do and talk about. Does Khal do shopping for him, for example? Doesn't your dad have a home carer to do that?'

'No – yeah, he does have a carer, and my wife and I do a bulk shop for him online, too, but Khal's good – he'll step in and get stuff at short notice.' He rubbed his dad's bare forearm, moving the silvery hairs over the red skin. 'Like, he'll buy him milk if he's short. Tunes in his TV if something goes wrong.'

'Good. Anything else? What about gardening stuff? Flower seeds and that.'

'Och, they do wee projects. Like clearing out the greenhouse.

145

That was last year's job. The boy gave him a hand with that. And planting up sweet peas.' Rob looked at Allan. 'I'm a joiner, but I'm self-employed. You've got to take the work when you can get it. Sometimes it means I'm hardly around.'

'So, what was this year's project?' Allan put his phone back in his pocket.

Rob scratched the back of his head. 'To be honest, I don't pay that much attention.' His eyes went from Allan's to Sam's. 'But he's a good lad. Well, my dad's good to him, too. It works out well for both of them, you know? Especially with Khal's dad being the way he is. Old Bob here's a good role model, you know?'

Allan didn't know but nodded as if he did.

'Wait!' Rob said. 'There was something. Dad was telling me he'd given the boy cash to buy compost so they could plant up bulbs, that was it. I warned him about giving the boy his money.' He gazed for a long time at the old man on the bed, before looking back up at first Sam then Allan. 'But he was convinced Khal could be trusted. He's usually a good judge of character. Are you telling me he got it wrong this time?'

'No, no – I think there's been a mix-up. Listen, would you be able to give DC Abouwaye here a written statement?'

'Sure. The old guy's not very talkative, anyway.' He smiled.

'Great.' Allan motioned Sam over to the corridor. 'Would you do the paperwork and make the calls to get Khal released?'

'Sure, Boss. Are you going back to the office?'

Allan was evasive. 'Not yet. I've got to be somewhere. I'll see you later.'

Chapter 32

The nurse wasn't someone you'd mistake for the stripper at your stag night, but she was down to earth and friendly, and more to the point, efficient. She picked up the signs he really wasn't into this. He really didn't have time for this. Well, he told her.

'Sit your ass down there,' she said in response, indicating a chair. 'Do you think anybody in this building wants to be here?' When he gave in and sat down, she leaned in close to his head, and said, 'and that's including the staff.' She dragged a grey swivel chair towards him and sat heavily. 'Right – jacket off and roll up your sleeve.' A scent of something pink and floral emanated from her throat and chest, and the curls of her yellow hair tickled his cheek as she depressed a vein with her fingertip and released it. 'That's the one,' she said, then inserted a needle with an everyday efficiency into the crook of his elbow.

He watched her draw off a phial of his blood, then put a stopper on the needle, leaving it sticking out of his arm for next time.

'Right. This goes off to the lab. I'll be back in half an hour for another one. Meanwhile,' by now she was holding a needle upright and squeezing the plunger till two or three drops dripped out, 'I'll inject you with this. You might feel a rush. Some people do.'

'Woohoo,' he said, dryly. 'Something to look forward to.'

'Okay?' She looked him in the eyes while she rubbed the site with a swab.

He was almost disappointed. 'That it?'

'Right, see you in half an hour. Don't go anywhere.'

She'd left him in a side room off one of the hospital wards. He wondered if it had been the smokers' day room. There wasn't a hint of smoke now, anyway. No grubby tarnishing of the paintwork on the walls, and no swirling fug billowing in the top third of the air in the room. He'd a sudden flashback. Fifteen. The stink of smoke in his hair, his school uniform, even off his anorak. Better than the stink that exuded from his mother. He blinked. Her stick arms with the skin hanging on them. Her gaunt ribs.

Enough of that. Half an hour, she said. He took out his phone and checked the time, then dialled Lorraine.

'Ho, it's me. How are you doing?'

'Okay,' she said. 'Did you speak to old Bob?'

He told her what had happened – how the old man was incapacitated, but by good luck his son had been there and had backed up everything Lorraine had claimed about him and Khal.

'Thank God for that!' she said, her voice surging. 'So, when can I get him home?'

'Sam's doing the paperwork now,' he said. 'We'll have to run it past the terror boys, but I can't see how they can hold him after this.'

'I should bloody well think not. Terror boys. Fuck sake, what were they thinking? Anyway...'

'Yeah, look – listen. Your neighbour's son mentioned something.' He swivelled on his chair, looking down at the plastic funnel thing sticking out of his arm. 'He mentioned something about Khal needing a mentor with the kind of dad he had.'

Lorraine didn't say anything. He imagined her mouth a hard line. Eventually she said, 'Was that Rob, then? What would he know?'

Allan weighed up whether he should press it. Decided yes. 'Well, he didn't drop any hints, but he did give an impression – that maybe things weren't good for Khal. And you.'

'Hmm. He's one to talk. He never goes near his father. I'm amazed he's actually turned up at his hospital bedside. If he's such a good guy, why isn't he up here, popping in every day to make sure his father's alright?'

Allan held the phone away from his ear. Watched the cars travel along the road outside the hospital. The seagulls cutting through the air. 'Yeah, but I wasn't talking about him. I was talking about Khal's father.'

But Lorraine had grown angry. 'The past's the past, Allan. Yeah, Khal's dad could be trouble. Nobody's perfect.'

There was a beep and Allan checked his phone screen. 'Got another call coming in, Lorraine. I'll need to take it. I hope the boy gets out asap. I'll get back to you.'

He cut the call and took the other.

'Hey, Boss. Breaking news. Turns out Thistlebank Academy and the Abriachan road are part of Mo Khan's regular Monday route, so he was definitely scheduled to be in the area when the boy was murdered. Whether he actually was there or not, we've still to find out. We've still to check customer signature records for the actual drops he did.'

Just then, the door opened and Nursey came in, that nylon sound of her thighs rubbing together inside layers of tights and leggings and tunics and apron. She clinked jars and phials into a tray and wheeled her chair over to him.

'Sound! Find out where he is and pull him in. If you draw a blank, go to the depot.' He sat forward, allowing the nurse to take command of his prepped arm. 'Keep me in the loop?'

'Will do,' said Jane. 'What's the noise? Are you still in the hospital?'

He was evasive. 'Aye, there's some kind of a blip. I'll not be long. I'll head to the depot as soon as I'm done here.'

The yellow-haired nurse was eyeing him. 'Some kind of a blip, is it?'

'Some kind of blip. Nearly done?'

'Just this next sample to take, but then you'll need to see the doctor.' She held his arm and pushed the empty phial into the funnel that was sticking out of his vein. Deep red blood squirted and started filling it up.

'Nah, no time for that,' he said.

'Make time for it!' The nurse tugged the phial out, capped it and started to withdraw the funnel.

'No – I'll catch him another day.'

She had a grip on his arm and pressed a square of cotton wool over the puncture site. 'Press this,' she said. 'Keep it pressed.'

Allan took over pressing it but started looking to his jacket as if he might have another couple of arms that could slip it over his shoulders to speed up his exit.

'Keep pressing it! Otherwise you'll be bleeding all down your arm with the excitement.'

'I need to get away,' he said. 'Work to do.'

'You'll do your work a lot better if you speak to the doctor about treatment.' She took the cotton away and applied a tiny plaster.

'What kind of treatment?'

Again, she leaned in, her face sideways as if talking to a child who should know better. 'If I knew that, would I be on a nurse's salary?'

He made a face while he pulled on his jacket. 'I'm a police officer. Something's come up that I need to get to. If it's important, you'll get back to me, won't you?' He headed out the day room door, but she set off after him, nylon rustling.

'Look, Mr MacIntyre. I don't know what this test is going to show up – positive or negative. But I do know it's a serious one. And you need to take it seriously.'

By now he was half-way down the corridor, heading for the lift, and she was straggling behind.

She skipped a few steps and caught his sleeve. 'If it's positive, you'll be on medication for life!'

'If it's negative, I'll not be,' he said. Then, registering the exertion on her face, as well as the concern, he said, 'I'll come back. I will come back. Promise!'

Chapter 33

They'd checked his mobile and tried to make contact through the van's radio, but Mo Khan wasn't answering. Ross felt a flicker of excitement at the prospect of picking him up. Could there be any doubt he was the teenage boy's murderer? It didn't look like it. Not now they'd confirmation he'd a paedophile past and his delivery route took him past the murder scene on Mondays. And Ross was the one who was going to track him down and pull him in. He could almost visualise himself on the TV news footage.

Traffic was building up around Inchmarsh Industrial Estate, so Ross radioed the PCs in the marked car behind them to take the lead and clear a path. As soon as the siren started wailing, the lanes of traffic in front split in two, with cars scurrying over to either side of the carriageway. 'Get in!' Ross said, eyes on his wing mirror, watching for the white, blue and yellow of the squad car to pull out and manoeuvre in front. As it drew level he flicked his indicator and spun the wheel to join it before any wide boys could try the same. In seconds, they had cleared the blockage and were headed round the roundabout and into the estate itself.

'You've a great future ahead of you in rally driving,' Jane said, holding her seat belt.

'Aye.' Ross grinned.

Without needing to be told, the boys in the marked car pulled over to let the DCs back in front.

'Where to?'

Jane had already been there with Allan. 'Up ahead,' she said. 'Over to your right. The door's round the back.'

Ross swung the wheel and the two cars pulled up sharply in the Q-buster car park.

The front door was locked, so Jane buzzed the intercom for access. Their arrival caused alarm: she heard it in Cathy Coates' voice when she answered, though that might have been the office manager's permanent state. Ross and the two PCs from the other car followed Jane into the entrance and Cathy Coates with her anxious face and tousled brown-grey hair was waiting for them, peering myopically through the reception window.

'Police,' Jane said, again, showing her ID this time. 'I need to speak to Mr Thompson. Urgently.'

'Yes, yes,' Cathy said, nodding her head and swapping her glasses for the other pair that hung from a brooch on her cardigan. Her thin arms and hands were trembling. 'If you'd like to wait I'll tell him you're here.'

'No – we'll come through,' Jane said, and gave a quick glance of disbelief to Ross, who returned it. 'Let us in, please.'

Cathy nodded and made her way to the door to let them through. 'It's just – we don't have a lot of room for four of you.'

'We'll breathe in. So – Mr Thompson?'

The older woman pressed a shaky finger on her telephone. 'Could you come through, please? The police are here.'

Immediately, the door at the back of the office opened and Hugo Thompson appeared. He looked taken aback, possibly at the sight of the uniformed officers. He looked guilty. He ran a hand through his white-blond hair, nodded, and gestured the way to his office.

'Will I make tea?' Cathy asked.

Jane gave a curt shake of her head.

'No thanks, Cathy,' Thompson said. 'Hold my calls.'

Close up, the man's pale skin looked pasty. He motioned Jane to the seat she'd sat in before, but she declined. 'I'll just get straight to business, Sir. We want to speak with one of your employees, and as you know, you were good enough to give us a note of his schedule, but he's not where you said he would be.'

A look of disbelief passed over Thompson's face. 'That's it? It needed four of you to disrupt my office to tell me that?' He was standing behind his desk, now, like a man trying to disappear into a trench. 'The vans have radio. All you needed to do was phone Cathy and she would have radioed him.'

Jane stared him out. 'We tried that, Sir, but he didn't answer. Didn't answer his mobile, either. Do you know where he is or why that might be?'

Thompson eyed a clock on the wall. 'Sometimes a man's got to do what a man's got to do. Radio doesn't extend to public toilets. But he's due back any time.'

'We'll wait for him.'

'As you will.'

'Thank you.' She sent Ross and the two PCs outside to watch for Khan's van coming in.

Jane looked around the office. There was no trace of the cutting she'd photographed – the cutting about the bin explosion. She made a mental note of the carpet, the noticeboard on the wall, and even the plants on the window ledge.

'What's this about, anyway?' Thompson said, shuffling papers from one pile to another. 'Is it connected to Q-busters, or something specifically about Mo Khan?'

'I can't discuss that, Sir,' Jane said, 'but I may need access to Mr Khan's vehicle and any personal locker or work space here.'

'Anything I can do to help,' he said, and shrugged, regaining the poise of his former suave self. Jane left to join the others.

~~~

Allan reached the depot in time to see a Q-busters van screech to a halt and begin reversing back out on to the access road. Two uniforms and Ross scattered for their cars but Allan braked his Alfa to cut the van off, steeling himself for a crump that didn't come. Khan jumped out of the driver's seat and ran off across the grassed area towards the main road. Allan shot after him, happy to see the two uniforms and the leggy Ross quickly out-pace both him and their target. Grabbing one arm each, the PCs marched Mo Khan back towards Q-busters and the police car.

'Well done,' Allan said, clapping Ross on the back before leaning his hands on his thighs to get his breath back.

'Do you want him taken in for questioning, Sir?' It was Jane. She'd left the building just as Khan had spotted the police car and tried to escape.

'Let's have a look around first.'

'What's this about?' Khan said, his arms held rigid behind him.

'Mr Khan,' Allan said. 'We'd like you to help us with our enquiries connected with the disappearance and death of Jamie Brooks. You're not under arrest at this moment, but that is under review, you can believe me.'

'But that's nothing to do with me,' Khan said. 'I told you that at the mosque on Saturday.'

'No?' A small crowd had gathered, made up mostly of workers from the distribution centre and surrounding premises. Allan leaned in. 'So why did you run?'

'Victimisation. That's why.' Khan spat at the ground.

Allan looked at Jane. 'Have you had time to check inside?'

'Not yet, Boss. I warned the MD we might need to.'

'Good. Mr Khan, I'll ask you to sit in the car with these officers for a few minutes. They'll explain your rights to you and make sure you're comfortable.'

Thompson had come outside and was standing with the others. Allan acknowledged him and the two men approached each other.

'Mr Thompson, we've had information that could implicate Mo Khan in a very serious crime. I'd appreciate your full cooperation.'

'Of course,' Thompson said, fully restored to charm and suavity, his blond eyelashes glowing in the autumn sunlight. 'Anything I can do.'

Allan nodded. He looked back to where his Alfa and Khan's vehicle blocked the road. 'First things first. I'll need access to that van.'

154

Chapter 34

'I'll move the van,' Thompson said.

'Ross. Go with him,' Allan said. 'Keep an eye on him. Don't let him do anything other than park it.' He took the keys to his Alfa from his jacket pocket. 'Get the keys off him and move mine once you've secured the van.' He grabbed the DC's sleeve and dropped his keys into his pocket. 'Damage it and I'll damage your under-chassis.'

Jane was studying him. 'How did it go at the hospital?'

Allan wondered how she knew, then realised she was talking about Old Bob. 'Fine,' he said. 'As I told you, the old guy's out of it, but his son was there and his statement corroborated what Khalil Buchanan and his mother told us.' Thompson had climbed into the van and was bringing it round into one of the spaces in front of his office, next to the squad car. Ross walked the route and took the keys from him as soon as he jumped down.

'So, he's no longer a suspect?'

Allan stared at her. 'The Buchanan boy? Not for now. We'll keep an eye on him, but Sam's doing the paperwork to get him released.'

Thompson approached. His staff were still huddled on the office doorstep and around the distribution doors. 'Alright for my staff to get back to work?' he asked.

'Certainly,' Allan said. 'But you'll be available for the next hour or so?'

Thompson nodded and headed back, holding his arms out to sweep up his staff, his near-black suit making him look like some kind of pastor.

'And what about you?'

Carol McKay

'Eh?'

'Are you okay?'

Allan was in no doubt as to his depute's powers of interrogation. Her eyes didn't budge from his, giving him no room for obfuscation. Almost. 'I'm fine! Why would you think otherwise?' He broke away to take his car keys from Ross.

'Right,' he said. 'Let's get Khan back and processed. Ross – I want you to have a quick look in that van. Gloves on. And get someone down here from Forensics.' He leaned into the window of the squad car and told the uniforms to head back to the station. 'So,' he said to Jane. 'What was it like when you got here? What do you think of this Thompson guy?'

Jane leaned against Ross's car and told Allan how agitated their visit had made Cathy. 'But Thompson looked shocked, too. Shocked and anxious. At the sight of the uniforms, I think. Could be nothing, but you'd think a guy in his position wouldn't sweat it unless he'd something to feel guilty about.'

'Yeah. He's hard to read, that one.'

'He regained his composure once I told him it was Khan we were interested in. But he was definitely squirming before then.' They heard Ross call to them. 'He's definitely up to something. Could be totally unrelated, but I don't know –'

They started moving off towards the back of the Q-busters van. 'What have you got?'

Ross had opened the back doors of the van. Inside, there were shelves down both sides, and empty space in the middle. Ross was squatting deep inside the van. 'Found this,' he said. He held up a small roll of carpeting.

'Looks like a prayer mat,' Jane said.

'Right – get Forensics to check if it matches the hair and fibres.' If Khan had driven this van to Jamie Brooks' school and parked it on the zigzags the day Jamie went missing, there was more than enough room on the floor to molest the boy.

'No sign of blood or anything, Boss. But he's had plenty of time

156

to clean it.' Ross put the carpet roll back where he'd found it and the three were silent while he jumped down and secured the doors.

'He must be our man, surely?' Jane said.

'Time will tell. Hope so. That would be a neat finish.' Allan looked at the sky. 'But maybe too neat.' Clouds were gathering again, making it seem later than it really was. He looked at his watch. The office staff would be finishing up any time soon. 'I'm going to have a word with Thompson. Jane, come with me. Ross, you stay with this van till you've sorted it with Forensics. I don't want it left here, because there's probably another set of keys and I don't want anyone driving it away – either innocently or on purpose.'

They buzzed into the office to find Cathy dithery with agitation. The two other office workers were putting on their coats. 'Mr Thompson in his office?' Allan asked her.

'He's just popped over to the shop floor. Do you want me to ring him?'

'Yes, please,' Allan said.

Cathy rang and they waited. There was no answer.

'Bye, Cathy.' The two women left, Cathy nodding without looking at them. At least, she might have been nodding. It was hard to tell because nodding was a normal part of her body language.

'Tsk. He's just not answering,' she said, pushing her glasses up her nose to see the DI clearly.

Allan feigned impatience. Actually, what he really wanted was a seat, but she didn't offer.

'I'll try his mobile.' Cathy looked up a file on her computer and dialled a number from it. She waited, then shook her head. 'No, it's just ringing.' She hung up and screwed up her nose. 'Maybe popped to the loo with all the excitement.'

Allan heard Jane restrain a laugh. She turned away. 'Could you maybe pop through to the floor to see if he's there?' Allan asked Cathy. 'Not into the loo, of course,' he said, winking. 'I know you take your work seriously, but that would be beyond dedication, eh?'

Cathy's face was transformed by her smile. She looked younger, prettier. 'I'll do that. You don't mind waiting?'

'Not at all,' Allan said, channelling effort into smiling fulsomely back at her. 'I appreciate your time.'

The office lights hummed while she skirted the desk and headed to the door. Allan looked at Jane. As soon as Cathy disappeared, both looked at the screen. Cathy had left Thompson's details up on it. 'Looks like the boss has a schedule of his own,' Jane said.

'See if you can find out where he was the day Jamie disappeared,' Allan said.

The two bent, scrolling down to look through the info. They straightened quickly when they heard the turning of the door handle. Allan shifted to conceal Jane restoring the page to the precise spot Cathy had been looking at. He gave Cathy another smile. 'Success?' he said.

Cathy touched her throat and smiled. 'He's just coming. Why not take a seat in his office?'

'Great. Thanks!' Allan said. And, as if making small talk. 'Is that you finished for the day?'

'Och, I'll hang on to see if Mr Thompson needs me.' Her brow furrowed. 'In fact, can I ask you? Will Mo Khan be at work tomorrow?' She shook her head, setting her hair bobbing. 'Because if he's not, I'll need to rearrange his delivery schedule.'

'I think Mr Khan might be out of action for a day or two while he's helping us with our enquiries,' Jane said.

Cathy's frown deepened. She shook her head again. 'I don't get it. He's quite a nice person.' She sought Jane's eyes out. 'Really pleasant to work with. Does anything.' She looked to Allan. 'He's never any trouble.'

'Well, I'm sure he'll be relieved to know he can count on you if he ever needs a character reference,' Allan said, keeping his voice light. 'Will it be okay if we just go through, then?' He nodded towards the office.

'Of course! I said.'

'Thanks.' Allan paused. 'Any chance of a coffee?'

Chapter 35

Thompson floated through the door, on the face of it unruffled. He ran his fingers through his near-white hair, brushing it from his forehead. 'Sorry. Busy place. There's always something to sort out.'

Cathy came in with coffee. There was silence till she'd gone. Allan spooned in two sugars, stirred then drank deeply, finishing the cup in two goes. He sat back in his chair.

'So, Mr Thompson,' he said, discreetly dabbing his lips and watching while the other man and Jane sipped their drink. 'Mohammed Khan. How long has he been here? What can you tell me about him?'

Thompson put his cup down and bridged his fingers, elbows on the arms of his executive leather chair. 'He's been with us a while now. I can get Cathy to tell you precisely, but it must be close to a year. Maybe more than that.'

'A reliable worker?'

'I'd say so. What matters to me is he's got a clean sheet when it comes to driving. I wouldn't employ anyone otherwise.'

'Right. And what about any other kind of three point penalty – or more than three?'

'Like what?'

Allan edged forward. 'Pilfering, for example.' Jamie'd had that phone under his pillow. 'Maybe even using goods he's pilfered from your stock as bargaining chips. Did you know he's on the sex offenders' register?'

Thompson's nostrils flared and there appeared to be a struggle going on to control his breath and demeanour. Guilt or anger? If it was anger, was he angry at Khan for concealing his past, or angry at Allan for catching him out? The MD placed his palm on the desk, tapped his fingers a few times then stopped. It was the kind of trick a motivational speaker might teach in a mindfulness class. Or something. 'I run a professional business. An efficient business. This is my life. I have a young family, so I don't take risks. I take on employees because I trust them. I employ people because they merit it. If they work hard for me, I work hard for them. We're a team. I expect that's something you're likely to understand, being in the police force.'

Allan said nothing. Thompson hadn't finished.

'I also believe that people who do wrong deserve a chance to get back into society after they've been punished. In fact, they should be honour bound to get back into work to pay back. I'm a big fan of restorative justice. So, if Mo Khan did something wrong, showed remorse and served his punishment, in my books that gives him every right to a place in the workforce. And he's good. Believe me. He's a grafter.'

'You haven't said anything about pilfering.'

Thompson held his hands out. 'Where's your evidence?'

'Can you show me his locker?'

'Of course.'

Thompson rose abruptly and led Allan and Jane back out through the main office, past Cathy, and through to the shop floor, which was quiet and in semi-darkness, almost everyone having clocked off for the day. They walked past box shelves containing smaller goods and huge stacks reaching up ten metres, replete with white goods and other appliances. A fork-lift truck beeped and hummed down the aisles. Its operator nodded to his boss and stared at Allan. 'We have a small crew on overnight to restock. Delivery drivers are out on the road any time between seven in the morning and eight in the evening.'

At the end of the stacks they pushed through a door into the staff area.

'This is the men's rest zone.' Thompson pointed as he spoke. 'Toilets, vending machines, water, lockers. You want to see Khan's?'

'Yes, please.'

The yellow lockers were in one long line down the corridor, stacked two high. Thompson went halfway down the row and without hesitation stopped at the one numbered 22. 'This is it.' He opened it and Allan was aware of Jane, beside him, messaging him telepathically that Thompson had known exactly where it was, and had opened it without a key.

'I'll have a look in it, thanks. If you could just step back,' Allan said, pulling on gloves.

There was the standard clutter. A pair of trainers on the locker floor. A company fleece hanging from the hook near the roof of the box. Allan lifted it down. It was navy blue, with the spongy texture flattened a bit by wear around the neck and down the front. It smelled like a dog that needed a bath. Allan patted the pockets and had a quick feel through them. Pens, a tiny screwdriver, a sauce-stained paper napkin. He hung the fleece over the opened door and reached to unhook the 'bag for life' carrier that had been concealed by it. Bright orange, the bag was sturdy, which was just as well as its contents were heavy. Allan lowered it and held it open by its two handles so he and Jane could both see in. He glanced up at Thompson, who was standing with one arm across his waist and the other hand covering his mouth.

'You wanted evidence of pilfering?' Allan knelt, setting the bag on the floor, and he picked out phone after smartphone after handheld games console. He glanced up at Jane. 'Looks top of the range to me.'

'Anything other than a stone-age i-phone is top of the range to me, Boss,' Jane said, speaking quietly to the man on the floor so Thompson wouldn't hear. 'But yeah, those look good. Ross'll have a field day.'

Allan piled them all back in and stowed the bag back in the locker. 'I want no one near this locker,' he said to Thompson.

161

'Of course.'

To Jane, he said, 'Go and tell the boys from Forensics to have a look at this when they're finished.'

As she headed for the car park, Allan closed the door over and said to Thompson. 'Seems strange, to me, that you knew precisely where Khan's locker was. And that you didn't have to unlock it.' He met the man's eyes.

Thompson shrugged. 'I know my men,' he said. 'As I said, we're a team.'

Allan wondered if the man in front of him ever broke sweat. 'And what about your fingerprints? Is my team going to find them all over this?'

Thompson pale blue eyes held Allan's. 'I'm very hands on in this job.'

They waited in silence for a few moments till Jane returned with one of the forensics officers, who proceeded to bag up the contents of Khan's locker. 'Swab it, too, inside and out,' Allan said. 'Can we go back up to your office?' he asked Thompson. The question was rhetorical.

Cathy was still there, a silk scarf round her neck, her coat over her chair, and concern on her face. She jumped to her feet when Thompson and the police passed through.

'No need to hang around, Cathy. Everything's fine. I'll lock up.' Thompson's hand on her shoulder made the woman visibly relax. Her shoulders had been heading for her ears but a touch from her boss was enough to lower them. The tightly held skin on her face loosened and she almost smiled, nodding her relief as she picked up her coat, grasped the edge of her cardigan sleeve and pushed her arm in. Thompson held it steady for her while she slipped the other arm in its sleeve. She smiled at them all in turn, nodding in her usual way and pushed her glasses up her nose as she wished them goodnight.

Thompson led the way back into his office. Once there, he closed the door and said to Allan, 'So, what now?'

'Mr Khan will be out of commission for a while. How long, I can't say at this stage.'

'Okay.'

'And we'll be impounding his van.'

Thompson's brows twitched. 'Is that necessary?'

Allan sat forward. 'Khan might be guilty of pilfering, but right at this moment I've got my sights on a much more significant crime. So, is impounding one of your vans necessary? Let me tell you right now: if circumstances dictate, I'll be back here to impound every one of them.'

Chapter 36

It was late – past six o'clock – but Allan and Jane headed back to the office. Ross had supervised the uniforms arresting Khan and impounding the vehicle; the team from Forensics would stay on site at the depot collecting any evidence from there but would do a complete survey of the van once it was securely on police premises. Someone could go back the next day to ask Thompson for fingerprints – to rule him out, ostensibly.

Was Thompson implicated? Was there some connection between him and Mo Khan? Allan couldn't work it out. He found himself staring at bits of paper, seeing the photos of the dead boy and witness statements, but he felt brain dead, unable to hold on to the information long enough to compare and contrast and hypothesise over A or B. He knew, from experience, that the brain made intuitive leaps in its own time, even for something as basic as answers to crossword clues arriving in the middle of the night or remembering the name that went with a face three weeks after he'd seen its owner walk past him. This evening, though, he couldn't penetrate the fog to grasp the information presented to him in the first place.

'Coffee, Boss?' Jane handed him a steaming take-away cup.

He reached for it gladly. 'Is Khan in the cells?'

'Yep. Ross rang to say he's been processed and they're ready to start when we are.'

Allan nodded and drank. He set the cup down and scoured his forehead and eye sockets with his hands.

'Tired?'

'Yep.' He looked at his watch. 'Ross and Sam both on? They

can do the preliminaries. Give us time to think this through before the morning.' He picked up a photo of the dead boy. He noticed his hand was shaking. When had this tremor started? Too much caffeine? He pincered the photo top and bottom to keep it still. 'So, what do we know?'

'Seriously? Now? The boys are waiting for us.'

'We've a dead boy who hid an upmarket phone under his pillow. We've a guy on the sex offenders register who's found to have upmarket phones in a bag in his locker. And we're shown his locker – his unlocked locker – by his smarmy boss who says everyone who's done the crime and served the time deserves to be given a second chance, which is all very noble, but also pretty convenient.' He studied Jane. 'You noticed he went straight to that locker without hesitating, too, didn't you?'

'Yep. That was obvious.' Jane perched on the edge of the desk across from Allan's and sipped her coffee.

'And he didn't need a key.'

'Yeah – weird. And Cathy hadn't been able to find him when we turned up to talk to him. So he'd plenty of time to be putting those phones into that bag and planting it. But why would he want to do that? I don't get it.'

Allan glanced at the file on his desk and leafed through the previous witness statements and reports team members had completed from various visits. 'I've absolutely no idea. We've nothing on Thompson. He's not on the register. We've no reason to suspect him. Why would he want to fit Khan up? Why would he think I'd think he'd be implicated? Just because he's a smarmy bastard and I don't like him?'

'I don't think that would stand up in court,' Jane said, wrinkling her nose at him.

'You're right, there.'

The phone on the desk Jane was sitting on rang and she leaned over to answer it. 'Okay. We'll be straight down.' She hung up. 'Sam and Ross are ready,' she told Allan. 'Sam's going to take the lead, Ross says.'

Allan rose and tossed his empty cup at the waste bin.

In the interview room, Mo Khan was sitting with the duty solicitor. Impossible to say which of the two looked more hang-dog. Sam and Ross were avoiding the 'good cop, bad cop' routine, with Sam pursuing the line of questioning while Ross observed Khan's body language and facial expressions. Jane and Allan took up posts in the connecting room, watching it all via the camera link-up to the computer screen.

'When did you meet Jamie?' Sam asked.

Mo Khan's hands were clasped on the table in front of him and his face was angled down making it impossible to gauge his expression.

'You know my client doesn't need to answer that,' the solicitor said.

'Have you known him a while? How did you meet him?' Sam pursued. 'Was he a friend of a friend? Or did you see him at the school? He doesn't go to your mosque, does he?'

Khan's body twitched and he focused on Sam. 'He's nothing to do with the mosque.'

'No? So, did you make a delivery to him, then? A delivery to his house? Maybe he'd to sign for something, and he took your fancy. Maybe you told him you could get him something else. Something better. Something his mother couldn't afford. Something that wouldn't cost him anything – well, any money.'

Khan swung his head from side to side, grimacing.

'You don't need to answer that,' the solicitor told him.

'I'm innocent,' Khan said. 'I honestly haven't done anything.'

Sam sorted through some papers and let the silence build the tension.

'Check the signatures for the drops I did,' Khan said. 'I wasn't anywhere near the boy – or the murder site. Check it.'

Ross sat up and drew his chair in closer to the table. 'What murder site, Mr Khan? Do you know where the murder site is?

Have you something to tell us?'

Khan breathed out heavily. His eyes went to the camera. 'Of course I don't know the murder site.' He appealed to the solicitor. 'I've nothing to do with this. I've no idea where the murder site is. I just mean my time is fully accounted for.' There was sweat on his brow and on the thick strands of his hair. He wiped his hands over his beard and mouth. 'I'm innocent.'

'You haven't always been,' Sam said quietly, lifting his eyes from the file in front of him.

Agitated, Khan said, 'I'm finished with that. I've served my time.' He appealed to the solicitor again. 'That's why I volunteer. I've been trying to atone for all that. I wouldn't hurt anybody now. I don't know anything about that boy.'

The duty solicitor nodded and rested his hand on Khan's arm. The camera's red light pulsed as it recorded.

In the connecting room, Allan looked at his watch again. Jane saw it. 'D'you have to be somewhere?'

Allan flicked his eyes towards her. 'I've got this thing to do.' That nurse at the hospital had even texted him. How often did you hear that?

'They're nearly finished for now. I don't see them getting anything out of him till we get some forensics.' She leaned on her elbow and stared at Allan. 'I'm free tonight, so I'll stay on and debrief the boys. And you can take over tomorrow once we've softened him up a bit for you.' She tried a smile to see if Allan would return it.

He didn't. He had his eyes on the video screen that was focusing on the emotionally drained, sweating suspect. Straight faced, Allan said, 'He's still claiming he was fully occupied at the time of the murder.' He met Jane's eyes. 'He's said that since we interviewed him at the mosque.'

'Yeah, but do you believe him?' Jane said.

Allan rubbed his chin. 'We'll need to check that signature log in the morning. Need to make this watertight. He's quite easily distinguishable with the full beard and thick head of hair. Did we pick him up on CCTV anywhere near the scene?'

The look on Jane's face told him they hadn't.

'In the morning we'll need to have another go at it. The CCTV. At the school. Traffic cameras on the road to Abriachan. Whatever. We must have missed something.'

'Ross'll love that! He spent hours going square-eyed on it.'

Eyes. Khan's eyes were still bloodshot and his skin puffy. 'Yeah, but there must be something. Get him to pull in any more stuff. Further afield if he has to. Shop footage, if there's any left.' He folded the file with the dead boy's photo inside it and met Jane's eyes again. 'And pull in any footage near that bin fire 'explosion' and the streets around Q-busters to see if that was down to him – if he put Jamie's clothes in the bin and set light to them. In fact, the entire Industrial Estate. A place like that must be chocka with cameras. So far we've just got the fuzzy pics of two lads at the garage shop, but that doesn't prove anything. Let's extend the search back through time, as well. Let's look a good few hours before the fire even started.'

Chapter 37

The sun was setting in the west, beyond the wooded hills where they'd found the body of the young boy. Soft skinned and pink. The sky directly overhead was a deep and clear blue, but salmon-coloured clouds extended from the horizon, the texture of teased-out sheep's wool caught on barbed-wire fences. Nature, human nature – why was it all so bitter-sweet? Lights were coming on in the city: glowing spheres threaded the routes, while windows in the town's tenements fused into a glittering mosaic.

Allan turned the car into the hospital car park and cruised up and down the aisles. It must be evening visiting time and the parking was full. It was easier to sit in the car and wait. Preferable to stay out here in the twilight, rather than pull on the handbrake, activate central locking and take the walk through that doorway into the vaulted atrium to be with all those sick people and the ones who worried about them. Safer to be on the outside, in the mild autumn's evening air, than in there, facing the inevitable.

Hazard lights flickered and a middle-aged man with a paunch raised a hand to signal to Allan that he was returning to his car. He sat in heavily and reversed out, waving again as he vacated the space. Allan indicated and pulled in.

The text had said to go straight back to the ward where he'd been tested. The nurse herself was finishing just after eight and it was almost eight now. Allan took the lift to the fourth floor and walked through the doors, opened to welcome visitors. He pumped sanitising gel on to the palm of one hand and massaged it into both as he walked to the nurses' station. There were half a dozen

169

women there, grouped in a confab while the patients in the little rooms around them were occupied with their visitors, sometimes four round a bed, sometimes only one or two. In the subdued light, Allan had trouble making out which nurse was his, if she was still there, but she spotted him and came forward to the desk to greet him.

'You came! Good move,' she said. 'Can you wait two minutes? We're just handing over to the night shift.'

'Sure,' he said, still rubbing his hands together, but more for something to do, now, than necessity. He looked around, read the noticeboard, gazed idly at the pictures of the staff, all the different levels from head woman to minion. Read the list of names of the patients and what rooms they were in; what beds. The skin on his back crawled inside his shirt; crawled with the idea of having to be here.

'Ready?' The nurse with the sparking nylon thighs bustled out from behind the staff enclosure. She took him by the sleeve of his upper arm and guided him towards the same room he'd been in earlier.

'You taking me into custody?' he asked her, just to take the edge off things; making conversation.

'Nah. No need to worry. Unless you see me get my pink fluffy handcuffs out my locker.'

At the side room, she let him go, opened the door and flicked on the lights. It was enough to make him blink.

'In you go,' she said. 'Just take a seat for a minute and I'll go and get the records.'

'Records? None of that hip-hop or dance. I'm more of a Blur man, or Oasis.'

She smiled perfunctorily and he realised the woman had been working all day and was tired, and he was being a dickhead. That was anxiety making his heart motor. Along with his mouth. 'Get a grip,' he muttered aloud, adjusting his position on the chair and looking around him at a room that had been clinically scrubbed of emotional warmth or character.

The door opened abruptly and the nurse was there again, preceded by a younger, taller and thinner woman in plain clothes covered by a loose, unfastened white coat with a couple of pens in the top pocket. This woman was carrying the records, and none of them would fit on his dad's old turntable.

'Mr MacIntyre?' the woman said. 'I'm Dr Hall. Thanks for coming in.' She pulled out another of the padded lilac office chairs like the one he was sitting on and perched on it, placing the file on the table in front of her. From his angle, there were no photos of murder victims and no police reports, so he was probably in the clear. He swallowed, wishing he was on her side, reading the file the right way up and not on this side, devoid of knowledge or control.

'So, can I just go, Dani?' the nurse said. She was leaning in the open doorway.

'Of course, Lauren. Thanks! See you tomorrow.'

Lauren winked at Allan. 'Those handcuffs'll have to wait for another time.'

Funny how a woman could get away with saying that without being arrested for sexual harassment. He almost said as much to the doctor woman, who was engrossed in his file, but thought better of it, and just managed to apply the brakes to the banter wagon.

'So,' she said, looking up from his notes and smiling. 'How've you been feeling?'

He rubbed his palms in the space between his thighs. 'Och, okay, you know?'

'Uh-huh.' She waited. Blinked a few times while he said nothing.

He cast his eyes around. Caught a reflection of her back and himself in the glazed panel that gave sightlines over the corridor leading to the nurses' station. He looked jaundiced, but that was the artificial light. 'Well, I've been a bit tired. Easily tired. But my work can be quite active. Stairs to climb. That kind of thing. We've moved into a new building. I've been trying to avoid the lift. There's a poster beside the stairs that says if you climb them four times a day you'll have climbed a mountain by the end of the year. So I'm just unfit and trying to get fitter.'

'Okay,' she said. 'Easily tired. Anything else?'

'Och, you know.' He shrugged.

She smiled, brows raised. 'Not till you tell me.'

'Well, I'm not really coping well with stress, but again, that's probably just the job. But I shouldn't really say that. Not in my position.'

'You're a policeman?'

'Detective Inspector. Head of a small team. In the CID.' He grinned. 'We're the smart ones, rather than the PC Plods. But don't tell them I said that.'

'You've got quite a good tan, Mr MacIntyre. Have you just come back from holiday?'

He blinked and stared at her. 'No. Well, yes – but it was a while ago.' He looked at the back of his hand; pulled his jacket and shirt cuff up a bit so he could see his forearm. The sticky toffee tan was quite pronounced through the dark hair on it. 'I was in Spain a couple of months ago. Was doing the manly thing and resisting using suntan lotion, so I got a bit burned. Is that what the problem is? Is that what that test was for?'

The doctor had been looking at his arm, too. 'Do you have any scars – any recent cuts or scratches I could look at?'

He stared at her. Thought about it. 'Recent ones?'

'Uh-huh.'

He waved his hand vaguely. 'Well, maybe on my shoulder.'

She moistened her lips. 'Can I see them?'

He grinned, slightly embarrassed. 'Will I ...?'

She nodded and reached to tip the blinds before he slipped his jacket off and unfastened his shirt then pulled one arm out of the sleeve. She stood up to examine him, her facial expression giving nothing away. 'Thanks, Mr MacIntyre. You can put your shirt on again.' She sat down and wrote a note in the file. 'Did you notice those scratches have healed differently?'

'No.' He slipped his sleeve down again and angled his head to see over his shoulder.

'The scarring is brown rather than pink.'

'Is it? I can't really see.'

Once he was dressed again, she explained it to him. He felt like this was the moment she'd been waiting for; that this was the moment he'd been waiting for. It was like the build up to a performance, and now here he was, both audience and actor in the drama.

The blood test had measured the performance of his adrenals. The adrenals were glands on top of a person's kidneys, and when they weren't working properly that person was up shit creek without a paddle. On a one-way ticket to oblivion. Their number was up and they hadn't won the lottery.

He shook his head. 'So, what are you telling me?'

She pressed her lips together in a half-smile and looked at her hands. But then she raised her eyes to his and held them. 'Mr MacIntyre, you've a condition called Addison's. It's auto-immune in nature. That means your body is attacking its own tissues. In this case, it's attacking the outer layers of your adrenal glands, and that affects things like your blood volume and your blood pressure.'

Those eyes really weren't blinking. She went on, 'The damaged parts normally control the body's response to stress, for example.' She glanced at her file, then straight back. 'I mean physical stress, but mental and emotional as well. They respond to a signal from your brain. A chemical messenger?'

He nodded.

'So that, say you're fighting an infection, or break a bone or something, your brain sends a signal to your adrenals to step up a gear and produce more cortisol, but in Addison's Disease that part's damaged, so there isn't a full response.'

'But I haven't broken a bone or anything.'

She tucked a lock of hair behind her ear. 'No, but the decline in your health is gradual. It's an auto-immune attack and it takes place over a long time. So, just now, all you're experiencing is the low blood pressure – that's what's making you feel light-headed when you climb the stairs or rush about.'

He thought about how hard it had been to keep up with the others climbing that hillside. 'So it's not that I'm an unfit bastard?'

She smiled. 'No. And the tan and brown scratches are another sign. When the brain sends that signal to your adrenals to tell them to get a move on, it's not getting the response it wants, so it sends out more of the chemical messenger. And that has to go somewhere, so it ends up being excreted to the skin.'

'Like jaundice.' His mother had ended up jaundiced.

'Yeah – a bit like jaundice, but a different chemical messenger.'

'My mother had jaundice towards the end of her life.' So many years ago. More than twenty. Why was he telling her this? 'Liver cancer. I thought maybe I was going the same way.'

She nodded, as if she got it. They were silent for a moment.

He sat up and sniffed. Spoke louder now. 'So, what's the prognosis?'

She straightened up, too. 'A good one.'

They both nodded.

'JF Kennedy had Addison's Disease. That's what gave him that golden tan. He was one of the first to survive it.'

'Till the bullets got him.'

'Okay, till the bullets got him. But he was one of the first to get medicine. And he could run the world's mightiest country, so as I say, the prognosis is a good one. You'll just need to take the tablets. Addison's is controlled by drugs. You'll take them to replace what your body's no longer producing. It's a straightforward replacement therapy.' She blinked and fixed on his eyes again. 'I can't stress highly enough that this is serious, and you'll need to take these drugs regularly, every day – three times a day – without fail. If you don't, it's –'

'Curtains.'

From somewhere near her waist came a beeping sound. She

glanced at her pager and pressed a button.

'Someone wants you.'

She shrugged and frowned then looked in her notes. 'You're a policeman.'

'Mm-hmm.'

'Right.' She flicked through some pages and jotted down a few words. Then she met his eyes again, uncrossing her legs. 'I've written you a prescription for hydrocortisone. It's steroids, the drug of choice, chemically identical to what the normal body produces. Hydrocortisone's for your everyday, day-to-day management. You'll find it takes a bit of trial and error to get the dose that's right for you, but there's information in the pack, and I recommend you have a good read at the ADSHG website. It's a self-help group that does excellent work for survivors. That'll answer all your questions.' She passed him a post-it note that had a drug company logo on it and her blue hand-writing giving the web address. 'I'm also going to prescribe you an emergency injection kit. They're important for everyone with Addison's, but since you're a policeman, and could in theory be out there taking risks of falling or experiencing physical trauma, an emergency injection kit could be even more important for you.'

'What, like for diabetes?'

'Slightly. But different.'

'No – not with my work. I can't have that.'

The bleeper went off again. She raised her eyebrows. 'You'll have to.' She held his gaze, serious. 'Keep it with you. Read the information on it. Look on the website at the videos. Learn how to use it.'

She must have been five years younger than him. Ten, maybe. Late twenties? Early thirties? And here she was, giving him a death sentence. Well, he wasn't dying. He'd just been tired. That's all it was.

She started gathering her things, sweeping the file together, just the way he did in front of criminals. When he was in control.

175

'Look,' she said. 'I know this must feel a bit unreal.' Her eyes were deep blue without any kind of lines in them. In the sharp light in this room, her pupils had shrunk to pin heads. 'But you will need to take it seriously. It's not always identified so quickly, so you're lucky. I'll take you to the nurses' station and they'll put your prescription together. Take your first pill tonight and follow the dosing instructions from tomorrow. You'll need to go to your GP to get repeats. And it really is compulsory. Make no mistake about that, Mr MacIntyre: your blood work and the Synacthen test are totally convincing.' She'd stood by now, as he had. 'I'll send a letter calling you for a longer appointment in a week or two, so we can see how things are going for you, and we'll get the chance, then, to talk it all through.' She held out her hand to shake his. 'Good luck. I'll be in touch.'

Chapter 38

What to make of it? Best, nothing. Allan folded up information sheets the doctor printed off for him and stuffed them in his inside jacket pocket. At the nurse's station he'd to wait a few minutes till the duty pharmacist came up with six boxes – six boxes – of pills for him, and a couple of syringes. The whole scenario was laughable. The guy took time to show him how to use them, fully serious, but though Allan looked and nodded at what seemed like the appropriate points in the demonstration, his brain had put the shields up and was refusing to even countenance that any of this might actually apply to him. It wasn't going to apply to him. Full Stop. He nodded a final time, took the bag the pharmacy guy gave him and walked off.

It was only a bit after eight. The clocks hadn't changed yet and there was still some light in the sky. He could see it through the hospital windows as he made his way to the lifts. What to do? Go home and read this guff? That would be the sensible thing, but he was resisting sensible. It was overrated. The whole thing must be a cock-up anyway, because look – he was a thinking, breathing, Scotch-drinking human being who just needed to go to the gym more than once a year to get himself in shape. End of story.

He didn't want to go home. He should be thinking about Mo Khan, who'd just been arrested. But his thoughts were jumping like a kid on crazy paving, trying to avoid the cracks. He caught the lift in the midst of a melée of visitors who were leaving. The bell must have rung to get rid of them for the night. They'd only gone down one floor when there was a ping and the lift bounced, and the doors opened to let more people on. Something about the crush, backing him into the very furthest away part of the metal box, the smells of different perfumes and rattle of women's voices built up in him till he cracked.

'Sorry. Can't take this,' he said. 'Excuse me.' He shoved his way through the plump and scented fellow-travellers, onto the third floor. He'd find the stairs.

As the lift doors shut behind him, he recognised where he was. The sign confirmed it. It was old Bob's ward. The ward doors were still open and from the plaque it looked as if visiting hours were staggered, with this ward open till half past. There were still clusters of people who were part of normal life, wearing normal clothes, sitting round people who'd surrendered to going public in a state of undress. The fact of their surrender burned like bile in Allan's gut. He resented it, fearful of cross-contamination. No way he'd be giving in to it. Forcing himself, he swallowed the anger down and strode past the nurses' station to where he remembered old Bob's room being. The door was closed, but he could see old Bob through the observation window. He wasn't alone. Lorraine and Khalil were there. Allan's chest grew light. She was smiling; happy. He'd got her boy back for her, so he'd be in the good books.

Khal's face bore an open expression – youthful, innocent. Yes, innocent. Allan might be a cynical cop but he recognised that look straight away. Khal was holding his phone up to show Bob something, but he broke off mid sentence when Allan opened the door. Lorraine's bright look dulled.

'Hiya,' Allan said. He nodded to Bob, who clearly still hadn't got his speech back, but whose facial expression showed he'd been comfortable with his visitors till Allan arrived. Allan stepped to the bed and shook the old man's hand. He decided to introduce himself as a friend of Lorraine's, rather than by his job title. More prudent in the circumstances. 'How're you doing?' He bent to kiss Lorraine but she twisted her head, so his lips smacked her cheek rather than her lips. Very French.

Lorraine pursed her mouth like some Glasgow woman 'chewing a wasp'. She'd crossed her arms under her breasts, pushing them up. On a plate, as it were. Maybe. The mood he was in, he could put up with the wasp chewing. He needed the honey.

'Allan's the one who put Khalil in jail,' Lorraine said, pointedly loudly to Bob.

Maybe not. Obviously Allan's expectations weren't quite in touch with reality. But putting Khal in jail? That wasn't fair.

He scoffed. 'Not quite. I was instrumental in getting him out,' he said, addressing Lorraine directly rather than the others in the room. He still had the drugs in his hand, so he lifted the spare chair over from the window to the bottom of the bed and sat on it, tucking the drug bag underneath. Nobody spoke. So Allan spoke again. 'What's this you've got?' Allan asked Khal, indicating his phone.

'Nothing.' The boy had put the force field up around himself too. Not surprising. He still had dull patches on his face from the kicking the two local lads had given him. They were the ones who should've been taken in for questioning, and maybe even charged with race hate crimes, rather than Khal being investigated on suspicion of terrorism just because he had brown skin colouring, and a Muslim first name. Oh, and a bag full of the wherewithal for a five kilo nail bomb.

'Go on. Let's see it.' Allan leaned forward with his elbows on his knees.

'Are you asking him as a policeman?' Lorraine was straight faced. 'Is he obliged to let you see it?'

'Fuck, no,' Allan said, sitting back. 'I don't work all the time. I just wondered what the excitement was.' He stared Lorraine out. 'Look, I just noticed he was showing it off – when I spotted you through the window.' There was a pause when, once again, nobody spoke. Then Allan sat forward again and lowered his tone. 'And if you ask me, you could put in a complaint against those lads that beat him up – get them investigated for race hate crime.'

Lorraine's eyebrows rose. 'Really?' She looked at Khalil, but he shook his head.

'Leave it, Mum.'

Allan wiped the side of his mouth. 'Well, it's something to keep at the back of your mind.'

Lorraine thought about it. 'Go on, then, show him what you were showing Bob.' To Allan, she said, 'It's this Airplane Tracker thing he loves. He's always on it.'

Khal stayed at the far side of Bob's bed.

Allan stared at him. He was a skinny fifteen year old in clothes so baggy he could fit another one of him inside, and even from this distance he smelled of a pungent mix of deodorant and foot sweat. The bony arm that held the phone was brown and had a mesh of black hairs on it. Stubby black hairs punctured the skin at either corner of his upper lip, too. It took him back. At that age, Allan had loathed spending time hospital visiting, filling the dragging hour beside a bed where an emaciated loved one high on morphine barely rumpled the covers.

'So, what is it, then, this aeroplane tracker?'

Khal angled the phone as little as he could get away with to let Allan see it. It was big. Modern and expensive looking, with a large screen. On the screen was one of these map apps. Jane had tried showing him one, once, that logged where you went every time you cycled, or ran, trying to get him interested. That was a failure. This one looked different. It was the one he'd seen that night at Lorraine's house when they were showing Ahmed out. Khal used two fingers to scroll out a bit, and soon Allan could see a wide chunk of Europe.

'Oh, right. Like a travel map,' Allan said. His eyes flicked to Lorraine again. She'd crossed her legs and he'd had a glimpse of inner thigh.

'No,' she said, 'it's more about the planes, isn't it, Khal? Following what routes they take. What cargoes they have. That kind of thing.'

'Eh?' Allan said, suddenly alert. 'Is that a smart thing to have when you've just been interviewed on terror charges?'

The boy switched the screen off and slid the phone into his back pocket. 'Are we going to be long?'

'Don't be rude!' Lorraine's eyes flashed at him, then signalled that old Bob was still lying there, half awake and half dozing.

'Well, can I go to the shop?'

'Okay.' She looked at her watch. 'Just say goodbye now, because it's nearly chucking-out time. Wait at the shop and I'll get you.' She shook her head and rolled her eyes to Bob and to Allan, while Khal stepped through the gaps between bed and chairs towards the door.

Just as the door closed behind him, the bell for the end of visiting time rang out. Lorraine ignored it and exchanged a few more words with Bob, or, rather, told him a few lines about this neighbour or that window cleaner. 'And Khal's going to keep an eye on your plants,' she said. 'I'll make sure he waters them.' She started putting her coat on. Behind him, through the door, Allan could hear the clip of heels as visitors headed for the lifts.

They said their goodbyes and Allan gripped Lorraine's elbow on the way out. There was quite a crush in the corridor. 'What are you doing after this?' he asked, trying out some lingering eye contact.

'Going home. What else?'

Was she playing a game, blowing hot and cold? He couldn't work her out. He supposed it was because she was sober now. And maybe he was redundant now he'd got her son home for her. The four lifts were busy between floors and a crowd had built up around them. Still edgy, Allan couldn't wait. 'Want to take the stairs?'

'Sure.'

For some reason, he couldn't contain his inner policeman. 'Where did Khalil get his fancy phone from?' he asked her and she told him it was Mo.

'Mo Khan?' Allan stopped three steps from the bottom of the second flight. 'Ahmed's uncle?'

Lorraine stopped a step down and stared up at him. 'What about it?'

Allan shook his head and they started walking again. At the next landing, he came to a halt. 'You know Mo Khan's got a record?'

Lorraine shrugged. 'So?'

'He's on the child protection register. Did you know that?'

She sighed. An angry sigh. 'For fuck's sake, Allan. Folk like you can't ever let go of things, can you? That was years ago.' She set off downstairs again then thought better of it. 'You can't keep persecuting people and punishing them because they made a mistake once upon a time. Neither Mo nor Khal are in any trouble. Neither looking for it nor making it.'

She took the rest of the stairs on her own, ahead of him, but Allan's steps rang in the staircase as he clipped down after her. 'Seriously, Lorraine. Mo's not what he seems. You should keep Khalil away from him.'

She rounded on him. 'What are you like? Listen – he's my son and I'll look after him my way. I'll be the one who decides who is and isn't suitable company for him.'

Chapter 39

What now?

He watched her disappear along the corridor and into the atrium, and he stood with his hands in his pockets as he observed her reunion with the boy outside the shop. She fussed over him, tidying the magazine he'd bought into her bag and brushing something invisible from the back of his shirt. Khal was typically cool in his reaction. Allan would offer them a lift. He waited as they walked through the wide, open atrium, heading towards the doors. She glanced his way then pointedly blanked him. So be it; he wasn't going to run after her. Let her suffer a long drawn out public transport ride home. Hell mend her. He'd his scarlet Alfa crouched in the car park, waiting for him, and the choice between a smoky half bottle of Lagavullin or a bison grass vodka at home. He stood a moment or two, watching Lorraine and her son leave the building. Maybe he'd draw up at the bus stop. Give her a couple of minutes, the rain lashing down and that cold wind blowing. How could she resist?

Shit. He'd left the bag of drugs upstairs in old Bob's room and had to go back up in the lift to reclaim it. By the time he eventually passed through the hospital's wide revolving doors, there was no rain, no cold wind, just a mild October evening. And the bus stop was empty.

It was dark as he headed back to his car. There were plenty of spaces, now. He sat in and tossed the drug bag on to the passenger seat, then glanced at it, glowing dusty white and blue in the car park street lights. What the fuck was it all about? He should think about it. He should at least bloody look at it. He picked the bag up and threw it on the back seat where he couldn't see it then turned the key in the ignition and worked his feet on the pedals.

Mo Khan was in custody overnight and wouldn't be troubling anyone. Allan would have a good go with him in the morning. By then, they'd have enough to hold him on suspicion until Forensics could come up with something. He'd have a debrief with Sam, Jane and Ross; see if they'd got anything out of him tonight. Go over everything. Tell them to check the CCTV again. No, he'd said that. To Jane. Well, he'd reiterate it. Make sure they jumped to it. Something was going on in this case and he just had to find the leads to it.

He turned the steering wheel one-handed with the palm of his hand. Back on auto-pilot, on home territory, near the loch. The water was deep and cold and black as he drove along beside it. Inky deep. So much concealed in it. Life. Death. Monsters. Anything could be going on under the surface gloss of it. What was going on beneath Thompson's gloss? That was the other part of this puzzle. Something had spooked him, earlier. Allan recognised that startled look. That panicked look when someone who'd thought he was safe suddenly felt the solid ground he was walking on turn to water.

As for Khal and this aeroplane tracker – what was that about? He'd caught him looking up at the sky before, one night when he'd pulled away from Lorraine's in the car. Khal had been at the window. But the terror boys had let him go. He was just a kid, buying gardening stuff for his old neighbour. His alibi checked out. So they said, but did it? Did an old guy like Bob not already have a shed full of four inch nails and umpteen packets of fertiliser?

He yawned. What time was it? He was knackered. And he hadn't even eaten. Pity about Lorraine, but it looked as if that was a road going nowhere. He stopped at a traffic signal and watched a light winking from a boat on the far side of the water. It was over near Emma's house. The guy in the car behind him honked his horn and the Alfa leapt forward, responding to Allan's touch. He engaged dynamic mode and savoured the speed and G force pinning him in his seat as the distance opened up between him and the guy behind him on this long straight stretch.

~~~

'Emma? It's Allan. Can I come up?'

The buzzer sounded. By the time he'd climbed the flights to her flat he was breathing heavily. The door was slightly ajar, but he filled his lungs a few times before pushing it open. She was in the kitchen part of her big open-plan living space, reaching into a cupboard and bringing down a box. If she was surprised at his arrival, she didn't give it away.

'Cake? Or nuts?'

'Both.' He pulled out one of her leather dining chairs and sat.

She wiped cream and jam from the knife and licked her finger. 'You miss dinner again? I can make you a toastie? Or we could order in pizza?'

'No, it's good. Cake and cashew nuts. What could be finer?'

She set them on the table then stood looking at him with her hands on her hips. 'You're working too hard. You look shit.'

He fake-smiled. 'Cheers.' Helped himself to a piece of cake and licked the cream and jam from his thumb. 'How are you?'

'Wondering what brings you here at nine o'clock on a school night, without a text or phone call or anything.'

He tipped his head. 'Yeah.'

She sat at the table. 'You alright?'

It was Emma. He could tell Emma anything. He could tell her... He reached for her hands and held them. It was Emma with her dark brown eyes. He leaned across the table and kissed her. She opened her mouth. Didn't resist him. Kept silent while he put his hand between his knees and drew his seat closer. Then they were kissing again, deep, the passion igniting with suddenness and intensity. Her white silk top was up and off and she dropped it. Her breasts filled his hands. Her tawny nipples rose, hardened. He kissed them; felt her drag his shirt from his waistband and her hands on his chest and belly skin.

'Move,' she said.

He dropped a knee to the floor, feeling the strain of his trapped dick inside his clothes ease off as she released it, her hands enclosing the shaft, finding the groove, working it, massaging his balls then he was on her on her kitchen floor, her thighs up round his hips, her hands on his chest and back, his dick deep inside her. Holding her eyes till the relief came spiralling through him with each push.

~~~

Emma gazed at him for a long time after the session on the floor ended.

He was knackered and had the shakes when he tried to stand up. 'You took too much out of me,' he said, and she replied he must be getting soft. Which was factually accurate, of course, the evidence being there. But it was true, he really was knackered.

'Stretch out on the couch, then,' she said, frowning out of concern for him. 'You relax and I'll get cleaned up.'

He must have fallen asleep. When he woke up, she was back, moving quietly, setting out toasties and tea and a glass of wine each, and when they'd finished the food he caved in and told her what had happened at the hospital.

'You're kidding me on!' she said.

He gave his head the smallest shake.

'Jesus Christ, Allan! And you're still going to work?' She shoved her hands through her hair. 'This isn't manflu.'

He reached for his wine, not wanting her to see his face.

'So, where's the stuff they gave you?'

'In the car.'

'Go and get it!'

Together, they read through it and looked up the information online. He was still feeling shaky, even after he'd eaten, so she told him to take one of the pills. They sat on her sofa together, his arm looped over her shoulders with her cosying in the way she used to. They'd been good together when she wasn't hitting the drink. Not that he was completely innocent.

Emma poured them each another small glass and vowed, only half joking, not to look through his phone if he stayed for the night. And he did want to stay for the night. He wanted to stretch out naked in the bed beside her. Not so much for the sex as for the comfort; the companionship. But the sex had been good.

'I saw Khalil Buchanan up at the hospital,' he said, sitting up to set his glass on the coffee table then relaxing deep in the sofa again.

'Yeah?'

'What do you think about him and his pal – Ahmed?'

Emma lifted her head from his shoulder and studied him. 'Once a cop, always a cop, eh? You feeling better?'

He shrugged. 'You know them both, don't you? What do you think – good kids or trouble?'

She wrinkled her nose. 'Good kids, without a doubt. They've always hung about together. I'm not sure if they're related. Runs in my mind they are.'

'You know Khal was in trouble?' She sipped wine and nodded. He went on. 'He was released without charges because he had a legitimate alibi, but I saw him tonight looking at this thing on his phone – some kind of aeroplane tracker. And he's such a sullen wee bastard I can't help thinking I should be keeping an eye on him.'

Emma sat up and drew her legs up on to the sofa. Her face lit up with delight. 'Khal sullen?' She grinned at him. 'He's a teenage boy. Try teaching a class full of them!'

'You sure?'

'Och, to me, he's just normal.' Her face grew more serious. 'Though I'd say there is a problem with the two of them being the only Asian boys in the class. They've definitely been exposed to some low level bullying. It's just the way it is. If it wasn't them being Asian, it would be because they got straight A passes, or because they wore glasses, or didn't have the latest phone model.'

'Oh they've definitely got the latest phone model.' Allan didn't tell her about Mo Khan's thievery and the link he was looking for with the dead boy Jamie.

'Half the class have probably got better phones than me,' Emma said.

'You and me, both.'

Emma reached for hers and keyed in the passcode. 'Don't worry about that aeroplane tracking thing, though.' She tapped through a few screens then held her phone out for him to see. She was wearing that sleeveless white silk blouse, again, and her long arms were bare. It was almost enough to distract him, but he looked at the screen. 'See, look,' she said. 'Click on the little yellow aeroplane icon and a box opens up with all the details about it – where it came from and where it's going. What its number is and what make. Even what cargo it's carrying.'

'That's what I mean,' Allan said. 'Surely it's dangerous to be able to find out about that? What's the boy looking it up for?' He didn't tell her about the potential bomb making gear Khalil had been carrying.

Emma ran her free hand through her thick black hair. 'But this can't be classified or anything. It's like trainspotting. It's for nerds like the people you see at the entrance to the bus station, taking photos of different bus models. Honestly.' She stared at him. 'Anyway, there's a time delay. It's not live data. You could check that, but I'm sure some of the kids in school who were doing a project on it already discovered that.' She paused a moment. 'The planes are well moved on from where it says they are. Are you alright, Allan?'

'Me?'

'There's a funny look in your eyes.'

He grinned. 'I feel great.'

'Uh-huh?'

He took the phone from her hand and set it on the table. 'In fact, I feel fantastic.'

'Frisky?'

He ran his finger up the inside of her upper arm. 'How did you guess?'

'I'm guessing that medicine must be good for you,' she said, and moved in close to him.

Chapter 40

Allan arrived early next morning, all set to interview Mo Khan. First, there was the team briefing. He'd see if Ross and Sam had discovered more overnight. The three – Ross, Sam and Jane – arrived sluggish, having stayed at work late into the evening. Allan watched them file into the incident room with their double espressos and their drooping eyelids and shoulders and felt like laughing. Usually he was the dragging one, but one little hydrocortisone pill popped along with his tea and toast at Emma's house this morning and he felt primed and ready for action. On steroids, basically.

'So, how's Khan? Did you get anything further from him last night?'

Jane stifled a yawn. 'Not really. He seems genuinely convinced his conscience is clear. Says all that's behind him.'

'What about the stuff in his locker – all those phones and tablets?'

Jane pulled a face and looked to Sam, who shrugged and said, 'Claimed to know nothing about them.'

'What about Forensics? Did they find any prints on them?' He looked around his team. No one seemed to know. 'Anyone?'

'Sorry, Boss.'

Allan scratched the back of his head roughly. 'No one from Forensics? How can I get anything out of Khan at interview if I don't have anything to pin to him?'

'I'll check it out, Boss,' Jane said. 'I will. I'll speak with them. But it IS only nine o'clock. And we are allowed time off to sleep.'

Allan turned to the board behind him. 'Yeah, that's fair enough.

But look at this boy – this thirteen year old boy.' A picture of Jamie, the dead boy, was at the centre of a spider diagram. 'This boy should be keeping us off our sleep.' One spider leg pointed to a picture of Mo Khan with a question mark beside it. 'So, are you telling me we've turned up no connection between Jamie and Mo Khan?'

There was silence in the room. The atmosphere was heavy.

'What about the CCTV?' He'd asked Jane to get Ross to look through it again. 'Any word on that?'

From the back row, Ross's voice came, cracked and indignant. 'Boss, we were in here till after eleven last night. We had a good look through some of the tapes again, but there's hours and hours.'

'This is ridiculous.' Allan could hardly sit still. He wanted to take each of his DCs and shake them. 'Look – get yourselves another coffee while I'm looking through these reports. Jane – find out where the hell Forensics are this morning, and what they're saying about that stuff in his locker while I'm having a word with him direct. Sam and Ross – get back on to that CCTV footage.'

Sam's phone sounded. 'I might know the answer to that,' he said after he rang off. He sat up, more awake, to tell them. 'That's a report come in about a small fire – described as "a bang and a blue flash" – in a bin at some school kitchens on the other side of Inverness.'

'When?'

'Just in. Staff on duty for the breakfast club heard it. Saw it. And phoned it in – 999 emergency. They evacuated the kids and staff. The fire service is on the scene now along with plod. So I'm guessing Forensics have gone along for the ride.'

'Well, we can't accuse Mo Khan of that. Presumably, then, he wasn't responsible for the Q-busters one.'

Surely it wouldn't have been Khal?

Just then, the door opened and a frazzled looking minor from the Forensics department passed Allan a file. 'Sorry, Sir. Two of the team have been called out to a bin fire at a school and the Sup's at a meeting. He asked me to hand you this.'

Allan squinted at the cover then nodded to the young man.

'Where's everybody else?'

'Two are on holiday and two have gone to a conference in Aberdeen. But just for the day.'

'Nice work if you can get it.'

'Tell me about it!'

'Okay, thanks.' Allan waved him away with the file he was holding. To his team, he said, 'It's the report on the fibres found in the prayer rug in the back of Mo Khan's van. And the rest of the van.' He skimmed the contents and shook his head. He looked up then read out to them. 'Okay, "Fibres from the prayer rug are not a match for the fibres found under Jamie Brooks' fingernails." Shit. Right, there's more. "Hairs found at the scene... originate from several different sources. DNA from the hairs does not match any DNA samples currently on record, other than Mo Khan's." And since it's his van, his hairs have a right to be there.'

'Did anyone check if Khan has pets?' It was Ross.

Allan disregarded him. 'Jane, pull your weight and get Forensics to pay a visit to Khan's house as soon as they're back from that school scene.' He frowned. 'Hold on a minute. It's a week since the fire in the bin at Q-busters, isn't it?' The others mumbled, and Allan rose to add another leg to the spider diagram. He took it right to the edge of the board. 'Obviously, Khan's in a cell. These two bin blasts are probably just kids with chemistry sets, practising for Guy Fawkes Night, but it's strange they're exactly a week apart. Keep an eye out for connections.'

His team didn't budge.

'That coffee not got to work yet?'

There was shaking of heads and mumbling.

'Right. Wakey wakey. Sam – get to that bin fire. I want a full report. Ross – get back to your CCTV investigation. I told you before, call in help if you need it. Jane – I want you to look into something. Hold on a minute.' He waited till Ross and Sam left.

'You okay, Boss?' she said, under her breath, while they were waiting.

'Me? Aye, I'm fine.' Allan continued drumming his pen against the folder he was holding.

When the door closed, he told her about Khalil and the aeroplane tracker app. There was that link between Khal's pal Ahmed and Mo Khan, too. 'Now I'm wondering about these bin fires. I know the terror boys let Khalil go, and I know the tracker app is just a bit of fun – or so they say – but something stinks here.' He stood and looked at the board, tapped the latest addition to it, about the school kitchen bin fire. 'Something's going on. Think links. Look for links between the two boys and Khan. Are they working for him – covering up for him? And when it comes to that – did we find out for sure about the drops Khan made that Monday? Customer signatures to verify them?'

'Not yet. I'll make sure we get that asap.'

'This morning. While we've got him in custody.'

Downstairs, Khan had been shown into Interview Room 2. Allan checked on him via the TV linkup next door to try to get a feel for his attitude through his body language. Khan sat very still, hands clasped in his lap, head angled down just like last night. The duty solicitor was with him, but it didn't look as if there was much communication between the two.

Allan pushed open the door and both looked up. Khan's eyes were lustre-less, giving Allan a glimpse into just how deep his mood had sunk after a night in the cells. The solicitor raised his brows to acknowledge Allan, and the interview began.

'Mr Khan, how did you come to have a bag full of brand new mobile phones and tablets in your locker?'

Khan looked dolefully at him. 'I told your man last night they're nothing to do with me.'

'Uh-huh.' Allan looked at his nails then engaged eye contact with the man opposite him. 'How do you suppose they made it to your locker?'

Khan's eyes dropped to his lap again and he shrugged.

'No idea?' There was no response. The solicitor was doodling on his pad. 'Do you know of any reason why anyone would want to fit you up? Why anyone would want to place those items in your locker, to make it look as if you had stolen them?'

Khan hesitated. Then he shrugged again.

Allan changed position in his chair. 'How do you get on with your workmates?'

'Fine.'

'No personality clashes?'

'Not really. Everyone gets on well enough.'

'What about racism?'

Khan raised his head. 'They've got used to me.'

'Okay. What about the boss. Is he a decent guy?'

A fraction of a second delay. Khan's face was beginning to glow with a film of dampness. 'He's alright.' He held Allan's eyes. 'Fair.'

Allan edged forward in his chair and glanced at the solicitor before focusing fully on Mo. 'Mr Khan,' he said. 'When we met at the mosque, you struck me as a bit anxious.'

Khan stared straight at him. 'Was I?'

'Oh, I think you know that. And your nephew was a bit – let's say protective of you.' Khan said nothing, so Allan went on. 'Now, I happened to notice that your nephew – that's Ahmed Atchi – happens to have a very upmarket phone.' He let that sink in. 'I've seen him use it. It's a very modern one.' The solicitor was looking at his client, now, and his doodles had turned to writing. The boy's name, probably. Allan cleared his throat. 'Do you happen to know how he came by that?'

Now Khan wriggled in his seat, clearing his throat and sitting more upright. There was a definite gloss on his face now, above the beard. 'A boy's entitled to a phone. They've all got them, nowadays.'

'Did you give him it?'

'That doesn't mean I stole it. Staff discount. I've probably still got the receipts.' He met Allan's eyes. 'You could check my wallet.'

'Okay. I've been told you also supplied a phone to another lad – Khalil Buchanan.'

A flicker passed over Khan's face, but he said nothing.

'And what about Jamie Brooks? Did you give him a mobile, too?'

The solicitor told Khan he didn't need to answer.

'Jamie Brooks had a very top of the range phone,' Allan said. 'But he kept it hidden from his mother. His own mother. As if it was a secret.'

Khan didn't speak.

'What do you know about that?'

Khan shrugged. 'What would I know about that? I don't know that boy.'

'You don't need to say anything,' the solicitor cautioned.

'I've got nothing to say, because I don't know anything,' Khan said.

There was a smell of sweat coming from the man. It was intensifying as the interview went on.

'My client says he knows nothing, so I expect you to charge him or release him,' the solicitor said.

There was a knock at the door and Jane popped her head in. Allan looked at his watch and stopped the recording. He excused himself for a few moments and went into the corridor with Jane.

'Mo Khan's in the clear. His time's accounted for,' she said.

'Shit.'

'His signature pad confirms his time was fully accounted for.'

'Can we trust it?'

Jane shrugged. 'It's electronic, and there are all sorts of different customer signatures.'

Khan was on the road or with other people over the entire time-frame when the boy was being picked up, abused, murdered and dumped. There wasn't a big enough window on his schedule for him to have done all that and murder the boy. They were going to have to let him go. But not yet. Allan returned to the interview room. He told the solicitor the interview was suspended and that Khan would be returned to the holding cell. They still had an hour to release or charge him.

~~~

Allan collected Jane and a plod and headed to Khan's house. They cut through the Victorian Market arcade, senses assaulted by fishmongers, florists, and shops selling cheap kitsch ornaments. The place was buzzing. They skipped between cars at the junction and climbed on to High Street. Allan never tired of the view the street gave, over the gentle brow of the hill towards the River Ness.

'Not far now, Boss,' Jane said.

A man in his early twenties was cupping his mouth and yelling a woman's name, head back while he directed his voice to the top floor flat. 'Angie!' he shouted. 'Angie!' but Angie wasn't answering. Four teenage girls skirted round him, laughing.

'Here we go.'

Khan lived in a studio flat on the top storey of a street off the High Street. The keys they'd obtained from him once they'd satisfied his lawyer they'd a warrant, were stiff in the close door and it took a good shove before they were able to enter the dingy stone entrance tunnel. Light from a skylight in the roof at least illuminated the stairwell at the far end. As they mounted the stairs, Jane remarked that Allan wasn't so out of breath as usual.

'Getting there,' he wheezed.

Khan's door was the middle of three. The keys slipped in and turned easily, granting them access straight into a large room furnished with the basics: a double bed whose quilt had been roughly thrown up, a pine table with two rickety chairs, a small screen TV on a chest of drawers, and – in a corner – a two-ring cooker, microwave and fridge. Jane pulled the greasy curtains apart and slanting sunlight came through tall windows that were speckled by grime and the work of raindrops. The flat reeked of vegetable matter dead in the food waste, but apart from that it was tidy.

There were no pictures on the walls, or photos in frames on the second chest of drawers. Allan had been in many flats and houses over the years, some of which were dingy and depressing, but although this one was devoid of human touches – tender human touches like ornaments and soft furnishings – it didn't have an air of utter despair. Judging by this room, Khan wasn't a man who felt alone. Whether that was because of his connection with his nephew Ahmed, or work and the mosque, it was clear that, at some level, he had the comfort of believing he belonged. Allan recalled the misery in Khan's eyes in the interview room. Was that a recent plummet? Sorrow at returning to the misdemeanours and depravity of his past?

'What are we looking for?' Jane asked.

Allan bent to eye some books and papers stacked at one end of the table, being careful not to touch them while he gloved up. 'Anything to suggest that Jamie – or any other boy – might have been in here. And the usual porn. Laptop. That kind of thing.'

Jane's phone rang. 'Forensics are downstairs.' She pushed the entrance button to let them into the building.

Forensics bagged Khan's laptop and two tablets they found under his mattress. There were black hairs in the shower and sink, so they took those, too. Jamie may have been murdered on the hill, but those fibres in his hair were witness to him being attacked elsewhere first. Conscious he hadn't yet found that locus, Allan made the Forensics team spray and swab walls, carpet and sofa for any suspicion of blood, but the test was clear. Jamie's murderer had used his hands as weapons, so they weren't looking for objects as such. Blood, hair and fibres, yes.

'Sir?'

Allan popped his head round the shower-room door.

The minor from Forensics, gowned and hooded in white, was holding a phial of some kind of medicine he'd taken from the open cabinet.

'What is it?'

'Looks like a sedative.'

'Bag it and log it,' Allan said. 'The victim was drugged.'

It was something, but it wasn't enough. Allan told Jane it was time to go. The twenty-four hours was almost up and Khan would have to be released. They couldn't hold him longer. Only blood spatter on the walls or furniture would've made a water-tight case for extending the custody time.

'You'll send me a full report asap?' Allan said in the doorway.

The Forensic lead gave him a nod.

'And don't forget to check the bed.'

Chapter 41

Back at the station, Allan went through the formalities to have Mo Khan released, including going through a checklist of what he was obliged to do as a convicted paedophile. It was important for Khan to be seen to be behaving himself, and it was just as important that he was kept under close watch. There was also the danger that Khan could be 'outed' and face the revenge of a vigilante public, even though they'd found nothing on him – so far – to link him to the Jamie case.

There was no sense of elation on the man's part. None of the triumphalism Allan expected from seasoned crooks who crowed over getting one up on the legal system. Just a heavy-hearted forbearance. At the desk, Khan signed for his pocket contents and shoelaces, and Allan handed over his keys to him, warning him that Forensics had taken a few pieces in for examination. Khan signed the document acknowledging it all, accepting this infringement of his liberty with uncomplaining resignation.

Back in the office, Allan checked for any news from Ross about the CCTV footage, but there was nothing. Sam had come back from the bin fire while Allan and Jane were at Khan's flat. The fire had been directly outside the school kitchens. 'One of the cooks saw a blue flash through the window.'

'Who did you speak to?' Allan said.

Sam pushed a folder across the desk. 'I conducted interviews with all the catering and janitorial staff. Some of them saw it, some didn't. I checked out their movements before the blast.'

'Blast?'

'That might be a bit strong, but they definitely gave the impression it was a whoosh, if not an all-out explosion, Sir. And the fabric of the bin itself melted, even though the jannie got to it with a fire extinguisher pretty quickly.' Sam waited for a nod of response before going on. 'The contents of the bin were incinerated. The Forensics guy's preliminary impression was that whoever did it must have used an accelerant.'

'So it was definitely a planned fire, and not just something careless?'

'No doubt, Sir. This was nothing to do with burnt toast or a careless cigarette.'

'Right. And what school did you say it was?'

'Thistlebank Academy, Sir.'

'Thistlebank? That's Jamie Brooks' school. That's got to be more than a coincidence.' Allan tipped up his cup, but it was empty. He'd been buoyed up all day but felt crumpled again like every day before this. Four o'clock. Should he take another pill? 'Right. Good work, Sam. Thanks for that.'

The young officer tried to hide his pleasure by keeping his face down.

'When are you on till? You're owed time from last night?'

Sam looked up. 'Yes, Sir.'

'Why don't you spend an hour helping Ross nail who did it by watching the telly? But finish at five so you're back tomorrow morning, rested?'

The young man grinned.

'I'm convinced those two fires are connected,' Allan said to Sam and Jane. 'Not to Khan, by the look of it, but to each other, and maybe to this.' He tapped the file for Jamie's murder case. 'Remember those fibres in the wreckage of the first one – that could've been linked to the dead boy's clothes and trainers?'

Taking advantage of Sam and Jane heading away from his desk, Allan reached into his inside pocket and slipped a pill from its foil. He caught sight of Jane watching him on her way back and concealed it in his fist.

'Headache?'

Dead pan, Allan said, 'Why don't you and I go over to the mosque before we finish?' He checked his watch again. 'Just there and back – arrange a quick forensic sweep.'

'At this time?' Jane said. 'They'll not be very happy to see us turn up now. Better to wait till morning?'

'I'm thinking of us getting nowhere with the carpet fibres.' He let that sink in. 'I'm thinking about all the plush carpets there.'

'Fair point – but that's a major job. Forensics'll not be able to cope with that if they've got two off on holiday and two away at a conference. And it's after four o'clock in the afternoon.'

Allan looked at his watch again. 'Well, that young Forensics guy was quite cooperative. And keen.' He flashed a smile to Jane. 'So he might be happy to make a start on it. Only thing is, it's a bit sensitive.' Allan picked up his phone and contacted Forensics to see if the lad or anyone else was available. Then he phoned his boss to arrange for him to pull strings. 'Smooth things over with the community,' Allan said into the phone. 'You mean maintain good community relations,' echoed back.

On the way out, they had to endure a media scrum. Word had got out that Mo Khan had been released and the baying mob weren't pleased. Journalists and cameramen were an unhappy throng surrounding the police office steps.

'Is it true you let a convicted paedophile go, DI MacIntyre?' one 'keen' young journalist asked, forcing his mobile phone on voice recorder under Allan's chin.

'No comment.'

'What lines of enquiry are you pursuing now?'

Allan and Jane pushed through. As they stepped free, Allan turned back and addressed the media. 'We're pursuing several lines of investigation, and I'll arrange a full briefing for you tomorrow.'

That seemed to satisfy them for a bit, and when Allan looked back they were talking into their mobiles and dispersing to their cars.

'That worked,' Allan said.

'Yeah, but what are you going to tell them tomorrow?'

He raised an eyebrow. 'We'll need to tell them something. They're absolutely right about the convicted paedophile. Would you want to be living in the same close as that?'

Once they were seated in the car, Allan blew out and tried to dredge up energy from somewhere. His nerves were shot from having to face down those journalists. Journalists! All he wanted to do was lie down and hide from everything. Get his breath and his energy back.

'Are you alright, Boss? You're all up one minute and down the next.'

He glanced sideways at her. 'Story of my life.'

'Uh-huh. So why don't you take that pill you were going to take earlier till you saw me clocking you about to swallow it?'

Allan frowned at her. He sat with his hands in his lap for a minute then reached into his inside pocket again. 'You should join the police. You'd make a great detective. Now, pass me that water from the back seat.'

He was going to have to tell Jane about it. The doctor at the hospital – and Emma – were right. In his line of work, this wasn't something he could keep to himself. He thought about that emergency injection kit. He would tell Jane for now. After that, he might go on and tell the others. Make it official. It was only fair since they were a team and he'd need to be full strength at all times so they could trust him to have their backs.

'And while you're at it,' he said, 'open that glove compartment and bring out the medical box. I need to show you something.'

Chapter 42

Next morning, Forensics sent a full crew out to the mosque, and Allan arranged to meet up with PR man Jason Bonar to brief him and for advice. Standing too close as always, and with his breath stinking of mint, Bonar told Allan he'd get a grip on it quickly, 'Before the racists and anti-paedo vigilantes fall in league and attack the mosque.' He drafted a quick statement and called the media and press to come to the station for eleven o'clock.

It went well – Jason took the lead and Allan read a brief statement then fielded questions. He ended with an appeal to the community for information, and for calm. 'At the moment, we're pursuing several lines of inquiry,' he reiterated in conclusion. 'We've every reason to believe this is one man acting alone, and we'd like to assure the public that we're focusing all available resources in identifying Jamie's murderer and bringing him to justice. It's crucial that the public trust us with this, and don't try to take matters into their own hands.'

When Allan returned to the office, Ross looked up. 'Boss! D'you want the good news or the bad news?' Seeing the look on his boss's face, he went on, 'Okay. The bad. Khan didn't report in when he was supposed to. We sent a car to his flat and there's no sign of him.'

Somehow, that didn't really come as a surprise.

'But there's good news! Come and see this.' Ross angled the monitor towards Allan, knocking empty paper cups and drink bottles off the desk then bending to clear up the clutter while Allan drew over a chair. 'It's footage from earlier in the night before that first bin fire. The original one at Q-busters?'

203

Allan nodded. The only 'hit' they'd had so far had been from CCTV in one of the streets nearby of two skinny male figures who might, just might, have been Khalil and Ahmed. But the quality was so poor, and so circumstantial, that there wasn't a hope of it standing up in court.

'I went back several hours and found this.' He hit a few keys and the grainy footage sprang into action. The clock in the corner of the screen read 3.31am. First there was nothing happening – a scroll of packing paper billowed across the black tarmac with the random breath of the wind. Then a blurry figure came into shot.

Allan peered closer. This was one single person. A man. Bigger built than either of the skinny boys. What was he carrying? A box? Bulky, but, judging by his body language, not particularly heavy. The footage jumped from frame to frame, skipping to other locations around the Industrial Estate. When it returned to directly outside Q-busters, the box had disappeared – presumably inside the giant bin – and the figure was checking back and forward that he wasn't observed. The last image was of the top of his head.

'Grey hair?' Allan said. 'Or blond?'

'Do you think it's Thompson?' Ross asked, voice boyish with excitement. 'I'll bet it's Thompson!'

Allan stood up, pushing back the chair noisily. 'See if you can find the same guy at the kitchen fire.'

Thompson had every right to be putting stuff in the Q-busters bin. But at 3.31 at night? And why would Thompson be disposing of Jamie Brooks' clothes? Allan swivelled in his chair, looking out through the full wall of windows. Cars manoeuvred in and out of the car park. Leaves on the young trees were yellowing up thanks to early frosts. Sometimes, he had an irrational dislike of people. Something about them rubbed him up the wrong way. It might be a sneer. A casual remark. A certain style of dress. One thing that got right on his tits was smarmy gits who made him feel inadequate just for trying to make his way in life on the same planet. Irrational. But that was it.

'Sam?'

DC Abouwaye looked up.

Allan tapped his pen on the open file on his desk and rubbed his chin with his other hand. 'See if you can find anything on Hugo Thompson. Just to rule him out. And while you're doing that – Jane – why don't you and I pay him a visit right now?'

~~~

There was no sign of Thompson's car in Q-buster's car park. Inside, Cathy confirmed her boss had gone. She fumbled, cleaning her glasses with the edge of her cardigan. She peered short-sightedly up at Allan's eyes. 'A family emergency. He told Jess.' She angled her head to indicate one of the other members of staff, who nodded from behind her computer screen. 'I don't think it was anything too serious. I hope not, anyway. He just said he had to go home.'

Allan wasn't familiar with the address. He punched it in on the SatNav and followed the route across town and into the suburbs. At the roundabout he turned left, giving his car its head to take the steep hill past cul de sacs clustered with large white detached houses. 'The only thing this scheme's missing is a gated entrance. What number are we looking for?'

'15.' Jane whistled as Allan pulled up outside a big modern house set back from the road. There was a sleek silver Porsche parked in the driveway and a people carrier, with baby blinds, next to it.

Their feet crunched on the gravel as they approached the broad front door. While they waited for it to be opened, they heard music – something esoteric; Indian, maybe – and the sound of a child having a tantrum.

Rosie Thompson was flustered when she opened the door to them, and her round cheeks were flushed. In one arm, and balanced on one hip, she was carrying a baby that was neither walking sized nor tiny. The tantrum noises were coming from further inside the building. Rosie Thompson stared at the two police officers and pushed loose curls of hair back from her forehead. 'Yes?' she asked, frowning.

'DI Allan MacIntyre,' Allan said, showing his pass. 'And this is my colleague DS Jane Coburn. I'm looking for Mr Thompson. I understand this is his address?'

The frown deepened. 'He's not here. He's at work.' The screaming moved up a gear. The woman raised her voice, directing it into the house behind her. 'Lou – Mummy's busy. Be quiet!' She looked at Allan. 'You'll find him at Q-busters Distribution Centre in the Inchmarsh Industrial Estate. He'll be in the office.'

'Are you his partner?'

Rosie's forehead frown deepened. 'Yes. It's Hugo you're looking for?' The sounds from behind her grew even louder and now the baby was beginning to join in.

'We've just come from Q-busters. They told us he was here. Can we come in for a minute? Sounds like someone in there needs his mum.' Allan made the suggestion of a move forward, a technique he found usually worked when the person in front of him was harassed or on the back foot.

'Come in.' Rosie Thompson moved back to let them enter.

Jane closed the door behind her and they walked through a spacious, light-filled, double height hallway towards where the screaming was coming from. Jane and Allan met eyes. The woman who'd shown them in may have been dressed in a washed out and baggy black top, and chinos slashed across the knees, but this was serious money. The floors were creamy marble and the walls and paintwork on the doors were cream coloured with white cornicing. The rooms glowed with light which came in from wide, high window panels. Allan and Jane crossed behind the statement staircase, following Rosie Thompson towards a door that opened out into a room whose end wall was made entirely of glass. These floor to ceiling glass doors gave views out on to a large, enclosed garden dressed with russet coloured acers and flowering shrubs. At one side, water trickled over slabs of slate and scree. On the other side was a patio with a raised pool and generous table and chairs that could easily seat eight. Beyond it was what looked like a bespoke wooden playhouse and climbing frame, complete with slide. A small child of indeterminate gender was slumped against the closed glass doors, clearly keen to get out.

'Lou, get up. I told you you couldn't get out while I'm feeding Ollie.' Rosie turned to the officers and waved a hand towards one of two oversized, slouchy sofas whose tapestry covers and lumpy padding could be described as lived in. 'Do sit down. Do you mind if I finish this?' She removed the muslin square from her shoulder as she sat down, hand automatically going to liberate her breast from containment.

'Not at all,' Allan said, averting his eyes. He and Jane used the time to appraise the pattern of the sofa and their surroundings. At their feet was a large naïf style 'ethnic' rug in colours and patterns that brought to mind alpacas and Peru. There were wooden sculptures and coarse pottery on white plinths, and two huge canvases of naïf art daubed in primary colours adorned one wall. Allan wondered if the larger child had painted them. Opposite, the lower part of the wall was dressed with a band of black paint which someone had chalked squiggles on in pinks and greens. The older child continued to growl and kick its feet. It was dressed in woollen clothes with stripes and patterns that suggested South America, too. It had long curling hair and wore trousers. 'I think your son wants out,' Allan said, raising his voice to be heard.

'No, Lou's alright, thanks.' Pointedly, she said, 'And it's "Lou". We don't do gendered terms in this house.'

'Sorry?'

The baby sucked noisily. Rosie adjusted her position, kicking off fleecy slippers and tucking her feet up under her on the opposite sofa. 'You were telling me about my husband.'

Allan focused on the mother's face. 'The office manager said he was taking a few days off for a domestic emergency.'

Rosie's eyes widened barely perceptibly then she looked away. 'I haven't checked my mobile. It's probably a misunderstanding. Cathy can be – excitable.'

207

'Indeed. Do you know when he'll be back?'

'Well, no – I didn't even know he'd gone. He's very independent, my husband.'

Allan felt Jane's fingertip gently prod his leg. Then she said, 'Mrs Thompson, could I fetch your phone for you, and you can tell us if your husband's sent a text or tried to call you? You're a bit busy, there.'

Rosie flushed. She glanced around. 'It's probably in the kitchen.'

Jane disappeared and returned a couple of minutes later with the phone in her hand. She passed it to the mother, who skimmed it and shook her head. Was that a deeper flush? 'He's obviously been caught up in work.'

'Does he often disappear without telling you where he's going?' Fighting against Lou's rising wailing, Allan's voice had an edge in it.

'We're not joined at the hip, if that's what you mean!' Rosie called back. 'He's a busy man. Just as I'm busy here.'

'Absolutely.' Allan let a moment pass. 'So, you've no idea where he's gone or when he'll be back?'

'No.'

'And he does this often?'

'Lou, be quiet!' She shook her head and wiped her upper lip with the back of her hand. 'Not often. I'm sure he'll be in touch as soon as he can.'

'Is that his Porsche in the driveway? He couldn't be in the house without you realising? In one of the upper rooms, or the garage?'

Riled, Rosie scowled. 'I'm not that busy.'

Allan looked around. They were getting nowhere. There were no clues lying around this room to suggest any kind of life Hugo Thompson had. This was the family's informal living space but – apart, maybe, from the art – it showed little evidence of the father. 'Does your husband have an office here?'

'At the other end of the hall. Why?'

Allan rose to his feet. 'You're busy. I'll check if he's got something written in his diary that explains where he might be.' Again, he used the power of suggestion in his body language. 'Jane, why don't you tell wee Lou a story or something? Help Mrs Thompson out.'

The office wasn't locked. Allan flipped through paperwork but it all seemed genuine – orders and leads and even conference papers connected to distribution companies and the local business scene. He powered up the laptop, but it needed a password. He tried 'Lou' And 'Ollie' And '10u' And '0ll1e' And various combinations but nothing got him into it. Where was Ross when he needed him? A calendar on the wall was purely business – a Q-busters advertising freebie with nothing in the least pervy in its pictures. It showed nothing interesting happening today, and there was nothing to suggest anything untoward on the day Jamie disappeared, or the day the bins went on fire. The guy was either clean, or an expert in concealment.

He heard Jane's voice, raised, alerting him. 'Mrs Thompson! Mrs Thompson!' Just in time, he closed the lid of the laptop.

'Are you finished?' Thompson's wife was standing in the doorway, watching him.

'Just, thanks.' Allan made his way to the door and stepped through, making her automatically step back. He kept up a stream of talk to keep her thoughts occupied so she wouldn't think to complain about him ferreting through private documents without having made it official. Jane was by the outside door. She opened it as Allan said their goodbyes. 'And please let me know as soon as you hear from your husband – whether that's because he's arrived home, or because he contacts you to tell you where he is.' He stopped with his hand on the edge of the door. Could he take the laptop? Too obvious. 'Your husband isn't in trouble. We need to rule him out, that's all. It's important you get in touch with us as soon as possible – for his sake. You understand?'

Chapter 43

'"We don't do gendered terms in this house"?' Allan couldn't resist chuckling then he caught a look in Jane's eye and shook his head. 'Maybe I really should put our names down for more Sensitivity Training.' He and Jane crunched back over the gravel towards his Alfa.

'Yours, anyway.'

They settled into the car. 'Poor kids. Still. Man, that house has serious money.'

'Where do you think it comes from?' Jane asked. 'All legit?'

Allan shrugged. 'No reason to think otherwise.' He belted himself in. 'There was no trace of anything dodgy in his home office – no porn, no kiddy porn, no sign of any suspicious contacts.' He rapped on the steering wheel. 'His laptop needed a password, though, so I couldn't get on that.' He hummed and hawed for a moment. 'I was so close to taking it for Ross to look at.'

'Tsk, tsk, Boss. Angel on your shoulder change your mind just in time?'

He grinned. 'No, I just didn't have pockets big enough.'

Allan put the car in gear, drove out of the driveway and headed back to base.

'She certainly didn't seem to know about any kind of family emergency,' Jane said.

'No. That was clearly made up. I wonder where he's gone. And what he's driving. She'll be on the phone to him right now.'

'Aye, his ears'll be burning.'

'I liked the way you tried to get her onside at the end, telling her

210

to contact us for his sake.'

Allan glanced at her. 'You think that was made up?'

'You mean you were sincere?'

He tilted his head. 'Well, we've nothing to suggest he's done anything wrong.'

'True.'

They drove in silence for a while then Allan sniffed. 'Is that you or me?'

Jane dug her phone from her pocket. 'Hi Sam. What's up?' She nodded a few times. 'Okay, I'll tell the boss. Hold on.' To Allan, she said, 'Thompson had a record as a student. Demos – but violent behaviour. Anti-capitalist. Anti-fox-hunting. Been clean for ten years, though.' She looked at him. 'Grew up?'

'Tell Sam to keep digging. I want his full record. Tell him to find out where they lived before they moved to Scotland, and where the fuck he might have gone now.' He turned the car one and a half times round the roundabout.

'Hear that, Sam?' Jane hung up and put her phone away. 'What about us, Boss? Where are we going?'

'Back to the depot for a proper look.'

There was still no sign of Thompson at Q-busters. Judging by the comings and goings in the car park and at the warehouse entrance, business was going ahead as normal. Allan parked up and he and Jane rang for entrance to the office. Cathy was on duty, as ever. She didn't seem surprised to see them back, though it was hard to tell because, for her, a high level of anxiety seemed to count as normal behaviour.

Allan took the chance she wasn't up to date on what level of inquisitiveness a police officer was permitted to show. He flashed his pass and motioned to come through. 'We're concerned about Mr Thompson's welfare and need to trace his movements,' he said. That was enough for Cathy's finger to scurry to the entrance button. The buzzer sounded and they pushed their way through. 'We'll need access to his office.'

'Of course.' Cathy resettled her glasses on her nose. 'Is Mr Thompson alright?' She unlocked the office door and stepped back to allow them through.

'We'll have to wait and see.' Allan looked from her to Jess, the other worker in the office. 'But it's important that you don't pass our concerns on to anyone. For his safety.'

'Of course,' Cathy repeated. She nodded a few times while Allan and Jane filed into the room.

'We'll call you if we've any questions,' Jane said, and closed the door, shutting Cathy out.

Here, too, Thompson was meticulously tidy. There was nothing lying around that might suggest anything out of the ordinary. Anything suspicious about the man or his behaviour. They checked his desk drawers, the little bit of paperwork he had left on top of it, and skimmed through the labels on the box files on his shelving, but it all gave the impression of a man whose sole interest was running an efficient company. Cathy brought them coffee and logged into his computer for them, and yet still there was nothing in the recent files or in the photos or emails to suggest anything other than a decent, honest businessman doing his utmost.

'So, remind me.' Allan was sitting in Thompson's padded leather executive chair. He put his feet on the table, coffee mug in hand. 'Why are we after this guy?'

Jane laughed. 'You tell me.'

He sipped from his drink, thinking. 'You saw the cutting about the bin fire.'

'But that might just have been natural interest, given it was outside his premises.'

'Yeah, but cutting it out of the paper?'

Jane nodded.

'And that blond or white haired guy throwing the box in the bin at the back of three a.m. the night after Jamie was murdered and before the bin fire right outside.'

'Yep.'

'The fact he was dodgy when we brought Mo Khan in. I mean really dodgy. The shock was all over him. And he didn't need a key to get into Khan's locker. He could easily have stashed that stuff in there to frame Khan while we were busy looking for him.'

'And now he's disappeared.'

Allan took his feet off the table. 'Could all be circumstantial. Coincidence. I mean – look at this place. There's nothing. Nothing here. Nothing in his office at home.'

'Maybe he's too tidy, Boss.'

'What's the motive, though? What's he guilty of? Looking guilty and raising my hackles? That's not enough to warrant tracking him down or arresting him.'

Jane took the cups through to the main office and went to use the toilet before they headed back. Meanwhile, a suspicion wouldn't let Allan go. His eyes were still roaming the room, just looking, taking stock, checking for any tiny unconformity. He found it just as Jane came back into the room. He was on his feet, close to the bookcase.

'Found something?'

Allan moved to examine the side edge of the bookshelves. It was a double-shelf unit, six feet tall, light coloured and Scandinavian-looking design. A fairly heavy beast with the box files on it. Yet it would be a lot heavier if the shelves were full. He glanced back at Jane, and behind her, to verify that the office door was closed. 'What do you think of this unit?'

'What about it? We had a glance at the files. D'you want to take them back for a thorough check?'

He put his hands in his trouser pockets and nodded down to the floor. 'What do you think of the carpet?'

Jane considered it. It just looked like normal carpet. 'What about it? Are you thinking about the fibres Forensics found under Jamie's nails? I thought we'd ruled that out?'

Allan crouched down, his knees clicking. 'No, but look.' He ran his hand over the carpet in the middle of the shelving unit then squinted back up at Jane. 'D'you not think there's a bit too much wear there?'

Her facial expression confirmed what he'd been thinking. He stood up and moved to the side of the unit again. Jane lifted some of the box files off and put them on the desk, and Allan gripped one edge of the unit and walked it into the room, opening it like a door. And there behind it was a genuine door.

'Fuck me!' Jane said.

Allan tried the handle. It was locked.

'Boss.' Jane was pointing at the floor. There was a strip of dark blue carpet showing on the threshold.

'Right – stand back.' Allan booted the lock. The door swung inwards and he caught it on the rebound. The room was in darkness but there was a light switch on his right. He flicked it on and they saw a small room filled with shelving down one side. There were phones, game consoles, tablets. But there were bits, too. Electronic bits. Allan lifted one and turned it over in his hand. 'I'm no expert, but why do you need computer gizzards in a distribution centre? They don't do repairs here.'

'No,' Jane said. 'Even if they did, they wouldn't do it in a room closed off behind a bookcase. As for that carpet...'

'Thick blue carpet?' Allan said. He knelt and felt it. 'Are you thinking what I'm thinking?'

'Jamie?'

The office door opened. Cathy rushed in, flustered. 'What are you doing?'

'Stay back, Cathy.' Jane steered her to a seat.

'You can't go in there. That's breaking and entering.'

'It's hardly breaking and entering. Just sit there for a minute.' Jane phoned HQ and called out Forensics.

'Did you know this room was here, Mrs Coates?' Allan had come out of the room to interrogate her.

'Of course I did, but it hasn't been used for years. We stopped using it years ago.'

'Someone's been using it. When was it blocked off by the

214

shelving unit?'

Cathy shook her head. 'About a year ago? Mr Thompson said we didn't need it any more. But we'd to keep it in case of expansion.'

'I'm going to have to ask you to show me Mr Thompson's diary. I need to know his movements over the last couple of weeks. Can we do that in the front office?'

They closed off Thompson's office, leaving everything as it was till Forensics arrived. At Cathy's desk they went through the boss's online diary. It showed he was out of the office for hours on the day Jamie was killed. There was no record of where. 'Family emergency?' Allan said, heavy with irony. When he realised Cathy might cry, he gripped her shoulder and asked if she was alright. She dabbed a tissue to her nose and eyes, and as he waited for her to recover herself, he spotted another tab on the on-screen spreadsheet.

'What's that?'

Cathy pushed her glasses further up on the bridge of her nose and peered at the screen. 'The log for the vans and drivers.'

Allan thought of the Porsche parked in Thompson's driveway, and the easy way he'd taken over Mo Khan's van to park it properly the day Khan was arrested. 'Does the boss ever drive a van? Has he got one today?'

Cathy shook her head. 'I wouldn't think so.' But she pulled up the information on the screen. 'No, they're all accounted for. The drivers are all using them.' She looked up at Allan, who was standing bent over at her shoulder so he could see the screen. 'We usually have a spare, but we've had to use it because you impounded Mo Khan's van.'

'But Mo Khan's back at work?'

Her brow wrinkled. 'No, he phoned in and Mr Thompson told him to take a few days off.'

Allan met Jane's eyes over Cathy's head. 'So you should have a spare van?'

'Well, we'll have got a spare driver in.'

'No, but Cathy –' This was Jess's voice. She spoke up from across the office, enunciating her words slowly and clearly as if she was talking to a child. 'Remember one of the boys phoned in sick.'

Cathy didn't say anything. Her fingers tripped over the keyboard. 'There should be a spare van.' She half rose to her feet and peered out through the window to the parking area across from the office building. 'But it's not there just now.'

Allan spoke quietly. 'Can you look a couple of weeks earlier?' She pulled up that screen. 'See that day, Cathy.' He pointed to the log for the day Jamie was murdered. 'Who was driving the spare van then?'

She wiped her nose with her tissue and pushed the hankie back up her sleeve while she digested the information on screen. Then she shook her head. 'I can't see,' she said.

'What do you mean?' Allan asked her.

She met his eyes. 'I can't see it listed. It's there, but there's nothing logged for it, except "OUT". Look. And no initials or staff number to say who drove it or authorised it.'

Chapter 44

They waited till Forensics came so Allan could outline their suspicions for the hidden room. Not only were they to take a look at the electronics – interesting because of the bin fire 'explosions' – but they were to examine that carpet.

There was no obvious blood as far as Allan could see, but then, Jamie's skin had been largely untouched except for some lacerations the report had suggested happened in the woodlands where his body was recovered. He was murdered on the hillside, but the fibres suggested he'd been attacked somewhere carpeted. Forensics had gathered samples from the mosque yesterday; today they'd gather samples from here. Allan was pleased – or more accurately relieved – the investigation finally had some drive. As for the missing van – Thompson had probably steam-cleaned that.

Jane was on the phone to Traffic with its description and licence number when Allan felt his own mobile vibrate. It was Lorraine. He was still talking to the Forensics guy, and he was tempted to ignore it, but when she rang a third time he answered.

'Hi, Allan, it's Lorraine,' she said. Her voice was hesitant; not at all what he expected from the queue of calls. 'Are you doing something just now? Could I have a word with you?'

'On you go,' he said, perching on Thompson's desk.

Lorraine stuttered over something then drew breath and said, 'This might be nothing, and I don't want to cause any upset, but Khalil says he can't get in touch with Ahmed, so we're a bit worried about him.'

'What do you mean? How long has he been trying?'

'Well, a few hours? I've not said to his mum, but it's not like him.'

Thompson was missing; Khan was missing. Now Ahmed?

Allan looked around the room. He could leave the slog to the Forensics guys. He raised his brows in a signal to Jane as he walked into the main office. 'Are you at home? Stay there. We'll come out. '

In the car, he took another pill. 'This is when I'm supposed to take it,' he said to Jane. 'So don't say anything. Got it? Routine.' She held her hands up to show she wasn't going to protest. As he drove, Allan could feel the drug kicking in; feel it flow through his veins like caffeine. Or super strength lager after a strenuous afternoon. He'd never done hard drugs but he wondered if this was how junkies felt when they got their fix.

'So, this Lorraine,' Jane was saying.

'Uh-huh?'

'Is that the woman you've been seeing?'

He cast a sideways look at her. 'Who, me?' changed gear and turned right at a busy junction. 'I'm saying nothing.' Soon they were in Lorraine's street and Allan drew up outside her house.

'No need for Satnav, anyway.'

'I tell you,' he said as they got out, 'you've got great powers of observation. You'd be brilliant in the police force.'

Lorraine answered the door and there was a moment of awkwardness when she expected Allan to kiss her and he clearly didn't. She showed them into the living room. Khalil was there, propped on the arm of the sofa.

'Hiya,' Allan said. 'This is Jane. DS Coburn.' The adults stayed standing. 'So, Khal – d'you want to tell us about Ahmed?'

Lorraine jumped in while the boy struggled to produce words, as if he had to disgorge them. 'The two of them are usually on their computer game. Aren't you, Khal?' She addressed Allan. 'You know what they're like – never off it.' To Jane, she said, 'I don't know how it works, but they can both be on the same game at the same time, even when they're in different places. Show them,' Lorraine said, nudging her son's shoulder. 'Show them on the screen.'

Khal thumbed a few buttons on his gaming console and a list of names and scores came up on the TV. Allan glanced at Jane for acknowledgement she too had spotted Jamie's name on the list.

'But Ahmed's not been on it for hours,' Lorraine went on. 'Eh, Khal? You haven't seen him?'

'No,' the boy said.

'When did you last see him or speak to him? In the real world or the computer.'

Khal blushed and shrugged his gangly shoulders. 'Not since last night. Well,' he squirmed, looking at his mother. 'Not since the middle of the night. About five in the morning.'

'Five in the morning!' his mum tutted. 'No wonder you can't get up for school.'

'It's an in-service day. There's no school.'

'Right,' Allan said. 'And you've not heard from him since?'

Again the boy shrugged. More a sign of embarrassment than truculence. 'He was going out with his mum but he said he'd be back on after that.'

'Have you spoken to his mum?'

Lorraine answered. 'I saw her for coffee at ten. She was on her own. She said Ahmed had gone to my house to see Khal, but when I got back Khal said there'd never been any sign of him.' She was standing with her arms folded, swaying slightly from side to side. Her eyes went from Allan to Jane.

'I tried phoning him,' Khal said, 'but he didn't pick up.'

'D'you want to try him again, now?' Allan stood up and moved closer to Lorraine, shepherding her to one side, out of Khalil's earshot. 'Are you genuinely worried?' he asked her. 'You told me there was nothing to worry about.'

Lorraine frowned. 'I wouldn't have phoned you if I wasn't worried. D'you think I was just trying to get you over, or something?'

'You weren't exactly pleased the other day when I mentioned Mo Khan.'

Now it was Lorraine's turn to blush, but this time it looked like anger.

'No answer,' Khal said.

Allan whipped round. 'Try his house phone.'

'What if his mother answers?'

'Tell her you'll get him on his mobile.' When it was clear the boy wasn't at home, Allan looked at Lorraine. 'Could you put the kettle on?' She left the room as Khalil ended the call. Allan told Jane to help Lorraine and, when she left, he closed the door firmly. 'We need a word,' he said to the boy.

'What about?'

'Mo Khan.'

Khal's eyes dropped.

'He's the one that gives you the games machines and the phone, I'm guessing?'

Khalil shook his head.

'Come on – it's him, isn't it? That's where you get them?'

'I'm saying nothing.'

Annoyed at him being a smart arse, Allan lunged, pulled the boy off the perch on the sofa arm, and held him by the front of his sweatshirt. 'I've pussy footed round you enough, son. I saw Jamie Brooks' name on that gaming list. Strange pal to have, given you called him a wee prick-teasing dick, if I remember correctly. Now, tell me about Mo Khan. He's Ahmed's uncle, yeah? How involved is Ahmed in Mo Khan's racket?' He gave the boy a shake, more theatrical than physical. 'I'm waiting.'

'Ahmed's got nothing to do with it.' He tried to tug Allan's hand off, but Allan held tight. 'Mo's not as bad as you think.'

'But he gives you the electronics, eh? How does he expect you to pay for them? How did Jamie pay for them? For Ahmed's sake, you'd better tell me.'

Khal struggled, but Allan kept a hold, winding the cloth of his sweatshirt tighter in his fist.

'You know Mo Khan's got a record? A paedophile record?' Allan's face was up close to the boy's now. He could see the sweat on his upper lip and smell whatever the gel he used on his hair.

'Leave me alone!'

Allan laughed. 'Leave you alone? You think this is bad? You want me to take you back in for questioning?' He threatened a head butt.

'Wait!' Khalil spluttered unswallowed saliva. 'He gave Ahmed and me the phones and stuff.'

'Where does he get them?' No answer. 'Where does he get them?'

'From his work.'

'And Jamie, too?'

'Probably!'

Allan relaxed his grip a fraction. 'Now we're getting somewhere. How is he involved with Thompson? What else does he get up to with Thompson?'

'I'm not telling you!' The teenager's voice squeaked.

Lorraine shoved open the door. 'What are you – ? Leave him alone! He's fifteen years old!' She thumped Allan's arm on repeat. He released the boy and she grabbed her son close to her.

'Calm down! I wouldn't hurt him. But maybe you can get it out of him since he's never going to spill to me.'

'I didn't realise I was walking into a domestic.' Jane glared at Allan. She set down the laden tray and looked around. 'A break, eh? Everybody sit down.' She waited while they all dropped into seats and took up their broody, crossed arm positions. 'Right. What's going on? Lorraine.'

Lorraine sighed and made a face at Allan. 'He's not likely to spill to you, because he's not likely to spill bad stuff about his dad to anyone.'

'Thompson?'

Lorraine tutted, arms still crossed. 'For God's sake, Allan! I thought you were a detective?'

There was silence.

'Mo Khan? Mo Khan is Khal's father?'

221

Chapter 45

'How did I miss that?' he whistled to Jane when they went into the hall for a confab, leaving Lorraine and the boy in the living room.

'Well, maybe with Khan's record they don't tend to broadcast it.'

Allan rubbed the top of his head. When he thought about it, not even Emma Gough at school had seemed to know, though she'd said the boys might be related. 'Right. This Ahmed going missing. I think we'll need to take that seriously and not wait the twenty-four hours. Can you phone Ross and ask him to run a trace on Ahmed's number? Khal will have it. Get him to check Mo Khan's while he's at it.'

Back in the living room, the atmosphere was calmer. Lorraine was sipping tea and Khal was studying his phone. 'Don't go putting the word out,' Allan said to him. 'In fact, let me have that. I'll give you it back later.' He passed the phone to Jane who took it out to the car.

Allan perched on the arm of the chair opposite the boy, giving him space. 'Khal, I understand, now, why you feel such loyalty. I get it.' He let that sink in. 'That's a decent quality. One that says a lot about you.' Khalil said nothing, but his body language softened, his shoulders losing some of their tension. 'But I think we all have concerns your dad's involved in something. Something he shouldn't be, and I need to put a stop to it, okay?'

Khal, hands in the pockets of his slouchy joggers, slumped from the arm of the sofa on to the seat.

'Okay?'

He shrugged, keeping his eyes off Allan. Lorraine was looking from one to the other but held her tongue.

'And that means you need to tell me everything you know about him and Hugo Thompson.' Allan took a slow breath in. 'For a start, do you know where your dad is right now?'

The boy looked up. 'At work or in his flat, I guess.'

Allan's phone rang. 'Ross is on it, Boss,' Jane said. 'He'll get back to you direct any minute.'

He placed the phone on the coffee table. 'Have you ever been in Thompson's office?'

'No.' Khal's expression was innocent. 'Why would I?'

'Okay. So, do you know if your dad takes the games machines and phones as and when he wants them, or do you think he has a stash? Maybe in his locker at work? Or maybe bigger than that – like in a special room?'

Both Lorraine and Khalil's faces were blank.

'No?'

Lorraine shrugged. She rubbed her eyes. 'I've no idea about any of this, Allan. Mo's a law to himself.' She looked at her son. 'He always has been.'

Allan nodded. 'Okay – I have to ask this. The boy Jamie. He had a top of the range phone.' He focused in on Khal, excluding Lorraine. 'Do you think your dad might be the one that gave him it?'

The boy said nothing. Allan switched his look to Lorraine, but she raised and lowered her shoulders.

'Khal – it's important.'

Khal looked as if he was going to vomit. At last, he said, 'Probably.' He met Allan's eyes. 'But none of this has been my dad's fault.' He sniffed and appealed to his mum. 'It wasn't my dad that was grooming Jamie. It was the other way round. Jamie was playing him. Jamie was desperate for anything he could get.' He broke off then flicked a glance at Allan with the last words. 'He got what he deserved.'

Throttle the boy? Allan pushed his hands firmly into his pockets.

'Nah, nah, son – Jamie Brooks was a kid. Your dad was the adult. You're victim blaming. I'm not having that.'

The phone buzzed and skated about the table. Allan grabbed it. It was Ross.

'We've tracked Ahmed's phone to an area between Paul Street and Bowker Place, off the main road. We're narrowing it down. No trace yet of Khan's.'

Jane appeared in the doorway.

'Jane and I'll head over. Get me some support.' Allan put the phone in his pocket and told Khal, 'I'll get yours back to you,' as he rose. To Lorraine, he said, 'Not a word to anyone. For Ahmed's sake. Not a word till I tell you.' She nodded, rising to her feet and following him and Jane to the front door.

As they got into the car, Allan said, 'Paul Street? Isn't that near the mosque?'

'Yep.'

It was lunchtime and the roads were busy. Traffic queued through the town and on the bridges. 'Come on.' Allan tapped at the steering wheel as they waited to turn by the river.

Jane's phone rang. It was Ross again. 'It is the mosque,' she told Allan, 'nearest they can pinpoint it.'

'They're going to love this. Forensics were there yesterday; we're turning up again today.' In the background, he could still hear Ross's voice. 'What's he getting excited about?'

Jane put him on loudspeaker. 'Khan's phone must be switched off, but I checked his mobile number against Jamie's phone and it's there. It's there, Boss! Khan definitely knew him. They were in regular contact.'

'Thank Fuck – a firm connection! Organise a warrant for his arrest.' Finally the filter light lit up and the Alfa roared on to the open road ahead of it.

Two squad cars were already at the mosque when they arrived, and the PCs followed Allan and Jane into the building. There was no one in the entrance to stop them, but Allan told Jane to wait. She wasn't happy. 'Are you telling me I'm barred?'

He took her to one side. 'You know the rules. And we don't want a PR catastrophe. You can be backup. I'll call you if I need you. And if you see Khan or Ahmed leaving – grab them!' He told PC Welsh to wait with her, and took to the corridor, leaving the two women standing, arms folded.

As the men strode down the corridor, three others came from a room, chatting amicably. Allan recognised one from before and flashed his identity badge at them. The tallest introduced himself as Iqbal, a committee member.

'I wonder if you can help me,' Allan said. 'I'm looking for a young lad who comes here. His name's Ahmed Atchi. I've seen him here before, helping in the canteen. I'm concerned about his whereabouts and I want to confirm he's alright. Is he here just now, can you tell me?'

'I haven't seen Ahmed since yesterday,' Iqbal said. 'And he'll be at school today.'

'Is it not an in-service day? I was told the boys are off,' Allan said.

'Really? My kids are at school.' The first man tugged at his beard, twisting a lock of it round his finger. 'But I really don't think he's been in today. I haven't seen him. Have you?' The other men signalled they hadn't.

'We're also looking for Mo Khan, his uncle.'

The mood changed. 'No, he's not been in, either.' The man frowned, suddenly, at the officers. 'Look. What is this? Your people were here yesterday doing a search. Now this. We've been really supportive but this is beginning to feel like harassment. Do you turn up mob-handed for every teenage boy and his uncle?'

'For every teenage boy whose safety we're concerned about,' Allan said and cleared his throat, buying time. 'Let me be straight. We're carrying out an investigation into the death of a teenage boy. Now I'm concerned another teenage boy's gone missing.' He let his words sink in. 'I'm talking about Ahmed Atchi, a boy you know well in this mosque. This is the last place his phone was traced to. I'm happy to leave it to you to look for him, but if you can't find him, soon, I'll be carrying out a detailed search. He has to be found.'

While the three men conferred, Allan tried Ahmed's number on his phone. It rang out. The men showed Allan and the PCs into a side room and offered them tea while they carried out their own search around the building. Allan took advantage of the pause to phone Ross again.

'No, Boss, the signal's strong. It's definitely in those premises. Definitely. I guarantee it. And there's still no sign of Mo Khan. It looks as if he never went back to his flat.'

Allan phoned his boss. Within minutes, Iqbal came back and reported that no one had seen Ahmed since yesterday. 'In that case,' Allan said, rising to face him, 'I'm sorry, but I'm empowered to carry out a full search of the building.'

They split into teams, getting word to Jane and PC Welsh to go through the women's section, and carried out a top to toe search of all the public areas and the rooms on the upper floor. There were classes in one of the rooms, but none of the five men there had seen or heard from Khan or Ahmed. In the canteen, those men clearing up after lunch looked blankly at the intrusion of uniformed police and said nothing. In the library, an elderly man at the desk told Allan he'd seen Mo Khan that lunchtime.

'Serving food in the canteen,' he said, his thin right hand trembling slightly as he rested his arm on the desk.

'Are you sure, Uncle?' Iqbal said.

'Yes, I'm sure. He told his nephew to give me an extra portion of chicken.'

Allan stepped in. 'His nephew? The young lad Ahmed?'

The elderly man's head wobbled as he raised it high enough to see Allan properly. Thin strings of skin stretched at his neck. 'That's the one.'

'Thank you, Uncle.'

A look passed between Allan and Iqbal. On Allan's part, it was frustration that the men in the canteen had lied to him, but Iqbal shook his head. 'He's old; he gets mixed up.'

'What's through that door?' Allan asked, indicating a door on the back wall of the library.

'The library store. And toilets.'

'Can we go through?'

Iqbal took out a bunch of keys and led the way. The door led to a staircase surrounded by white painted brick walls. The men's footsteps echoed as they descended an uncarpeted stair to a service area. There were several doors off a corridor that ran under the library. In one, books, scrolls and newspapers were ranged along floor to ceiling shelves. In another, there were cleaning materials and a sink. A third opened to reveal stacked tables and chairs. Allan phoned Jane. 'Any joy?' he said.

'None, Sir. No trace of him. No one's seen either of them. Or so they're saying. But they probably wouldn't have been in the women's section. What about you?'

'No sign of them, but an old guy claims he saw them both at lunchtime. Keep looking.' Once again, he tried calling Ahmed's number. The sound of a ring tone came from close by. 'Check the toilets.'

No one was in them, but there was a small red smear on the outside edge of a sink. 'Sir!' PC Smith said.

Iqbal looked shocked. 'That definitely shouldn't be there. Unless it's paint.'

Allan knelt. 'No, it's blood.' He scanned the floor. There were red spots and the bin was on its side with a scatter of used paper towels issuing from it. 'Check the cubicles for the phone,' he told Smith. At the end of the corridor Allan tried the last door. It wouldn't budge. 'What's in here?'

Iqbal stared at it, his face screwed up. 'Electrics? Meters and fuse box.' He pumped the handle. 'It's not usually locked.'

'Well, you've got the keys.'

While Iqbal tried a few, Allan dialled Ahmed's number again.

227

The phone rang behind him. PC Smith put his head out of the toilets door. 'Found it, Sir.'

'Step aside,' Allan said. 'Smith –'

The door flew back and there was Ahmed, bundled on the floor with his mouth bound and his arms tied behind his back. They sat him up and untied him. He'd a gash on his forehead and a couple of bruises, but he was otherwise unhurt. 'I tried to stop him,' he said, near tears.

'Your uncle?' Allan said, passing him a couple of damp paper towels one of the PCs brought from the toilets.

The boy nodded. 'I tried to stop him. I told him he couldn't do it.'

'Did he hurt you any other way, Ahmed?' The boy was fully clothed. 'You can tell me, or you can wait and I'll get someone else for you to talk to. But you know you're safe, now.'

Ahmed looked from Iqbal to Allan and back again. 'He didn't hurt me. Just this,' he gesticulated, indicating the bumps and bruises. 'My uncle's been trying to do the right thing.' He bobbed his head at Iqbal. 'He knows it.'

'Iqbal?'

Iqbal was squeezing his jaw, twisting a lock of his black beard again. He nodded, concern in his eyes. 'We've been working with him – all of us – trying to keep him from going back, like, to his old ways? Insha'Allah.' He nodded again, a bond obvious between him and the lad on the cupboard floor. 'We tried, Ahmed. Didn't we?' He bent down and rubbed the teenage boy's shoulder. 'Did he hurt you?'

Ahmed blinked tears. 'I tried to stop him.' His eyes appealed to Iqbal and then to Allan. 'But he was angry. Frightened. He was too strong.'

'Is that your blood in the toilets?'

Ahmed said yes. 'Then he shoved me in here.'

'Where was he going?'

The boy didn't answer. He looked down at his hands and rubbed his wrists where the binding had left red indentations. On a hunch, Allan said, 'I've spoken with Khal. It was him that told me you were missing.'

'Khal?'

'Yep.'

'Khal told you?'

Allan nodded. 'He told me everything.'

'Khal?'

Allan held his breath.

'Khal told you everything?'

'Yep.'

Ahmed groaned. 'My uncle isn't into bad things. It's his boss that's forcing him.' The young lad's voice was earnest, but Allan wasn't having it.

'Come off it, Ahmed – your uncle has a record.'

'Not for the bomb thing!'

Allan inhaled a sharp breath. A thought occurred to him. 'On a plane? Is it that "airplane tracker" thing?'

'What?' Ahmed frowned. 'That's just a game. It's the bomb at school. That's why we didn't go today. I thought you said Khal told you?'

'The one at the kitchens? In the bins?'

'What are you talking about?' Ahmed said. 'Not that one. The big one.'

Chapter 46

Thompson.

Even if it was a hoax, they had to evacuate. Allan phoned the headteacher, Frances Wallace, then called his boss to raise the threat level and call out the bomb squad. All the while, he thought about Emma. Straight after, he phoned her mobile. 'Get it cleared,' he said. 'Make sure everyone gets away. Far away. You, too. D'you hear me?'

He left Ahmed with two officers while he, Jane and the others dashed to their cars. 'Thistlebank Academy,' he shouted to the PCs. 'Blue light. Meet you there.' He threw himself into the car. 'Get Ross and Sam out,' he told Jane. 'Wait – phone Sam first. See if he's found anything else on Thompson.' He groaned. 'This isn't a kids' prank. And it's not Mo Khan.' He'd been in jail at the time of the second bin fire.

'But why Thompson?' Jane said.

'How the fuck are those two connected? I mean, really connected?'

Driving, he pulled up Lorraine's number. It rang and he tucked the phone between chin and shoulder. 'Has Khan turned up?' It was clear he hadn't. 'Any idea where he's staying? Is he hunkering down somewhere? Maybe Khal knows?' He put his foot down to run a light as it changed to red, saw a gap open up just behind an HGV waiting to turn right, and engaged dynamic mode to push through.

'Jesus fuck, Allan. Put on the blue light if you're going to do that!' Jane braced herself against the dashboard with her free hand.

He was too busy concentrating to answer. 'Is Khal still there?

Tell him we've got Ahmed, safe and well. PC Welsh'll get in touch with his mother.'

'Who said men can't multitask?' Jane muttered down the phone to Sam. 'Any further word on Thompson? Boss needs to know asap.' While Allan drove, Jane listened, then hung up and turned in her seat to tell him. 'Word just in. Thompson had a suspended sentence for a "lively" climate change protest down south a dozen years ago.'

Allan flashed a glance at her. '"Lively"? What does "lively" mean?'

'Sam says "fireworks". It's him, isn't it?'

'What else?'

'He'd a night in the cells. A posh lawyer got him off.'

'Why does that not surprise me?'

They were nearing the school. All around, life was normal. People walked dogs. Mothers pushed buggies. Any minute that could end. How many pupils were there? Thistlebank was one of those megaschools.

'But why the jump, now? Why the move from climate change to kids? And why now? I don't get it.' Allan turned hard left. At lights, he tapped the wheel. 'Khal and Ahmed, that aeroplane tracker thing – that's pish, agree?' his eyes swept to Jane.

'Agreed.'

'Kids' games. But why were they off school today? Khal told me it was an inset day.'

Jane shrugged. 'Did you never dog school for the hell of it?'

'You think it's coincidence? Don't know if I believe in coincidence. Ahmed connected it with Mo Khan. I wonder if he and Khalil know something was planned and that's why they stayed away. Either to save their own skin, or to prevent it happening.'

'You think they're both involved, then? The boys?'

'Isn't it too big a coincidence that we saw two guys who might have been them on the CCTV near Q-busters the night before the first bin fire?'

'Boss, that could've been anybody. You know that. It wouldn't stand up.'

'But it could've been them. Doing what?'

'Covering up for Mo Khan? Ahmed's uncle –'

'– and now we know he's Khal's dad, too.' He drove off, the car surging forward, then braked hard when the car in front obeyed the speed limit. 'This is taking too long.' He reached out the window and attached the blue light, then the car leapt into a clear lane ahead of him.

'They'll evacuate the school before we get there.'

'Any word on the van? The Q-busters van? The one that went missing, that we think Thompson took?'

Jane checked in with Traffic. 'Picked up ten minutes ago on the expressway cameras.' She sounded breathy. 'En route to Thistlebank by the sound of it.'

'Get all available units after it.'

'What about Mo – isn't he still the murder suspect?'

'Ahmed said he was trying to stop him, and I don't think he meant carrying out another sexual assault. If Khan's connected with this bomb alert, it's under his boss's influence. It's Thompson we need to focus on. Repeat – Thompson's the priority. When we catch Mo, it's a bonus.'

Chapter 47

They turned into School Street. Pupils were streaming out in lines like navy blue ink, heading towards the far end of the sports pitches. It was a relief to see the building intact, and no black smoke billowing out of it. There was a big police presence already, with officers coming out of vans, and fire tenders on standby. There was nowhere to park. An officer waved Allan down and directed him to a driveway. He and Jane got out of the car and checked in with the lead officer. Bomb disposal officers had arrived with sniffer dogs and were making ready to enter the building. Frances Wallace was at the main entrance, patting each pupil on the shoulder as he or she left. Alarm was written all over the woman's plump face, along with a film of sweat. Her mascara was smudged.

'We'll get them all out, I assure you,' Allan told her.

'I know you will,' she said, her eyes dewy as she pushed locks of hair back from her face, her silver bangles jingling.

Allan sought out the lead bomb disposal guy and told him about the bin fires. 'The first – we know of – was a small one at Q-busters in the Inchmarsh Industrial Estate. We thought it was random, but it looked like it might be connected to a crime we've been working on – set to dispose of evidence? There was a second – here, this time, but round at the kitchen. First thing in the morning, before the kids turned up. The staff described it to my officer as a blue flash. Forensics said the first had a powerful accelerant, and there's the suggestion both were detonated remotely.'

All this time, babbling school students and teachers were pouring out through the doors, the janitor and head teacher tapping each on the shoulder as they passed, doing a head count. The sudden noise of a helicopter surprised them. It appeared directly overhead crossing over the building from back to front. Its blades beat the air and drowned out all but the highest squeals from the pupils, whose faces were more excited than scared.

'That's one good thing about it,' Jane said to Allan, remarking on the mood of the school kids.

Where was Emma Gough in all this? Allan searched the long stream of navy blue uniforms to the pool of dark blue two hundred metres away. Was she there?

'Can you stand back, please, Sir.' The last of the students had passed through, and the bomb disposal experts looked ready to go into the school. Two of them, holding back enthusiastic dogs, headed across the car park, making their way towards the kitchen block. The helicopter hovered in place.

'It'll be looking for the van,' Allan called out as he and Jane returned to where he'd parked. 'At least that means it's not here.'

'But that thing you said about detonating remotely,' Jane said. 'Is that what Thompson's doing with those computer parts in his secret room? Or is Khalil Buchanan back in the spotlight?'

Allan slammed his door from the inside and the helicopter decibel count reduced. He looked at Jane and started to speak but changed his mind. The street was awash with activity. Could Khal be involved in this? He'd ruled him out – ruled out the airplane tracker device, the fertiliser and nails he'd bought 'for old Bob'. Could there be a link? It would fit, but why? But then, what was Thompson's motive to blow up a school, or threaten it? 'No fucking idea,' he finally said. 'But for now we –'

Jane's mobile rang. 'They've picked up the van again.'

'Tell Ross to call in a team to follow us.'

The only way to get out was by turning the car in its own body width. 'Just when I don't need a twenty-three point turn,' Allan said, sweating as he wrestled his Alfa forward and back. Jane braced her hand against the dashboard again as the car lurched and braked.

'Feed me the details.'

'They're coming up on the screen,' she said, keying in the passcode. A map of the streets appeared, with their vehicle highlighted and the route they'd to follow. 'Last reported at the junction of Hazlitt and Falconer Street,' she said, and switched her gaze to the windscreen. 'Left here and left again. Shit, watch out for that – okay. We should have visual – there! There it is. See it?' She pointed to the blue van just as it turned the corner and they lost sight of it behind a double decker bus. 'Where the hell's he going now?'

Allan focused on driving. The town streets could be cramped and congested. No wide boulevard grid system here. It reminded him of the old parts of Glasgow. Real towns grew haphazardly. 'Good we got the kids out.'

Jane said nothing, her attention split between the animation on the screen and the streets where taxis were picking people up from the station and small delivery vans were scurrying to and fro with home deliveries. Where was their blue one? 'There!'

The van was waiting to turn right but there was too much traffic. Allan checked his rear mirror, indicated and changed lanes, the driver in the car he'd cut up leaning on the horn furiously. Thompson must have heard it. He hung a right across the junction, forcing cars both ways to brake. 'Damn. He must've seen the light on the roof,' Allan said, though it wasn't on. He lowered the window and stretched out. It was now. The siren wailed, deafening until he raised the window again. It worked. The traffic on all four roads into the junction drew up in ragged lines, leaving room for him to push through after the van. He turned right and pressed on the accelerator. 'This is where it pays to drive an Alfa.' The car outstripped the speed of the van less than a hundred metres ahead of them.

'Shit. Zebra crossing.' The lollipop woman skittered back to the pavement as the van sped through. The crossing was empty. Allan put the foot down and followed, catching an impression of open mouths on the pavement.

Jane twisted in her seat. 'They're fine. They're all fine.'

'He's turning left. Where does left go?'

Jane surveyed the screen. 'Full circle!' As Allan turned the car, she checked the window. 'The new industrial estate. They're still building it. It backs up against the school grounds.' She scanned the screen and raised her eyes to the streets ahead of them. 'There he goes – round to the right. See him? It's a dead end. He'll have to back out past us or go on foot.'

They were in an open landscape of empty building plots with only a couple of workers operating diggers. 'Did you call Ross?' Allan said. 'Get that back-up over here.'

The van ahead braked and veered round but the turning circle was too tight. It bumped against a high kerb sitting proud on the unfinished carriageway and rolled back, its engine stalling.

'He's getting out.' Allan accelerated towards the Q-busters van to cut off Thompson's escape through the driver's door. Too late. Thompson was out and running. Allan swung the Alfa into his path, side on, and Thompson seized up, hands on the bonnet. Allan undid his seatbelt and leapt from the car. He had cut Thompson off from the open landscape that led towards the school. Instead, Thompson ran towards a row of two storey brick buildings lying derelict.

Jane grabbed her phone and started running, gasping their location into the phone as soon as she heard Ross's voice. Behind her, she heard the sound of a siren wailing, and as she sprinted, she looked back and saw the uniforms' car turn into the road where they'd left the Alfa.

Thompson's height and agility had him covering the ground ahead of them. His blond hair flapped as he ran. At the brick buildings, he hesitated, then climbed in one of the holes where there used to be windows. Allan pushed himself to catch up. He was faster than Jane. He determined to catch this guy, clear in his mind he was guilty, or why was he running? He followed him into the building, leaping up on to the empty window frame and down again, his eyes taking time to adjust to the gloom. There were noises ahead. Thompson was kicking a door, searching for a way out through the back. Allan followed. The wooden door was hanging on its frame, hinges broken. Outside, they were in a concrete yard filled with builders' rubble. Thompson was legging it over a stack of bricks and broken pallets. Allan ran after, clambering almost on all fours over a burst bag of aggregate. His breath came fast and harsh, but he was closing in. Thompson glanced back as he topped the perimeter wall and dropped down into the scrub land.

'Back-up's arrived. They're right behind,' Jane yelled from the broken doorway as Allan dropped down from the wall after Thompson, who was disappearing uphill between birch saplings and whin bushes. Allan gave chase, gasping up the hill after the other man, gaining ground little by little till the side of his flapping suit jacket tangled in the curved stems of brambles and he had to tug it free.

Thompson tripped and fell his length but got up straight away and kept climbing. Near the shoulder of the hill, he stopped, hands on his thighs to catch his breath. Allan shouted to him, 'Police! Stop now!' but he turned and started running again, disappearing down the other side. As Allan reached the top, he looked ahead and saw the school playing grounds, coloured thickly with the navy blue uniforms of a thousand or more young people. 'Where the fuck are you going?' Allan gasped aloud as he started his descent.

Thompson went to the right. Weighing things up from the advantage of height, Allan chose a route through thicket, down steeper ground between hawthorns. Thompson was two metres below. Allan took his chance and leapt, grasping the blond by the shoulders, making them both plummet to the ground. Something the size of a mobile phone flew out of Thompson's pocket, clattering on the stony ground ahead of them. Allan's shoulder hit a boulder. The two men scrambled to their feet, Thompson pocketing the phone or whatever it was and taking off again. Allan followed in pursuit, but his shoulder was throbbing. He heard the uniforms plunge through the scrub land behind him. His shoulder was pounding. At least he'd slowed him. Had he slowed him? Something was slowing Allan. The air was a wall and he couldn't run through it. Uniforms burst past him; inch-thick shoe leather. Allan bent over with his hands on his knees. What was happening to him? His hands reached for the path. Stars twinkled on the periphery of his vision.

'Boss!'

Jane.

His forehead hit the ground. 'He's heading for the school.'

'What, Boss?'

He tried speaking again. Twisted to see her. She was searching downhill where Thompson had run off. There were leaves above her head. They were blurring. She was blurring.

'He's got a detonator.'

She leaned in close, hand on his shoulder. 'Say it again, Boss?'

His arms and legs were numb. The skin around his lips was tingling. 'A detonator.' He rolled on his back and everything stopped.

Chapter 48

He thought he heard a bird cry. A buzzard, high up, looking for a field mouse. A shrew, a baby bird, a young pine marten. They must be in the hills outside the city. There was a smell, now. Undergrowth. Dead leaves. Like being in the forest. Sparklers in his eyelids. Sweat stinging his upper lip.

Dappled light through yellow leaves. And then a face above him, indistinct. A halo effect from the sun through the trees behind her.

'Jane.'

'Well, hello. Decided to come back and join us, did you?'

Allan licked his lips. He was lying on the ground in the woodland, on a bed of crisp copper-coloured leaves. Jane was above him. Piece by piece, memory came back to him: the chase; the way he'd leapt downhill on top of Thompson; the way all vitality had drained away from him.

The ground was chilly under him. Chilly and hard. Thistledown floated across, a foot or two above his body. He propped himself up on his elbows. 'What the fuck?' No wonder he felt cold.

'Sorry, Sir.' Jane laughed. 'I had to!'

'Caught with my pants down.'

She was putting a used needle in a box. His injection kit – that pack the hospital had given him – was lying on the ground beside his bare thigh. She'd pulled his trousers down and injected him. 'Christ Almighty,' he said, lifting his hip and wriggling his trousers up so he could fasten them again. But it was too fast. Too soon. He lay his head back on the ground again. 'I'm beat.' He rubbed his shoulder. Watched her as she tidied up the kit – the tiny bottles and

239

the leaflet with the instructions. Was this the new normal? Could he do his job like this? 'What about Thompson?' he said. 'I seriously blew it.'

Jane sat back on her heels. 'No, you didn't blow it. You brought him down and gave the uniforms time to catch up.'

He'd no sense of time. No idea how long ago it had happened. But he remembered the uniforms. 'What about the detonator?' He thought he heard snatches of children's voices on the wind. Were they still out in the playground, waiting? What about Emma? 'Did they get him?'

'They caught him. He's at the school, now, so the bomb squad can deal with the detonator – which you told us about.'

Relief flushed through his body with the blood in his veins and whatever drug it was they carried. He looked up at the sky, and the yellowing leaves above his head. 'I think I should lie down like this after every job. It's quite peaceful.'

Jane smiled. 'What are you like?'

He squinted to see her again. 'I guess I should really thank you.'

'A wee glass of chilled rosé would be nice. Or a big one. But let's not make it a habit.'

Her phone sounded and she answered it. She nodded a few times, said, 'That's great, Ross. I'll pass that on.' She looked at Allan and added into the phone, 'Aye, he's fine now. Coming round.'

A leaf drifted down on him and he revelled – no, he floated – in the sense of calm. Then he thought he heard a noise downhill, and when he turned his head, he saw Emma in a blue dress and high heels, taking a big step up over the uneven ground, hauling herself up between bushes. She winced and rubbed at her wrist. 'This is your fault, MacIntyre,' she said, and stood a couple of metres away, still rubbing at her wrist, but her eyes supercharged, looking into his.

'Yeah, yeah,' he said, then held silent for a long moment, transfusing himself through that look.

'The bomb squad have deactivated the detonator, Sir.' Jane

spoke quietly and got to her feet. She nodded an acknowledgement to Emma and bobbed the emergency injection kit in her hand. 'I'll get this back to the car, now. Back in a minute.'

Emma perched on her heels beside him and put her hand on his shirt, on his chest. It was strange to see her in teacher mode, and sober, and worried about him. 'You frightened me,' she said. 'They told me you conked out. Spark out. Lifeless.' Her English-teacher voice cracked on the last syllables.

'Me? I'm fine,' he said, rubbing her hand. 'Bulletproof.' She had long nails. Long, polished nails. Blue like her dress. Not brown like her eyes. 'Did the kids all get away okay?'

'Yeah. I should still be with them,' she said. 'But I slipped away. Told Mrs Wallace what had happened to you. I think she must fancy you because she's never usually that nice to me.'

She grinned at him and he couldn't stop grinning back, no matter how he tried to resist it. A chuckle even forced its way out of him. 'I have that effect on women.' Almost as quickly, his mood grew sombre again and he thought about Jamie, the boy they'd found murdered in the woods. Jamie should be down there in the playground with his mates enjoying all the excitement, but he wasn't. And Allan shouldn't be lying here looking up at the sky under the falling leaves. He should be finding his killer. He struggled to sit up.

'Are you alright?' Emma brushed the leaf debris from the back of his jacket.

He remembered the elderly woman who'd found Jamie's body. The one who'd warned him about his skin colour. The one who'd lost someone she loved to Addison's. 'I've been worse. Been better, but been worse.' He rubbed his shoulder and circled his arm to test the joint.

'D'you need to get it checked out?'

'Nah, I think it's fine. Couple of paracetamol'll do it.' He met her eyes again. 'It must just have been this adrenal thing. This Addison's. I don't know how it's going to impact on work from now on.'

'You seem okay now. And didn't you say JFK had it? If he could run a country...'

He thought about it. 'Yeah, but I lost consciousness.' He stared at her. 'I mean, I was out of it. I don't even know what happened – to me. Jane must've taken my car keys and gone back to the car for the injection kit.'

Emma nodded. 'She did. She phoned Ross and told him. That's how I got to know.' She looked back up the hill. 'That's her coming back, now.'

'Do you need two women to get you up these days, Boss?' Jane said, hooking her arm under his.

'Never.' He brushed her arm off. Grimacing from one to the other, he added, 'but don't tempt me.' Then he made a point of getting to his feet unassisted. When he stood, he looked down at the playground, below. 'I think they're all being sent home.'

Emma stood beside him and looked at her watch. 'Yeah, they'll probably just dismiss them from there. I'd better get back.' She put her hand on his arm. 'Take care, eh?' She kissed him softly on his eyes and on his mouth and he let his hand linger on the thin film of dress over her buttocks.

'I'm good,' he said, and swallowed. 'You take care, too.' He watched her skitter on those high heels downhill between the bushes again, and when he was confident she had reached level ground, he turned to Jane. She was also watching her, and Allan recognised on her face the same emotion he was feeling. 'Right, DS Coburn. Almost time for that glass of chilled rosé, but first we better have a word with our suspect.'

Chapter 49

Back at the police office, Allan went to see his boss, reconciled to the need to inform the old man about his health condition since it was obviously going to affect the way he performed his duties. How was he to sound reassuring when his whole body felt whacked, and out of whack? He felt as if every bone and sinew had been dropped from a height then reassembled and held together by skin. In the toilet, before the meeting, he looked at himself in the mirror. He still had that glowing tan that made him look healthy. When he held his hands out, the tan was patchy as if it was fading, but that was presumably a good sign. And there was still a definite tremor. Once again he felt like a junkie and wondered when he should take his next dose. A quick search online told him the injection should be enough for now, and to wait and see. Actually, it said he should go to hospital for assessment, but he wasn't having that.

His boss was solemn as they sat in his office, his expression giving nothing away. He leaned back in his chair, elbow on the arm rest and hand covering his mouth while he listened to what Allan had to say.

'It's like diabetes. Or like thyroid deficiency. I'm kind of – on hormone replacement therapy,' Allan said, trying to keep it light.

His boss didn't seem convinced. Eventually though, he sat forward, the leather of his chair creaking. 'I'm going to refer you for a medical assessment.' He coughed, a gravelly cough. 'Don't know if you know this or not, but I've actually got diabetes, so I'm prepared to give you the benefit of the doubt. If you say you can do the job and follow whatever medical procedures you have to follow – to the letter – I'll trust you on that. But the minute I think you can't...'

When he came out the office, Allan bought a coffee from the canteen and swallowed a pill with it. Downstairs, Ross was overseeing Thompson being taken into detention. It was likely they'd get as much time as they needed to interview him, so there was no immediate rush to start now, which meant Allan could go home and sleep – after he'd bought Jane Coburn that glass of chilled rosé. He took a smug satisfaction in remembering seeing the urbane businessman appearing ruffled and powerless, angered at being confined to a cell. He wondered how police canteen food would go down with him overnight. It wasn't exactly what he was used to.

Next morning, Allan arrived at the office feeling refreshed and reinvigorated. He half expected the media scrum that had gathered, already, outside the entrance steps. As he locked his car and sauntered towards them, he steeled himself for their questions and for the photographs. He'd already decided to release a statement and had phoned Jason Bonar for a chat about it while he drank that coffee the previous evening.

He stood on the steps and reassured the public, through the media, that the man they wanted in connection with the fires and the bomb alert at the school was safely in custody. Investigations were ongoing, and they would maintain the enhanced police presence in the meantime. What he didn't expect was for them to ask him how he was. 'I'm fine,' he said. He indicated his tan. 'In fact, I'm glowing with health. So is the rest of my team. Nobody here needs to worry about me or my team or our ability to handle this issue.' With that, he drew the statement to a close. Inside the building, he went straight to Bonar's office. 'Did you tell them?' he asked the media man.

'Not me.'

'So how do they find these things out?' Allan said, leaning against Bonar's desk and skimming the reporting of the story in several of the media outlets.

'Probably eavesdropping on the phone call.' As soon as he

realised what he'd said, Jason added, 'I mean overhearing things when Ross took the call from Jane outside the school. Innocent enough.'

Fortunately, none of them showed a photo of him with his trousers down.

In the incident room, Allan gathered the team together for the briefing. Sam had been on into the late evening and had tried gleaning an informal preliminary statement from Thompson, but he hadn't been forthcoming, preferring to wait for his solicitor to spend hours travelling up from Edinburgh in the morning. It was decided that Allan and Jane would conduct a thorough interview after he'd arrived and spoken to his client.

Allan turned to Ross. 'How did you get on yesterday with the bomb team?'

Ross was on his second coffee. 'The school had a delivery the day before yesterday, with a second delivery expected yesterday afternoon. They'd had a big donation to supplement education authority funding and were planning a serious upgrade to their computer suite.' He tapped the papers he was reading from. 'Guess who was delivering the stuff?'

'Thompson?'

'Got it in one. I showed the office staff his photo and they've identified him. There's CCTV in the foyer area, and I reckon we should be able to pinpoint him.'

'Great work,' Allan said. Excitement and approval rippled through the group gathered there. 'At last we're on top of this.'

'Why, though? I just don't get the motivation.' This was Sam again.

'Fair point. We'll come back to that in a minute. Ross, what happened after that?'

Ross stretched his long legs out in front of him. 'The bomb squad already had the dogs sniffing round all the rooms in the school anyway, but when I heard about Thompson delivering the computer gear, I –' he bobbed his head to Sam, 'Sam and I got them to prioritise that, and believe me, those dogs get pretty excited.'

'Success?'

'The stuff's all been taken in by Forensics.' He straightened up in his chair. 'The bomb squad said it looked like there was enough explosive to blow the roof off. And if he'd blown it up while school was in, god knows how many deaths. Scary stuff.'

'A lot bigger than a blue-flash-in-a-bin caper.'

The resonances echoed round the room while everyone took this in.

'You did get the bomb squad to search the rest of the rooms just in case?'

'Of course,' Ross said. 'Well, to be honest, didn't matter what I said – they were doing it anyway.'

Allan rolled his pen between his palms. 'You guys do quite well when I'm having a nap on a hillside with my pants at my knees.'

There were grins all round, then Sam said, 'Aye, but fair's fair: we only caught Thompson because you threw yourself at him.'

'Kind of "Is that a detonator in your pocket, or are you just pleased to see me?"' Jane asked.

They all grinned then Allan caught sight of the picture of the schoolboy Jamie at the top of the inquiry board and his face straightened. 'Anyway. Good work, guys. Thanks for that. Let's move on. Sam – you were talking about motivation.'

Sam cleared his throat. 'We know Thompson has a history with activism, but it was ages ago. And why the move to targetting kids? And so many of them?' He looked round the faces of the others. 'I'm not saying he's not done it – I mean, he was caught pretty red handed. I just can't get why. Or how Mo Khan's involved with this.' Nodding to the board, he said, 'Or Jamie Brooks.'

'No, I'm with you on that. Right,' Allan looked at his watch, 'Jane – you and I'll have another word with Thompson's wife. Sam – go and have another look in Thompson's office, and see if you can sound out anything from Cathy and the other office staff. See if there's something we've missed.'

'What am I looking for?'

'Anything. The guy's a neat freak. Everything's tidy on the surface. We need to scratch under it.'

Sam nodded. 'Sure thing, Boss.'

'Ross, I'm sorry, but you know what I'm going to ask you to do.'

He grinned ruefully. 'CCTV?'

'Aye – but get PC Welsh to help you go through it. You can impress her when you finally find Thompson in the middle of the night setting up the school bin fire.' He was just about to leave when he had an afterthought. 'Actually – that woman that found Jamie's body gave me some pages from her notebook. It's only a dozen handwritten pages, but I've not had a chance to go over it. Have a look at that, too, will you? Even just to rule it out. It's on my desk.' He waited a second before adding, 'PC Welsh was the one who looked after her.'

He tapped his pen on the desk and considered for a moment then turned to Jane. 'I'm still confused about the delivery schedule on the day the boy went missing.'

'The Monday?'

'Yeah.' He looked at her. 'We've got all these signatures that prove Khan's whereabouts for that whole day, right? In theory. So, before we go to see Mrs Thompson, can you arrange for a squad car to take photos of Khan and Thompson round the drop off points to see if any of the customers who signed for things recognise – remember – who the driver was?'

They weren't the first to pull into the Thompsons' driveway. A squad car was already there, along with the young guy from Forensics and his senior officer. A full search was underway. Allan pulled on the handbrake and went to speak with them. 'I had a quick look round when we were here before. Couldn't find a thing, but he's cunning.' He mentioned the hidden room off Thompson's office at Q-busters. Forensics had already been over it with the nit comb, bagging everything, including carpet fibres, and sending it off to be tested at the main lab in the central belt. It was meticulous and methodical work and would take time. Meanwhile, Allan couldn't let the investigation lose momentum. He wished he'd taken Thompson's laptop back to Ross. As the two men moved away, transporting samples to their van, Allan considered the younger man, and evaluated his chances of persuading him to let him take the laptop now. He was so enthusiastic; so committed. He reminded Allan of his younger self, fresh faced and freshly out of police college. He'd a sudden flashback to the parade ground – how he'd polished his thick-soled shoes that day so much he took cramp in his arm. Almost. His ideals were so high, then, it would never have crossed his mind to do anything but follow procedures. Nowadays it was more pragmatism than anything else that kept him straight. After all, taking the laptop 'improperly' meant nothing they got from it would stand up in court. End of story.

'Okay, Boss?' Jane's eyebrows were raised and he felt the light touch of her fingers on his bent elbow. 'You were miles away.'

He blinked a few times. 'I was. But I'm back now. Let's get on with it.'

The senior Forensics guy came past again. 'By the way, his wife's in a state. Be warned. It's not pleasant.'

In the house, they went directly through to the room they'd been in previously – the one with the garden views and the comfy sofas. Mrs Thompson was a black mass against the white early November daylight that formed the external wall. Lou was playing in the garden and there was no sign of the baby.

'Mrs Thompson? Could we have a word with you?'

The woman turned round and her face came into focus, yet it still seemed dark to Allan and it was only as his eyes adjusted that he realised a huge bruise blackened her eye and cheek. Her face was visibly swollen. Through injury, or tears, he couldn't tell. Her breathing was irregular, anyway – shuddering.

'What now? Haven't you put us through enough?' she said.

No one made any moves to sit down. 'Mrs Thompson, as you know, we're investigating your husband.'

'Yes,' she hissed – she actually hissed – 'Of course, I know you're investigating him. But it's my house, and my life you're turning upside down!' Her face was contorted with rage. She looked beyond them, to where the young man from the Forensics team opened the door and came through, saying they'd need to start on this room now. As he approached Allan and spoke quietly in his ear, Rosie Thompson sniped, 'D'you want to do a strip search while you're at it?'

'Mrs Thompson,' Jane said. 'Please stay calm. We'll try to get this over with as soon as we can.'

Rosie Thompson glared at her. 'He's the one you should be investigating. Not me.' She looked at Allan. 'I mean, look at me.' She waved towards her face. 'Who do you think did this? I'm a victim in this.'

'Do you have someone who can look after your children, Mrs Thompson?' Allan said. He was aware of Jane turning to stare at him but kept his eyes forward on the woman in front of him.

'What do you mean?'

'Forensics have just emptied your husband's home office. They've found the laptop you tried to destroy. And believe me, they'll know it was you once they check the fingerprints on that hammer. Rosie Thompson, I'll have to ask you to come in for questioning with regard to aiding and abetting your husband in planning or conspiring to cause an explosion and to conceal evidence.'

She turned her face away, as if she was looking at the garden, but her hand formed a fist. When she turned to speak, her voice was on a choke chain. 'You can't take me in. I've done nothing. I warned him about what he was doing, but would he listen? He just can't stop himself. I told him. I said, "Give it up, and I'll get you away." My brother's got a private jet. I told him. But he never listens. All he cares about is his stupid obsessions.'

Allan was still trying to read her her rights, telling her she didn't need to say anything, but she was seething. Never again would she let him put her through this. Having to uproot themselves the last time was bad enough but now it was their children, too. 'But you won't take them away from me,' she told the police officers. As if finally realising what was happening, her voice was tinged with panic. 'You won't. I won't let you. My family won't let you. We know people!'

Allan felt a hot knife gore into his stomach and twist in it, but it was metaphorical. 'Your children will be taken care of,' he told her, as Jane phoned Social Services. He struggled to keep emotion from distorting his face, knowing full well the difference in the way posh children and poorer children were treated in the justice system. Or mixed heritage children. He only had to think of Khalil Buchanan.

Chapter 50

No matter the time of day, Interview Room 2 smelled like dust on an overheating light bulb. When Allan and Jane arrived to interview Thompson, it was two o'clock and the yellow painted room felt sulphurous rather than lemony fresh. The smell had been transported from the old police station along with the furniture. Thompson and his brief were already sitting on the snagged blue cushioned seats at the old Formica-topped table, each with a hand covering his mouth in the standard comforting gesture. Thompson's brief had files and folders in front of them, but they looked thin.

'Gentlemen,' Allan said. He introduced himself and DS Coburn for the men and the recorder. Thompson's lawyer immediately let it be known he believed his client was being victimised and harassed and had no case to answer. 'Well, that's what we're here to determine,' Allan said. 'And I take it that means he'll happily give us a full account of himself, since, from what you say, he has no reason to be reticent.'

The solicitor didn't reply and Thompson himself said nothing. Allan's chair rocked forward and back as he consulted his files, missing its rubber foot, and he silently cursed that he'd not remembered to request the chairs be replaced after he'd spoken with Jamie Brooks' mother.

'So,' he said, looking up and half-smiling to the man across from him. 'Hugo Thompson, Managing Director of Q-busters Distribution Company. Can you tell me why you delivered to Thistlebank Academy computers whose hard drives contained explosive materials which could potentially have caused serious damage to the building, and significant loss of life?'

'You can't expect my client to answer that,' the lawyer said.

Thompson's eyes almost grinned into Allan's. The rest of his face was expressionless. By now, he'd assumed a posture Allan recognised from visits to his office at Q-busters: both elbows on the table in front of him, thumbs and clasped hands taking the weight of his chin. More to the point, his chair was steady on all four feet.

'You don't think your client will answer that,' Allan said.

'No.'

Allan glanced at Jane. 'DS Coburn, can you play the accused and his brief video footage sequence number one? This is CCTV from inside the vestibule of Thistlebank Academy. The date and time recorded on the screen is two days ago.'

There was silence while the four watched the hazy footage of someone very like Hugo Thompson pushing stout boxes on a standard two-wheeled delivery trolley. 'Mr Thompson, do you deny you delivered computers to Thistlebank Academy two days ago?'

A look passed between Thompson and his solicitor then Thompson said, 'No.'

'No.'

Jane switched off the i-pad and laid it down.

'On a search of the premises yesterday afternoon, sniffer dogs discovered explosive materials packed into the computers you delivered. Perhaps you'd like to tell me how those explosives found their way into the computers which were delivered by you, from your company, Q-busters Distribution Company?'

Thompson moved his hands away from his mouth as if he was going to speak, but his lawyer said, 'My client doesn't need to answer that.'

'Mr Thompson?'

He cleared his throat. 'They could have been packed into them at any point. Before they reached Q-busters – we're just a distribution company, after all – or while they were at the school. Maybe someone at the school holds a grudge. There were twenty-four hours between when your CCTV shows me delivering them and when the dogs discovered the explosives.'

The lawyer made a note.

Allan fixed his eyes on Thompson. 'You were found, that same day, yesterday, to have a remote detonator in your pocket.'

Thompson sat back in his chair and slipped his hands into his trouser pockets. 'I found that on the hill outside the school when you were chasing me. You saw me pick it up.'

Allan wanted to laugh. 'I saw it fall out of your pocket, and then I saw you pick it up.'

Thompson depressed his almost white blond brow line. 'With respect, you were close to being unconscious, from what I've heard, so I don't think your testimony counts.'

'DI MacIntyre was fully conscious,' Jane piped up, 'and I was very close behind and saw exactly what happened.'

'Mr Thompson,' Allan went on, shuffling papers, 'can you say, for the record, why you keep explosive materials and computer parts in a room which has only one access point – off your private office – and whose access point is concealed by a very large shelving unit?'

Again, Thompson scanned his brief's face before answering. 'Look, it's in my interests to help with your enquiries. So I'm going to be honest with you. That room has nothing to do with me. Nothing at all. We decided a year ago it was excess to our requirements. You've been in my office; you know I'm not short of space. And if I was using it, I wouldn't have put the shelving unit in front of it to make access so difficult.'

'So what's your explanation? Don't you know what goes on in your own office?'

Now Thompson did laugh: a single, ironic laugh. He sat back in his chair again, his brow lightening. 'The only conclusion I can come to is I've been duped by an employee.'

The solicitor made another note.

'And Forensics won't show your fingerprints all over the contents of that room?' Allan said.

Thompson shrugged. 'I expect my fingerprints are all over Q-busters.'

Jane leaned forward. 'Mr Thompson – do you often carry out deliveries? Isn't there a team of delivery drivers to do that?'

'Needs must. Sometimes I lend a hand.'

'Right.'

'I told you before: I'm very hands-on in the company. We're a team.'

Allan slid two grainy photos from his file and turned them round to show Thompson and his brief. 'This is a photo of you, showing you behind the wheel of a Q-busters van, and this is one of a member of your staff: Mohammed Khan. Can you confirm that?'

'Not the most flattering.'

'Is that a yes?'

He shrugged his shoulders. 'Yes.'

'These were taken by traffic cameras a week ago last Monday. For the record – both photos are marked with the date Jamie Brooks went missing; the date the pathology report says he was murdered.'

Thompson said, 'I had nothing to do with that.'

'I'll tell you straight, Mr Thompson. I think you and your employee, Mo Khan, are working in collusion. You knowingly abetted him in covering up the rape and murder of Jamie Brooks, and in return, he colluded with you in preparing and testing explosives, as well as helping you prepare for the major blast you'd planned for Thistledown Academy.'

Thompson's brief had his head down. He'd occasionally been jotting down notes or one word comments. Now he sat up and addressed Allan. 'Why would my client do that? Why would he want to? What was his motive?'

It was what Sam had said. What was Thompson's motivation?

With good timing, Allan's phone rang. It was Ross. To the recorder, Allan said they would take a break and reconvene shortly then he and Jane left the room.

Chapter 51

'Smart bastard,' Allan muttered as the interview room door clicked shut behind them. 'He's right about the time delay, though. Twenty-four hours those computers were sitting in that school. Anyone could've got to them.' He checked to see Jane's expression. 'And he's right about the time before as well. Did anyone swab his hands when they picked him up yesterday? For forensics?'

'They did, but how many times would he have washed them in twenty-four hours? He's no grubby scheme boy.'

'True.'

Allan had redialled Ross's number. They walked along the corridor while waiting for him to answer, and opened the door into the observation room just as Ross got through.

'Irma Russell's journal pages are mostly about cascading leaves. "Ochre soft, shaken from the tree like a fox shakes water..."'

'Yeah, yeah, get to the point.'

Ross's grin was evident in his voice. 'One thing she mentions might be interesting. We know she found the boy's body on the hillside on the Tuesday, but she'd also taken a walk near there on the Monday. And she wrote in her journal that she'd seen, "A swarthy man driving a van." A blue van. And he was driving a bit erratically.'

'Swarthy?'

'We were wondering if that was poetic licence, or if she meant someone from a minority ethnic background.'

Allan looked at his watch. 'Good thinking. Have you had a chance to ask her what she meant by it?'

Ross sounded as if he was playing to an audience. 'We did,

though we didn't actually mention "swarthy". Just fired off some photos to her email address back home in England, and PC Welsh phoned her and asked if she could identify the driver.'

'Who did you send her?'

'Khan and Thompson.'

'And?'

'Khan.'

'Bingo!' To Jane, he said, 'We've a witness that someone fitting Khan's description was driving a blue van near where Jamie was found.' And of course, Emma had seen him too, outside the school. Into the phone, he said, 'Well done, you two. Get her to make an official statement. Anything else?'

'Yep. The search of the Q-busters delivery logs revealed something else that was interesting. Jamie Brooks took in a parcel for his neighbour, two months ago. He signed the electronic pad thing as a receipt for it. Mo Khan was the one that delivered it!'

'Got him!'

'That's not all.' Ross's voice rippled with excitement till he managed to quash it. 'Those cops Jane sent out to the customers who had deliveries that Monday... I gave them a bell. So far, they've only got three people in out of the twelve drops, but all three picked out Thompson. Not just because of ethnicity, but because it wasn't the usual friendly North West England guy that they all seemed to know and like. All three said it.'

'Great news.' To Jane, he said, 'Chinks in the armour. Thompson covered Khan's Monday afternoon route in Khan's van. He gave Khan an alibi – because the delivery roster and all those customer signatures made it look as if Khan was busy all afternoon, all over the area. Meanwhile, Khan could go and dispose of Jamie Brooks in the spare van.' He told Ross the PCs were to keep at it to get statements from as many of the customers as possible. 'And well done, you and PC Welsh.' He winked at Jane. 'What's her name – Anna? Take her out for a proper coffee instead of that machine guff. Once you get the statements sorted.'

Even Jane thought she could hear Ross blushing.

'Thanks, Boss.'

'Aye, but Ross?'

'Uhuh?'

'CCTV.'

'We'll just have to work on it together for longer.'

Back in the interview room, Allan confronted Thompson about covering Khan's route for him. He still denied it. He denied both the sex abuse and the explosives, even though his solicitor told Allan and Jane his client had no comment.

Allan rocked forward on his wonky chair again, and the metal leg scraped along the floor tiles as he drew it closer to the table.

'Who did it, then? You said you thought you'd been duped by an employee. Cathy?'

Thompson had been studying his hands. At Cathy's name, he sneered. 'Hardly. The woman barely knows what year it is.'

'Nice! So much for being "like a family". Who, then? Who duped you?'

'You don't need to say anything,' the solicitor said, but Thompson was used to being in charge. 'Mo Khan.'

Allan balanced his pen on the side of his index finger. When it fell off, he repeated what Thompson had said. 'Mo Khan?'

'That's what I said.'

'Why would Mo Khan want to blow up a school?'

Thompson shrugged. 'He was angry at himself. He's an abuser. You know that – he's got a record.'

Allan scraped his chair back and crossed his legs, feigning relaxed. 'You told me you believed in giving ex-cons a chance to come good and that's why you'd employed him.'

Thompson shifted in his seat. 'That's true.' He looked to his brief. 'That's exactly true.'

'So why are you dissing him now?'

'Because he's a murdering bastard, that's why.' Thompson ran his hand through his hair. 'He roughed that boy up in my office –

my office. God knows what else he did to him, and then he begged me to cover for him.' He shook his head as if he couldn't believe it. 'I refused. Point blank. Told him to get the boy out of there while Jess was at the dentist.' He shrugged. 'Or wherever she was. As for Cathy – wonderful, loyal Cathy, who was sitting there with a sandwich all the time. She waved the bastard in, didn't she?' He breathed an exasperated sigh, up towards the ceiling. 'Waved the bastard in, and the boy with him. The boy must've been drugged or something. He was out of it. But Khan went crazy. Took my goods – you know he had my business's goods in his locker; you saw that. He took my goods when I was out and ...' He looked from one to the other, pretty convincing if he was acting, 'and he must've rammed those computers full of explosives, knowing I'd to deliver them. So much for loyalty! Some way to pay me back for taking a chance on employing him!' He sat back then leaned forward again and pounded his finger on the table. 'He knew I was going to Thistlebank.' He looked at Jane. 'Thistlebank. That's the boy's school. That boy he killed. No wonder he wanted to blow the place up.'

Forensics would prove whether Thompson had handled the explosives or whether it was, as he claimed, Khan. Allan had no doubt there was a connection between the two men. There was a snag, though. Fingerprints on the bomb materials would prove involvement, but it wouldn't determine who was behind the plan. And forensics would take time. Allan was convinced Thompson was the mastermind. Khan was more of a foot soldier. Though Thompson did sound persuasive. And Khan was the one who was missing.

'Where is Mo Khan now?' Allan asked.

The man opposite him shrugged. 'How would I know?' He looked at his lawyer before turning back to Allan. 'You've lost him, have you? That was careless. A known paedophile?'

Allan felt bile rise from his stomach but swallowed it down. When was he due his next dose? It would be easy to lose track. He sifted through the papers on his desk in front of him, had a flashback to the evening in the hospital when he'd envied the doctor for being the one in charge with the papers the right way up. He caught sight of the note he'd penned about smartphones. 'You and Mr Khan work very closely together, don't you? Do you know he claimed you planted those phones in his locker?'

'And you take his word for it? A man like that?'

Jane said, 'I thought you believed in giving people a second chance, Mr Thompson? You're not sounding very charitable now.'

He flashed his blond eyelashes in her direction. 'He's not proven to be as reliable or trustworthy as I thought.'

'You can't get the staff,' Jane said.

It bought Allan time to focus. He straightened up again in his chair. 'You've claimed, before, that Mo Khan pilfered your stock. You said the goods in his locker were evidence of that. I put it to you, now, that Mo Khan groomed Jamie Brooks with items obtained from Q-busters, and that you found this out and used it to your advantage.'

'Why would I do that? What advantage?'

The lawyer spoke up again. 'I've already asked you to explain what you believe would be my client's motivation. But you haven't answered.'

Allan ignored him. Didn't even look in his direction. 'Mr Thompson. A team from Forensics has been going through your house this morning. They've removed your laptop and other items from your home office.'

Thompson looked straight at Allan but said nothing.

'Your wife has been taken into custody, charged with attempting to destroy evidence and to pervert the course of justice. She's being moved to Hallworth Women's Prison.'

A flush spread over Thompson's face. 'Who's got my children?'

'Your children are being taken care of.'

'Who's got them?'

'Ollie and Lou have been taken into care by the local authority,'

Jane said.

'I'm sorry, we need to stop, here,' Thompson said, and turned to his solicitor. 'You need to stop this. My kids need me. They need their mother.' He channelled all his authority into his posture and expression. 'You need to stop this. Now.'

'They'll be taken good care of, Mr Thompson,' Jane said.

'And your wife is less likely to get another black eye where she's going,' Allan said under his breath.

Chapter 52

As they walked along the corridor, Allan asked Jane to check up on progress in finding Mo Khan. When they arrived in the office, Ross and PC Welsh were sitting, outer edges of thighs touching, going over the CCTV footage. Allan pointedly signalled he was aware of the intimacy. 'Any joy?' he asked.

Ross took off his glasses and rubbed his eyes. 'Not yet.'

There was the sound of a distant boom. Fireworks. Allan clapped Ross on the shoulder. 'Keep going.'

At his desk, Allan unscrewed the two-day old bottle of water and swallowed a pill. Outside his window, the trees were almost entirely bare and the industrial estate car park was decorated with coppery carpeting. The clocks had changed, and the afternoon light was dimming. It was overcast, but the clouds were high, and buttoned like a continental quilt, creamy white. Good weather for Guy Fawkes Night. The streets and parks would be full of it. Explosions, fireworks, bonfires.

Allan flipped through the files in his folder. It wasn't looking great for the case against Thompson. He was convincing, and there was still that question over his motive. He'd been fazed by that news about his children, though. The man had a heart after all. Who could blame him? Forensics would say for sure who handled the explosives. He checked his emails to see if there was any news from them. There was. It was minor, but significant. The sweep of Khan's locker at Q-busters had revealed a new lead. He called out to his team members. 'Guys. Forensics found an exact match between the fibres found under Jamie Brooks' nails and Mo Khan's uniform.'

'Yes!'

They could definitely tie Khan down for this now. All they had to do was find him. Allan lifted his jacket from the back of his chair and headed for the exit. As he passed Jane, he asked what the situation was.

'He's definitely gone AWOL,' she said, looking up at him. 'No phone use, no bank card use.' She squeezed her bottom lip. 'You know what that means, usually?'

'Swimming with the fishes? The Loch Ness Monster got him?'

She twitched her eyebrows. 'Could Thompson have got him?'

'That's speculation.'

'Yep.'

Allan tapped his car key against his lips. 'No – I think Khan went to ground once we released him.' It was stupid to have let him go, but unavoidable. They couldn't control when evidence came to light. 'And I think Thompson's been too busy to have gone after him.'

There was another distant rumble. A whizz and a boom. Kids had already started blowing things up even though darkness hadn't fallen.

'Keep looking for him. He'll show up sometime.' He perched on a corner of her desk. 'In fact, I've thought of something. Get a squad car to bring Cathy in. She didn't believe what Khan was capable of – remember?' Jane nodded, brows down, questioning. 'Might she be giving Khan somewhere to hide? You heard what Thompson said – that she was there in the office that lunchtime when Khan brought Jamie in.'

'You think she colluded?'

Allan pursed his lips. 'More by accident than design, maybe. Anyway – time for the Coates collar to get felt.'

Jane smiled. 'I'll have her pulled in.' Then she looked at her boss; really looked at him. 'How are you doing?'

'I'm going for a word with Khalil and Ahmed.'

'That's not what I meant.'

'No?'

'You know what I was meaning,' Jane said. 'How are you feeling?'

Allan scanned round the busy office before coming back to her. 'I'm doing okay. I've more energy than I had a couple of weeks ago. My thinking's clearer. Most of the time. Kind of comes and goes, but I'm getting there.'

'Not ready for the desk job yet, then. Remember we talked about it – sitting with your legs crossed, dangling your high heel, filing your nails?'

'Hardly.'

She tapped his thigh. 'Glad to hear it.'

'Hey!' He stared at her hand. 'I could get you done for that.'

'If you perch on my desk, you're asking for it, darling.'

Outside, the wind was light but sharp. Allan fastened the middle button of his suit jacket and thought about unearthing his winter coat from the back of the wardrobe. His ears stung as he walked to the car. Once in, he turned the heating and the music up. By the time he reached Lorraine's street, the drugs were working, he was warmed through and the music lifted him. He felt fully human.

As he suspected, Khal and Ahmed were in the living room, playing video games. He saw them through the window. Lorraine couldn't have been home yet, because no one answered the door when he rang, so he made himself conspicuous through the living room window, screening his eyes with his hand so he could see inside and rapping on the glass with his knuckles so they could see they'd been discovered. Khal appeared at the front door, more truculent teenager than ever, his eyes shaded under an already impressive monobrow and the corners of his upper lip smudged with fresh growth.

'My mum's not in,' he said.

'It's not her I've come to see.' A boom followed by crackles sounded somewhere behind him. 'Can I come in?' He motioned forwards and Khal stepped back.

263

Ahmed had the same sullen look on his face. Allan asked them to turn the sound down and tried to ignore the colours flashing on the TV screen as the game looped on pause. He sat on the arm of the sofa, giving himself a bit of height in comparison with the two boys, whom he'd instructed to sit.

'Have you seen your dad, Khal? Either of you?'

Neither had seen him, or so they said.

'What about at the mosque?' Allan looked to Ahmed in particular. 'Should I get my team to ransack it a second time? There were good grounds the last time.'

'He's not at the mosque,' Ahmed said. He looked earnest. 'I'm telling you, there's not been any sign of him.'

'And what about your mum, has she seen or heard from him?' Allan asked Khal.

'Honestly, we've not heard anything.'

Allan let it stew for a minute. He folded his arms. 'So, where d'you think he's gone?'

A look passed between the boys before Khal spoke. 'I think he's gone to England. That's where he's from.'

'My team can't get any response to his phone. Do you have a new number for him?'

Khalil thought before speaking. He shook his head.

Allan cleared his throat. 'It would have been easy for him to get hold of a new phone.'

Khal shrugged.

'I mean, you could have given him one of the ones he gave you.'

Khal looked wide eyed at the older man.

'If I went upstairs and checked in your wardrobe, would there still be three new phones in their boxes?'

A guilty flush rose into Khalil's cheeks.

'And remember – I've still got that photo from CCTV of you and Ahmed near the Q-busters bin the night straight after Jamie Brooks was murdered.' Allan turned to Ahmed. 'You and Iqbal said you were trying to stop Mo Khan. You told us about the bomb. But you

264

pinned the blame on his boss, right?' Allan looked from one boy
to the other. 'Your testimony prevented the school blowing up, but
there's more going on. You told me you weren't at school because
it was in-service training for the teachers, but that was a lie. So,
what's going on, boys? Do I need to take you both in?' He looked
at Khal. 'You've already been held. This is important. This is way
more important than finding Mo Khan.'

Still, the boys said nothing. The room was growing darker. The
game on the TV screen flashed bright greens and yellows and reds
on a loop round the walls and their faces. Through the window, the
sky glowed with ruddy light from the setting sun, and the sudden
illumination of a firework.

'One phone call, and I can take you both in.' Allan reached into
his jacket pocket.

'Tell him!' Ahmed said, panicky.

'Shut up!'

'Tell him! They're not taking me into jail.'

'Khalil?' Allan said.

'We tried our best, man,' Ahmed said, his tone softening. 'Tell
him about White Spirit.'

Allan rounded on Khal. 'The white spirit, the nails and the
fertiliser? The stuff for old Bob, for doing "man-things"?'

Khal dropped his head into his hands and scratched his nails
hard over his scalp. 'It's not my dad's fault.' He looked up, anguished,
at Allan. 'It's his boss. I keep telling people that. It's his boss that
makes him do it.'

'That guy Thompson's a maniac,' Ahmed said. 'He forced us to
do it. He said if we didn't, he'd turn Mo in.'

'Will you make a statement about that? Will you come down
to the station and make it official? I need you – both – to tell me
everything you know. Everything you think you know. You might
get into trouble.' At this he focused on Khalil, 'but you were doing
things with the best motives, to get your dad free and make him
change.' Ahmed was wiping his cheeks. 'Tell us what you know and

it'll help us get Thompson. Come clean and a judge'll go easy on you,
I promise, especially since Ahmed prevented the big explosion.'

Chapter 53

Allan waited for Lorraine to come home, and then he took the three of them into the station and left them with the duty sergeant.

Back in the office, Sam was waiting for him. 'Guess what, Boss?' he took his phone out and pulled up some photos.

'What's this?'

'Press cuttings. From Q-busters.' Sam grinned, clearly pleased with himself. 'You told me Thompson was ultra-neat and I'd to scratch below the surface. Well, I uncovered something.'

'Let me grab a sandwich.'

As Allan ate, Sam explained how he'd gone over the files in Thompson's office and hadn't found anything but business documentation and invoices. Then he'd remembered Jane saying she'd seen the press cutting about the bin fire, but there was no trace of it, not in the drawers, or box files, or anywhere. 'So I asked Cathy,' he said, 'and it was as if I'd complimented her on having a beautiful baby.' He looked around, aware that the rest of the team were watching him. 'She smiled all over her face and reached for this huge ring binder off the shelf above where she sits in the front office.'

'What was in it?' Allan asked.

Sam pulled up the photo. 'Look at the size of it. She says she's kept press cuttings for all the years she's been there.' He told Allan he'd bagged the whole thing as evidence.

'Just because you found a cutting about a bin fire?' Allan said.

'No, Boss – I'm trying to show you. Look.'

Allan licked his fingers and wiped them on his trousers, then

267

took the phone Sam was offering him. There were several photos of dense text.

'Press cuttings from the local paper,' Sam said. He was itching to take the phone back because Allan wasn't seeing the information quickly enough. 'Scroll in!' he said.

But Allan had already done it. It was a letter. A letter in the local paper, signed 'WS' . 'What am I missing?' Allan asked him, handing the phone back.

Sam frowned. 'Look!' Exasperated, he turned to the others and then back to Allan. 'There's loads of them. WS has to be connected to Q-busters or Hugo Thompson. Why else would Cathy collect them? They don't even mention Q-busters.'

Allan threw away his sandwich wrapper. 'So, what are they about?'

'Recycling. Energy efficiency.'

'That's exciting. That'll really make someone's blood boil.' He glanced beyond Sam towards Jane and Ross and pulled a face.

Sam lowered his brow and evaluated his boss's reaction. 'You're just not getting this, are you?' When Allan quizzically raised a brow, Sam sat on the desk and said, 'It starts off with a simple complaint about a report in the previous week's paper. Cathy obviously went back a week and cut that out, too, so I know what it was. Over the weeks, the letters fly back and forward – there's a whole furore about it – and the tone of WS's letters becomes more and more irritated and sarcastic.'

Allan sat forward. 'I'm sorry, Sam, but I really am not getting this. What are you saying? Where does Q-busters come into this? And did anyone go and pick up Cathy?'

Sam sighed. 'Yes, they've picked up Cathy. But this – this isn't about Cathy. This is about a whole big argument, in the letters pages, between WS and Frances Wallace. He was sarcastic about the claims she made for a big project about energy efficiency.' He looked around them all. 'Does nobody get it?'

Allan looked to Jane, who looked to Ross, who looked to PC

Welsh, who blushed and looked at her lap.

'We were looking for motive, remember?' Sam went on. 'We know Hugo Thompson was done as a young man for "lively" protests at climate change demonstrations. This, here, these letters – they're from someone – connected to Q-busters – who holds this subject very close to his heart. It's been going on over the last two or three months. The letters back and forward get more and more venomous. Frances Wallace gives as good as she gets and WS becomes all the more irate. If it *is* Thompson, then, given his past, maybe fireworks were his next logical step.'

Allan smacked himself on the forehead. 'Frances Wallace! The headteacher at Thistlebank!'

'At last!' Sam said and slid into one of the new padded chairs.

'Well done, Son!' Allan said, rising to go over and pat him on the back, but stopping before he got there. 'But why "WS"?'

~~~

With the testimony from Khalil and Ahmed, and this new evidence that someone connected to Q-busters had clear animosity towards Frances Wallace, Allan was more optimistic his case against Thompson could hold. He arranged for the lawyer to come back in so Thompson could be interviewed again, and while he waited, he phoned Emma Gough. Partly, it was to ask if she knew anything about the newspaper correspondence. Partly, it was because he hadn't seen her since the school had been cleared and he'd taken ill; hadn't even phoned her.

She did know about the letters. She told him about gossip in the staffroom, Frances Wallace not being high on several of the teachers' popularity list. 'I probably shouldn't bitch like that,' she told Allan, 'but hey ho, that's how it is.'

The next port of call was the holding cell to see Cathy. The woman was as jittery as ever, trembling and touching her glasses. Her nervousness was obvious through the peep hole, even before he and Jane opened the cell door. 'Good cop or bad cop?' he asked Jane.

Carol McKay

'I kind of get the feeling saying "Boo" might be enough.'

The interview didn't take long. Cathy was more than ready to talk, to convince them about all of Thompson's good points. 'He's a wonderful man,' she assured them. 'He's fair, he's earnest, he's honest.' Her eyes were lit with something close to religious fervour. 'He gives all the staff Christmas bonuses. Not just the staff, but the warehouse men as well.'

'Mrs Coates,' Allan said, spreading his hands on the table and trying to bring her to a halt. 'Who is WS?'

Cathy fidgeted. Shrugged.

'You don't know?'

She pushed up her glasses. 'No.'

'Is it you?'

'Certainly not!'

'Okay,' Allan said. He let a moment pass. 'Then tell me the background to the newspaper cuttings.'

Cathy's eyes went from Allan to Jane and back again. 'I've always kept cuttings, ever since Mrs Thompson's father bought the company when we were still in the old town.'

'Mrs Thompson's father?' Jane said.

'Yes, he bought it – you know – as a kind of wedding present. Mr Thompson being a local boy. I think he thought it would be a good base for them. You know.' Her gaze jumped around the room, only just glancing now and then off the two police officers. 'After – well, there had been a bit of an incident. A prank. Mr Thompson – well, business people get to be business people because they're risk takers, aren't they?'

'And Frances Wallace? What's she got to do with anything?'

'Och, she's just difficult.' With that, Cathy sat back and pressed her lips together. Finished.

Allan and Jane looked at each other.

'Difficult?' Jane said.

'Difficult,' Cathy repeated.

'Would you like to expand –' Allan started.

270

Cathy leaned forward and tap, tap, tapped the nail of her index finger on the table between them. 'That woman always had it in for Hugh, ever since he started at that school. I used to know that boy's mother. And the misery she put that boy through was damnable. Damnable!' She sat back again.

'Frances Wallace?'

'Frances Wallace.'

Allan shook his head. 'I'm confused. Why did Frances Wallace treat Hugo Thompson badly as a child at school?'

'Because he was clever! Because he was different. Teachers like her don't like it when a pupil gets ideas about himself. But that's the kind of people who go on to make a difference in the world. People like Hugh, who take risks. Providing jobs. Tackling injustices.'

'Hugh?' Allan said.

Cathy blinked. 'Hugh. That's what we used to call him.'

Hugh. Hugo. And possibly also WS. Thompson seemed to be an expert at reinventing himself. There was silence while Allan took that in. He turned to Jane. 'Any questions?'

She shuffled through her paperwork, buying thinking time. 'That was all a long time ago, Cathy, yet this correspondence in the local paper – that's recent, isn't it? What would you say started that up?'

Cathy took a deep breath and sighed. 'He'd put it all behind him – all that animosity from his school days. Went away to uni and did really well for himself.'

'Apart from his wee foray into anti-capitalist rioting, you mean,' Allan said.

'He was young. He's been on the straight and narrow ever since. Till she started antagonising him with those letters,' she said.

'Hugo Thompson? Or WS?'

Cathy cleaned her glasses on the hem of her jumper.

'They're one and the same, aren't they? Hugo Thompson and WS?'

Eyes down, she nodded.

'Why do you think he rose to it? Retaliating like that in the newspaper?'

'Och, he's got all that pent-up fury at her. I tried to calm him, but he's spirited. He's got strong views and feelings!'

'Yes, we've seen something of that,' Jane said, thinking about his wife's black eye. 'So, how far did you think Thompson would go with his fury? Did you think it would go as far as explosions?'

Cathy shook her head.

'Explosions at a school full of pupils?'

Cathy said nothing.

Allan took his turn of questioning. 'And what about Mohammed Khan?'

Cathy's face flushed. Quiet, she said, 'He seemed a nice man. The customers like him.'

'You know he's got a record?'

'Mr Thompson –' she swallowed – 'Mr Thompson believes work helps rehabilitate people. That people deserve a second chance.'

Allan edged forward in his chair, not taking his eyes off the woman opposite. 'Mrs Coates, even if that's true and Mo Khan deserved a second chance, you let him blow it. You let Khan – a known sex offender – take a vulnerable young boy into Hugo Thompson's office.'

The woman's mouth turned down. She took off her glasses and wiped her eyes with bony, jittery fingers.

Stinging with outrage, Allan continued, 'Beyond that, you let him take the boy into a hidden room – a locked room hidden by a bookcase. But it wasn't a secret to you. You turned a blind eye to him, that boy. You could've saved him!'

Cathy covered her face and they watched her shoulders shudder on a long outbreath. 'I made a mistake,' she wailed, 'I admit it. I know I shouldn't have. But Mr Thompson had a special relationship with Mo. He was looking after him. He was trying to rehabilitate him. He told me to let Mo have more leeway than other workers. Mo and that boy loved gaming machines. Mo just wanted to share his passions.'

'No,' Allan said, reining in his voice with extreme difficulty. 'Mo Khan's passions were very different from that boy's.'

Chapter 54

Allan was still furious by the time he got back to his office. He'd need a clear head before he interviewed Thompson again. But Ross was standing waiting for him.

'What's up with you?' Allan asked, edging him out of the way so he could get past to his desk. He opened the drawer and fumbled for his pills.

'There's been ... a bit of bad news from Forensics.'

Allan gulped from his water bottle then shot him a look. 'Well – tell me!'

Ross looked shame-faced. 'There wasn't enough to blow up the school.'

'What?'

'It was just made to look that way.'

Allan shook his head. 'The dogs sniffed it. The bomb squad found explosives packed into the hard drives.'

The young DC's voice quivered. 'Yeah. They thought that. But it was subterfuge. The dogs sniffed something, and it looked like proper explosives when the team opened up the computers. But it was fake. There were only traces – just done up to look and smell like the real thing.'

'Shit!' Allan said, standing with his hands on his hips, trying to take it in.

'I've emailed you the report.'

Allan nodded, dismissing him. Then he swivelled round on his chair and looked out through the window, letting his eyes rove over the cars in the car park, and the trees and shrubs that were mostly bare, now, only some of them still with yellowed leaves clinging to them. He didn't really see them. One fell as he watched. Noises came from the rest of the office behind him. Someone laughed. A phone rang. There was the sound of the distant elevator. Allan rubbed his eyes. What the fuck was Thompson's game? Why WS? And why all these blue flashes and attention seeking?

Before he knew what he was doing, Allan rose and went to his locker. In a heap on the bottom was a pair of trainers and the running gear he'd been planning to use since the summer. He picked up the tee-shirt and sniffed it.

'Back in a minute,' he said to Jane when he passed her, speechless and with her eyebrows raised, in the corridor.

For half an hour, Allan ran alongside the river, stopping every couple of minutes to walk and regain even breathing before stepping it up again. His feet beat on the tarmac with a rhythm he loved but had forgotten. His steps echoed as he crossed and re-crossed the bridges. When he paused for breath mid-way over, leaning bare forearms on the metal railings, the low sun gleamed on the mirror surface of the Ness and brought him clarity. Well, a hunch. He had to make a call before he and Jane went back in to interview Thompson. He had to make a call now. He took out his mobile and started running.

It was late in the afternoon, but Frances Wallace was still at her desk. He pictured her, fragrant and jingling, powder puff and paint, slightly breathless. There was a darker side to her nature that Emma Gough and Cathy Coates had talked about, but he put that out of his mind.

'When the bomb disposal people came to the school, did they check your office?' he asked her.

She hesitated then said, 'I'm not actually sure. Should they have?'

He stooped, head down, leaning one hand on his knee. 'I don't want to panic you, but could you move into one of the areas they did check out, and wait there till I can arrange for someone to come and vet you?'

Then he phoned Ross to call out the bomb disposal team. 'Be thorough,' he said. 'Make it stick. Tell them to check her office, and her house and car.' He set off running towards base again as a bright light sparkled on the horizon. 'This might be bonfire night, but I don't want Frances Wallace going up in smoke.'

Chapter 55

Back in Interview Room 2, the lightbulb still smelled dusty. The high, rectangular window was black, but glowed intermittently with white, red and green flashes. There was a rumbling backdrop to the interview as the city's official firework display got underway. In the artificial light, Thompson looked sickly pale, concerned for himself, or his children. The evening had brought new seriousness to his face and body language.

The first thing Allan did was address the question of motive. He spread out printouts of the most recent letters.

'I think you could say there was a level of animosity between you and Frances Wallace,' Allan said.

'Fanny W, eh? Well, you've no proof they're from me,' Thompson said, but, compared to before, his performance was lacklustre.

'You think there's no paper trail just because they're signed WS? Cathy seems to think they're from you. And I'm sure the editor at the newspaper will agree.'

'Sticks and stones,' Thompson said. He looked at Jane. 'Names'll never hurt me. That's just an argument. It's a big step from arguing to ...'

'Taking direct action?' Allan interrupted. 'Like the direct action you took in London ten years ago, that got you a criminal record even though Daddy's big lawyer got you off with a caution? Or should that be "your wife's daddy's big lawyer"?' Allan slid forward a photocopy of a newspaper report. In the grainy photograph someone fitting the description of a younger Thompson was hurling a flaming missile in a crowded square. 'Pretty incendiary, I'd say,'

277

said Allan.

Thompson gnawed at the inside of his lip.

'You weren't too keen on this project the school were undertaking, were you?'

'Everything they did was superficial. Still is. They're just paying lip service. Not prepared to call in any experts to do it right.'

'And you had a personal grudge against the headteacher.'

'The woman's an idiot.' He ran his hand through his near-white hair. 'All that crap about being "plastic-wise" in the school foyer. *Every day* they're using single use cutlery and cups in the dinner school. Have you seen the waste all over the playground? And the litter in the streets outside the school? I tried to tell her.' He looked at his brief. 'That's what the letters were about in the paper. Frances Wallace is a fool. She's not interested in real change, or real education. Just ticking the boxes.' He flashed a glance at Jane, who was doing her best to draw Allan's attention to a note she'd typed on her i-pad.

Allan squinted at it. 'Mr Thompson, I'm sensing a bit of misogyny on top of everything else. You must really hate a woman to go to these lengths. To try to blow up a school with a thousand kids inside it? Call yourself some kind of anti-capitalist eco-warrior? Waging some kind of climate change guerrilla warfare against a thousand children?'

'I admit I was exasperated,' Thompson conceded, brushing back his hair. His solicitor touched his arm and shook his head, but he disregarded him. 'But to suggest I'd hurt her, or those kids, is crazy. Why would I do it? What have I to gain?'

'Attention?'

'Oh, come on – I've grown up in the last ten years,' Thompson said, sliding the photocopy back across the table.

'Maybe,' Allan said. He lifted the photocopy and looked at it. 'DC Coburn has better eyes than me. She's been able to read the caption. Which gives your nickname. "White Spirit". If you've moved on so much, why are you still using it?'

Thompson smirked and Allan recognised the smug schoolboy who thought he was better than anyone else. Thompson knew there wasn't enough explosive in those computers to do any serious damage. He was playing them. He knew it and Allan knew it.

'If you've no further questions for my client I expect you to release him.' The brief gathered his papers and tapped them, edge-on, on the table top then reached for his leather bag.

It wasn't even clear it was Thompson who'd stuffed the computers. Ahmed and Khal could be in the frame for that. Allan checked his watch. All he could pin on Thompson was wasting police time for masterminding a bomb hoax and making it convincing with that crazy car chase.

'So – if we're finished...?' the brief said.

Allan's phone vibrated in his pocket. 'I have to get this.' He rose to his feet then half turned and pointed straight at Thompson. 'Sit there.' He let the door click shut behind him.

'Word just in, Boss.' It was Ross. 'We've found another package and we've tested it. Just the one. And it's for real. The bomb squad have confirmed it. Thompson's fingerprints are all over it. Not only that, but a neighbour witnessed him delivering it.'

Attempted murder. Allan came back into the room dead pan but exultant. It had never been about the school. It had always been about Fanny W.

Disregarding Thompson, he spoke directly to his brief. 'Bomb disposal officers have found an explosive device left by a very blond Q-busters delivery man at the back door at Frances Wallace's home address. Hugo Thompson, I'm arresting you...'

~~~

Over the next hour, Thompson confessed he'd come to an arrangement with Mo Khan, knowing his predilection for boys, and Allan had him arraigned on a whole list of charges. 'In effect,' Allan told Sam and Ross, in the office, once Thompson had been taken away and locked up, 'while Khan groomed Jamie Brooks, Thompson was grooming Khan, overlooking his pilfering to keep him sweet, to give him an alibi. The weird thing is,' he said, sitting forward and stretching his back, 'it's as if he felt some kind of loyalty to him. I genuinely think he was shocked to discover Khan in the back room with Jamie that Monday lunchtime. Until we have Khan in custody, we can't know for sure, but to me it looks as if Khan acted on the spur of the moment, taking the boy from school. He knew Cathy would be a pushover, and maybe he remembered the other staff were away at the same time, at lunch or the dentist, or whatever. Anyway, it looks like Thompson was livid; told him to take the boy in the other van, and Thompson did his deliveries for him, which gave Khan an alibi in return.'

'Did Cathy confess?' Ross asked.

Allan laughed. 'From what I could make out through the snot and tears.'

'That's a shame.'

'No, it's not,' Allan said. 'She let Mo Khan take a schoolboy into the back office, knowing Khan had a record. She knew Thompson did, too. She'd been there for years, remember. What is it they say? All that's needed for evil to thrive is for good people to do nothing?' He looked around his team. 'So don't give Cathy your pity. Or Khan, or Thompson.'

'How long d'you think he'll get, Boss?' That was Sam.

The glass wall to the corridor reflected a scatter of gold and silver from the fireworks still going on outside in the city. It caught Allan's eye and he was slow in replying. But there was someone moving behind it.

'Boss?'

Allan looked at Sam. 'Not long enough. Certainly not long enough if he'd actually blown the school, or Frances Wallace, up. But at least he showed some kind of character with the plea bargaining.' His eyes went, once again, to the glass wall between the office and the corridor and he rose from his seat.

'He'll plead guilty so his wife gets off with a lesser charge,' Jane said.

'Yeah. Right. It's been a long day and it's time to go home. Who's staying? You, Ross?'

Ross took off his glasses again and rubbed his eyes. 'Yeah, I want to crack on and get this CCTV finished.' He let his eyes rest on PC Welsh.

'Okay dokes. Well, I'm off, guys. See you in the morning,' Allan said, and scooped his jacket off the back of his chair. In the corridor, Emma Gough was waiting for him.

Chapter 56

The air was hazy and there was a tang of smoke from the fireworks as he and Emma made their way across the car park. She slipped her hand inside his to slow him as another rocket streaked dull orange across the black sky then burst into a globe of a thousand silvery sparkles.

'It's like a fairy clock,' Emma said. 'A dandelion seed head! Make a wish.'

Allan wrapped his arms round her. 'Can I come to yours?'

She brushed his mouth with her lips. 'That was the right kind of wish.'

'My car, though.'

They drove alongside the river. Its surface reflected the kaleidoscope of colours still scattering across the sky. At the junction, they stopped to pick up ready meals and chilled fizz. Allan was in the mood for celebration, relieved to have a result against Thompson, despite the idea of Khan still being at large straining to find inroads into his thoughts. Tomorrow was another day. For tonight, he wanted to relax. He needed to relax.

Emma locked the door and scooped her shoes off her feet and into the cupboard while Allan hung his jacket on a chair and rummaged in her kitchen units for champagne flutes.

She padded through to stand beside him while he poured and she prepared the food. 'Ten minutes in the microwave or half an hour in the oven. How hungry are you?'

He ran his eyes down her body. 'I can wait.' He smoothed a hand round her waist and nuzzled into her.

'Let me get it in!' she said, squirming while she tried to remove the cardboard wraps.

'Let me get it in,' he mimicked.

Eventually she gave up and raised her mouth and eyes to his, encircled her arms round his neck, and clung to him.

With Lorraine, sex had been easy and uncomplicated. But he needed this. He needed Emma. He nuzzled her ear, pushing back her black hair. In her room, she eased herself backwards on the wide bed and he followed her, eyes on her eyes, gripping her waist and moving in close.

'I love you,' she said.

He didn't reply. He just looked at her.

~~~

He woke in the night in blackness. Emma was shaking him.

'Allan! Your phone's going.'

He'd been subterranean. He still felt subterranean.

'That's the second time it's rung. You'd better take it.'

Two missed calls. The phone light blinded him. He screwed his eyes up and asked her to put the lamp on.

Two missed calls from Lorraine. And here he was with Emma. 'I'll need to take it,' he said, pushing his legs free of the covers, away from where they'd been interlocked with hers. 'I'll go into the living room.'

He propped on one of the dining chairs. 'Hello?' he said.

'Khal's heard from Mo, Allan. Mo wants Khal and Ahmed to meet him. I don't know what to do. He wants to go to him. I don't want to let him. I had to get in touch with you.'

He rubbed his brow. 'What time is it?'

'After midnight. Were you sleeping? You sound dopey.'

He swallowed a yawn. 'Where does he want to meet?'

'The back of Q-busters. You know it?'

'Yeah.'

Khan.

Allan struggled to take it in. Khan wanting to see the boys. After

283

midnight? I'll come and get them. I'll come to yours, and we can pick up Ahmed on the way.' He stood up, now, more awake. 'Don't let them go before I get there, d'you hear me?'

He cut the call and went back to the bedroom. Emma was still under the covers, but she watched him dress. 'I have to go,' he said, forcing his fingers through his hair. 'It's a big development at work.'

'At this time of night? Will you be alright?'

He paused to look at her. 'I'll call it in but I want to be there. I'll come back. Or I'll be in touch with you.' He bent to kiss her.

'Should you take your medicine?'

'Eh? Probably.' He thought about it. 'Yeah, probably.'

He grabbed his jacket, pulled the front door shut behind him and skipped down the brightly lit stairs. Outside, the sky was still black and there was a faint veil of smoke in the air. He remotely unlocked his Alfa and sat in, reaching for his drugs from the glove compartment. He wasn't sure how much he would need, but he didn't want a repeat of what had happened on the hill when he went after Thompson, so he swallowed two then called Khan's appearance in. He put his foot down, speeding through the deserted streets, keen to reach Lorraine's before the boy chose to risk it by himself.

Lorraine was watching for him. She opened the door as he walked up the path and hugged him as he stepped into the hall.

He brushed her off. 'Where is he?' Allan asked.

Khalil appeared in the living room doorway, already wearing his jacket.

'Let's go.' To Lorraine, he said, 'I've called out a unit. Go back to bed.'

'That'll be fucking right,' she said, and gave her boy a death-squeeze hug.

Khal had contacted Ahmed. He'd sneaked out of the house and was waiting for them at the corner, under an overhang of almost bare tree branches. The streetlight showed the ground at his feet silver with oval cherry blossom leaves and long wooden sticks from firework rockets. Ahmed slipped into the back seat and none of the three spoke till they were close to Q-busters.

Allan slowed the car on the approach to the industrial estate. He pulled on the handbrake and looked at the boy in the passenger seat. 'What did Khan tell you he wanted?'

'Just to talk to me,' Khalil said. 'I think he's going home. Down south. And wants to see us.'

'You sure about that? You don't think you're in any danger?'

Khalil shrugged. 'I don't think so.' He sniffed. 'He's my dad. He'd never hurt me.'

Allan looked over the skinny, elongated limbs of the two fifteen year olds, and at their angular faces. 'We got Thompson,' he said, and their faces flickered with interest. 'He's confessed about the explosions. So Khan's in the clear, as near as damn it, as far as that's concerned. You can tell him.'

'Okay.'

'And convince him to hand himself in. Or why else did you call me?'

'That was my mum.'

'She knows it's best that way, son.'

They looked out of the window. They were a hundred metres away from Q-busters, and there was no sign of anyone else around. No moving vehicles, no cars parked with their lights on.

'Here's what we're going to do. I'll phone the squad car and tell them we're going in first and they're just back-up for if your dad tries to run. But I'm going to let you two go in and have a word with him.'

There was the sound of a distant firework. It cracked then wailed like a siren. Ahmed jumped visibly, and Allan felt his heart surge, but refused to give it any more attention. The three of them walked quickly to the front of Q-busters. The floodlights in the car park made the whole scene two-dimensional and the surfaces metallic. Mo Khan was nowhere.

Khal's pocket buzzed and he took out his phone. 'Hello? Right.'

He tucked it away again. 'He's round the back.' He paused. 'He just wants Ahmed and me.'

Allan nodded. He put his hand on Khalil's elbow and pointed towards the far corner of the building, just past the bins. 'That way.' They rounded the corner. Allan eased his head out to check. There was no sign of anyone. No lights except the glare of the floodlights. A fox hesitated. It stared at them, its long tail held out behind it, then walked past, headed for the bushes. A little further along, a human stepped out. Mo Khan.

'Wait here.' Allan pushed Khal by the arm and stepped forward.

'Mo Khan, I'm DI Allan MacIntyre of Police Scotland. We met before – at the mosque.' They'd also met in the interview room, but Allan thought better to skip that. 'There's a unit on its way. You need to give yourself up. Thompson's in custody. He's been arrested. He's made a full confession. But we need you to give yourself up and confess to murdering Jamie Brooks.'

'I want to speak to my boy first.'

The unit was on the way. Khan was out of shape – heavy round the belly, typical of someone who drove for a living. What harm would it do? Allan could take him if he had to – outrun him. He'd done it with Thompson. Did a doubt creep in? No. He wouldn't let it. He could definitely take him.

'Please, Allan.'

It was the first time the boy had addressed him by his name.

'A couple of minutes.'

Allan moved to the wall and let the two boys go forward. Khalil hugged his father. Ahmed joined in. Khan ruffled the tops of their heads. Allan could hear the catch in his voice: the hiccupping grief and self-reproach, evident in whatever it was he said to them.

Allan's phone vibrated. To his left, he could see car headlights move slowly along the approach road. 'Surround on foot,' he whispered into his mobile.

Khan was pushing the boys away. 'Go home. Look after your mother.'

The PCs would be moving in. They'd be fanning out behind and around him.

Just then, Khan shouted. 'Mr MacIntyre, I'm not coming in. I won't let you take me.' His voice cracked and he wiped his sleeve across his face. 'But I did kill him.' He peeled away. 'I got to know him. Groomed him with the phones and games. Drugged him.' His voice wavered. 'I just couldn't resist it. Couldn't restrain myself.' He sniffed loudly. 'But it's finished. Not happening again. I'm not doing it.' A firework whizzed in the sky behind him. 'Get back, boys. I told you. Go home to your mother. They're decent kids, Mr MacIntyre. They deserve better.'

Allan heard police boots on the tarmac behind him.

'Dad!' Khal said. Allan gripped his upper arm.

'I tried to fight it, but I couldn't do it.' Khan took something from his pocket. 'I hate this part of myself. Only one thing'll fix it.'

Heavy round the belly. It jolted Allan like a current. A freeze-frame in the floodlights: the two boys; the PCs; Khan with his thumb on the detonator. Allan yelled. He shoved the boys back.

Khan's belt exploded.

Acknowledgements

First, I'd like to thank the informal 'team'of individuals who form my writing support network and sustain me through the ups and downs of this craft. They are many, but I'd particularly like to thank Donal McLaughlin, Jacqueline Smith and Leela Soma.

Profound thanks to Keith McKay my publisher for his enduring strength, reliability and focus. Thanks to all my lovely family.

I've a lot to thank the UK's National Health Service for right from the start. The 'flying squad' rushed to my birth in the living room of our council flat in Glasgow's huge Drumchapel scheme on Christmas Day 1955. They saved my mum and me by cutting the umbilical cord that had wrapped itself round my neck. In 2010 the staff at Hairmyres A&E recognised the signs of Addison's Disease in me and again saved my life. And for all interventions in between and since – thank you! You are taken for granted yet much loved.

Addison's Disease is real, and dangerous. When I was diagnosed, and realised how close to death I had been, I felt very alone. The Addison's Disease Self-Help Group charity comforted me. They gave me information and company. Groups on social media helped too, and I'm thankful for these bonds. The author royalties for this book will go to ADSHG.

Last but not least – thank you to everyone from Moniack Mhor: Scotland's Creative Writing Centre near Inverness, and to the people of Inverness, whose city I love but have carefully fictionalised for this novel.

What is Addison's Disease?

Addison's – aka Primary Adrenal Insufficiency – is a rare condition in which the outer layers of the adrenal glands are damaged and can no longer produce hormones including cortisol and aldosterone which we simply can't live without. Cortisol regulates blood sugar levels and food metabolism; aldosterone regulates sodium levels, blood pressure and the body's fluid balance. In a healthy person, hormone production ticks away nicely at low levels. When we are put under physical or emotional stress, healthy adrenal glands are stimulated to increase these hormone levels to help the body rise to the challenge. In Addison's Disease, the damaged adrenals don't respond, which can lead to collapse and even death. Addison's is kept under control day to day fairly easily by taking replacement steroid hormones in tablet form. 'Addies' should also carry an emergency injection in case of sudden stressors such as falls or car crashes, and should wear a medical alert information bracelet or similar. More information can be found on the NHS and ADSHG websites.

The Addison's Disease Self-Help Group makes a range of authoritative, informative and supportive resources freely available to everyone via its website. Membership provides an opportunity for deeper connection through further resources and the personal touch of online forums and face-to-face meet-ups.

www.addisonsdisease.org.uk

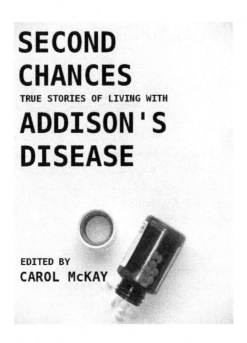

SECOND CHANCES

TRUE STORIES OF LIVING WITH

ADDISON'S DISEASE

EDITED BY
CAROL McKAY

How does it feel to be diagnosed with a life-threatening health condition?

Addison's disease is a rare auto-immune condition which can be fatal. Diagnosis is often made in an emergency. In this book, sixteen people describe the impact Addison's disease has had on their lives. Drawn from the USA, Canada, UK, Australia, South Africa, Belgium and South Korea, these men and women describe in their own words the difficult journey they've taken, from illness, through diagnosis, to living a full life, thanks to the second chance modern medicine has given them.

Compiled and edited by Carol McKay. Published by PotHole Press, 2012. Available on Kindle.

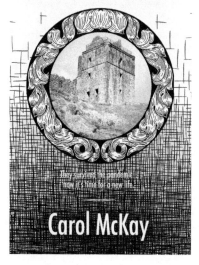

INCUNABULUM

Carol McKay

The internet's dead. The phone's dead. Alice wakes from flu to find the world dead. Or is it?

Choosing a few special photos, she sets off in search of other survivors. They've made it through the worst pandemic. Now it's time for a new life.

Set in Scotland, *Incunabulum* gets to grips with issues including social class and the Scots language. And when the social order crumples and it's every man for himself, what happens to equal rights for women?

'a visceral, wild ride set in Scotland... pure braw' MM

A post-pandemic novel for our times.

Published by PotHole Press, 2020. Available in print and Kindle.

Printed in Great Britain
by Amazon